CONTENTS

TO TELL THE TRUTH

CHAPTER ONE

The taxi tires crunched through the plowed streets, snow mounded in high walls on either side. The milk-gray sky blended with the snow-covered slopes of the Sierra Nevada, fat crystalline flakes gently falling from the clouds. A group of skiers walked into the street in front of the taxi, skis in their hands, the tips resting against their shoulders. The driver pushed on the horn and they scampered laughingly out of his way. Then the tire chains clinked to a stop in front of the ski lodge.

"Here you are, miss," the driver announced. The chill of a December afternoon in Squaw Valley swept into the warm interior as he opened the door and slid from behind the wheel.

Andrea Grant got out of the taxi and waited on the snow-mounded curb while the driver removed her luggage. Her arrival didn't go unnoticed but no one was particularly curious. In fact, no one seemed to recognize her and she felt a blissful sense of freedom with each breath of mountain air that filled her lungs. An entire week without sly comments being made behind her back, Andrea thought. She hadn't realized the gossip had bothered her.

A smile curved the fullness of her lips. A large flake landed on her nose and she wanted to laugh. How glad she was that John had suggested she take this vacation, the first one she'd had in more than three years.

John, always wise and understanding, had stepped in when she had so unexpectedly lost her father soon after cancer had taken her mother. He had offered his helping hand again when her engagement to Dale Marshall had been broken. *Face it,* Andrea scolded herself sternly, *Dale dumped you.* But that was in the past. She breathed in deeply. She would not let that bitter memory make her unhappy now.

The taxi driver was standing on the curb, her suitcases tucked under his arms. The sparkle of anticipation came back to her hazel eyes and Andrea turned toward the lodge entrance.

The lobby was crowded with skiers who had called it a day before the cloud-hidden sun settled behind Squaw Peak. The hum of voices and laughter was nonstop. Andrea noticed that there was a contagion in the easy friendliness that abounded. Her own smile was warmer and more natural as she thanked the driver, adding a generous tip to the fare after he had set her luggage in front of the registration desk.

"It was *my* pleasure," he responded, as his gaze swung admiringly over her figure.

Andrea missed the driver's look, but she saw the ones directed her way by the male skiers in the lobby. She ignored them as she ignored all the other looks that had come her way since Dale.

That faint air of aloofness only increased her attraction, but it did succeed in keeping men at arm's length. There was no coolness to her beauty, although her skin was pale. Wide and bright hazel eyes were fringed with thick lashes and flecked with a warm olive green. Dark blond hair was swept away from her face, its shiny medium length swirling into thick curls angling away from her ears and neck for an attractive windblown effect. There was a model's uniqueness rather than perfection to her prominent cheekbones, although her figure was more curved than the pencil thinness of a model's.

"May I help you, miss?" The tightly polite line of the desk clerk's mouth relaxed into a smile.

"Yes, I believe you have a reservation for me. Andrea Grant."

Looking into the computer screen in front of him and scrolling down, he stopped. "Andrea Grant from Oregon. We have your reservation right here. You'll be staying with us for a week, is that right?" At her answering nod, he smiled and slid a registration slip and pen toward her. "Fill this out, please, and I'll find someone to help you with your luggage."

Not an easy task, Andrea thought to herself as the clerk's attention was immediately claimed by a family waiting to register behind her. With her head bent over the registration form, she became conscious of being watched. She glanced to the side, and encountered the alertly appraising look of a pair of brown, nearly black eyes. The lean, handsome face revealed little concern that he had been caught studying her.

"Hello." His low, husky voice vibrated around her. Black hair gleamed with melted snowflakes while amusement deepened the creases along the corners of his mouth.

Slightly nonplussed, Andrea stared into the strongly masculine face, feeling the leap of physical response to his unquestionable attraction. What was more, he knew her reaction, or sensed it at least. She guessed that his virile charm had breached the walls of more than one feminine citadel.

"Hello." She returned the greeting evenly and reverted her attention to the form.

"May I have my keycard, Mike?" The request was addressed to the desk clerk as the man seemed to pick up on Andrea's subtle hint that she didn't wish to indulge in any idle flirtation.

"Sure thing, Mr. Stafford. There's a message for you, too." The keycard and a slip of paper were placed on the counter.

The hand that reached past Andrea was brown and strong. A brief, sideways glance at his face caught a thoughtful expression. That recklessly attractive look had vanished. He cast not one look her way as he moved away from the desk. She watched him leave, taking note of his tallness and his deceptively lean build that tapered wide shoulders into slim hips.

Something about the commanding way he carried himself told her that he was accustomed to being in charge. Of what or whom, she didn't know. Mr. Stafford, the desk clerk had called him. The name wasn't familiar to Andrea, but she hadn't really expected it to be. However, there was more than surface charm to the man and she wished now that she had not been quite so aloof. She would have liked to find out more about him.

Only for curiosity's sake, she assured herself. She wasn't interested in him as a man.

Then her view of the disappearing stranger was blocked by a young man with two of her bags tucked under one arm as he reached for the key from the desk clerk. The informal atmosphere of the ski lodge was enhanced by the lack of uniforms on the staff, but Andrea guessed that this was the bellboy in his stag's-head sweater and brown slacks.

"Art will show you to your room," the desk clerk told her as she slid the completed registration form to him.

"Could you recommend a restaurant?" Andrea asked.

"Check out the Olympic House. You have your choice, from a steak house to sandwich or pizza shops. All of them serve good food. It all depends on what you want." He shrugged.

"Thank you," she said with a smile. "I think I'll decide after I unpack."

The accommodation was more spacious than she required, but it had been the only thing available when she had made the booking. Andrea decided that before the week was out she would probably be grateful for the relative privacy and comfort of the living room with its fully equipped kitchenette and the separate bedroom loft.

The memories it brought back of previous vacations at Squaw Valley with her parents, staying in a room very similar to this one, were happy memories. Most of the grief she had felt at the deaths following so closely on one another was gone now. She could look back without pain and sorrow.

Time was a healer. She could even think of Dale now without wanting to dissolve into tears. She knew part of her bitterness had been because his defection came so soon after her father's death. She had barely recovered from the shock of that when he had left her.

John had told her that he had once loved and lost himself, but he had recovered. He'd assured her that there would be a time when she would trust again and love again. Andrea wasn't nearly so sure. True, there had been moments recently when she had wanted a man's arms around her and his kiss on her lips. But those feelings were only physical desires.

Mentally she shied away from men, unwilling to risk experiencing that deep, abiding hurt again. No one she met had possessed John's strength of character she so admired or the feeling she could depend on him no matter what. How very lucky she had been that her father had possessed a friend like John.

Partially unpacked, Andrea left the opened suitcases on her bed and picked up the phone. John would be worrying about whether she had arrived safely. She decided not to even think about the high hotel surcharges for a long-distance call and punched in the number in Oregon. Her fingers tapped impatiently on the table. The housekeeper answered on the second ring.

"Mrs. Davison, this is Andrea. May I speak to John?"

"He's in his study . . . waiting for your call." The housekeeper's hesitation before adding the last phrase increased the impression of reproof at Andrea's tardiness. Before Andrea could explain that she hadn't even unpacked, John's voice came over the line.

"Hey, Andie. Good to hear from you. I was

MAN OF MINE

JANET DAILEY

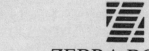

ZEBRA BOOKS
KENSINGTON PUBLISHING CORP.
http://www.kensingtonbooks.com

ZEBRA BOOKS are published by

Kensington Publishing Corp.
119 West 40th Street
New York, NY 10018

All Kensington titles, imprints, and distributed lines are available
at special quantity discounts for bulk purchases for sales promotion, premiums, fund-raising, educational, or institutional use.

Special book excerpts or customized printings can also be created to fit specific needs. For details, write or phone the office
of the Kensington Sales Manager: Attn. Sales Department.
Kensington Publishing Corp., 119 West 40th Street, New York,
NY 10018. Phone: 1-800-221-2647.

Zebra and the Z logo Reg. U.S. Pat. & TM Off.

First Mass-Market Paperback Printing: July 2007
ISBN-13: 978-1-4201-3581-7
ISBN-10: 1-4201-3581-3

10 9 8 7 6 5 4 3

Printed in the United States of America

WHENEVER YOU'RE AROUND

She didn't know how long Tell held her in his arms, crushing her against him as if there was satisfaction in just holding her. And after all the time they had been apart mentally and physically, it was almost enough for her, too.

Then, slowly, his mouth began moving along her hair to her face and she knew the moment had to climax with the searing fire of his kiss. She moaned softly in protest at his slowness. His possessive kiss, when it came, was as glorious as she had known it would be, sensually exploring and masterful. Then, drawing his head back, he studied her face with lazy thoroughness, the ardent fire in his half-closed eyes touching each beloved feature. "I love you, Andrea." His deep voice caressed her. "Whenever you're around, I know that all over again."

from "To Tell the Truth"

beginning to worry." He seemed to reach across the distance and take hold of her hand, the warmth and gladness in his greeting lightening her own heart.

"I just arrived, John. I'd started to unpack and decided to call you first. It's so beautiful here. There's fresh snow falling and everything is so pure and white, like a Christmas-card scene. You would love it. I wish you'd come." Her enthusiasm ended on a wistful note.

"I'm too old to keep up with you, Andie," he said, laughing.

"Will you stop harping about how old you are?" Andrea scolded lightly.

"I am old. Much older than you."

Behind his humorous tone, she caught the note of seriousness. Immediately a picture sprang to mind of him sitting behind the large walnut desk in his study, backed by shelves of bound books and richly paneled walls. His hair was dark brown but the sideburns were frosted with silver. The touch of gray made him look distinguished, not old. He had a wide powerful jaw, a cleft in his chin and warm gray eyes.

"Do you know—" Andrea laughed despite the lump in her throat "—I think I'm getting homesick?"

"No way. Don't even think like that. This vacation is going to do you a world of good. We both know you were letting the talk from some small minds get to you. You needed to get away."

She smiled to herself. "You're right as usual. You're so wise, John," she sighed.

"I wish I was always as positive about that as you seem to be," he observed dryly.

"I still miss you," Andrea stated, deliberately making her voice light.

"Maybe you won't be so anxious to rush back when I tell you that I finished another chapter today," he said. "Thanks to your research notes, I'll probably have several more scribbled down and ready for you to go over when you get back."

"Hmm. I wonder if I can extend my stay for another week," she said, responding in kind to his teasing remarks.

"Are you handing in your notice as my research assistant, my personal secretary and my right arm?" John said, laughing.

"No. One week of sun and snow and skiing will be all I'll want," she assured him.

"Okay. But call once in a while so I won't start imagining you with a cast on your leg."

"I will, I promise."

"Enjoy yourself, Andie. Be young and foolish while you can."

"At twenty-two, I sincerely hope I'm past that stage," Andrea answered, more sharply than she had intended.

"Yes, you are very nearly over the hill, aren't you?" But John didn't allow her an opportunity to respond to his mocking observation. "Have a good time, honey."

"I will . . . and take care of yourself."

There was a tightness in her throat when Andrea hung up the phone. She refused to give in to the cold shiver of apprehension that ran down her spine. It was senseless to feel this odd depression. John wanted her to enjoy this holiday, and she really did need it.

In a flurry of activity, Andrea finished unpacking, bathed and changed. Skipping the standard sweater and jeans, she chose a camel-tan tunic and matching, wide-legged pants. A cream-colored silk blouse added a dressy touch to the outfit. She considered wearing the locket John had given her before deciding on a gold braided chain necklace. Her suede parka was the same camel shade as her outfit.

Outdoors, the mountain air sharply revived her appetite, reminding her that she had not eaten since late morning. Walking alone while everyone else was in pairs or groups, Andrea avoided the more crowded restaurants, choosing the steak place in the Olympic House where her solitary state might not be so noticeable. The last thing she wanted was to fend off some guy's advances the first night she was there.

Like nearly all the other eating establishments, the steak house was crowded. Andrea waited at the front entrance while the host seated the couple who had been ahead of her. She was vaguely aware of someone entering the restaurant and stopping behind her. Since she knew no one, Andrea didn't bother to glance around.

"Well, we meet again," a familiar voice said.

A startled look over her shoulder revealed the stranger she had seen at the desk who had aroused her curiosity for a moment. Well, hello, Mr. Stafford, she thought. The ski suit was gone, replaced by a white ribbed turtleneck sweater and a dark blazer. If anything, his looks were more arresting than before, especially in view of the sexy smile that softened his lean, chiseled features.

"Hello." Andrea inclined her dark blond head in acknowledgment.

"Have you settled in for the weekend?" She nearly explained to him that she would be staying a week, then decided it wasn't necessary.

"Yes, I have."

"Hi, Tell. How are you tonight?" The host approached, smiling widely at the man standing behind Andrea.

"Just fine, Kyle," the man answered.

"I have a table for the two of you right over here." The host started to walk away and Andrea realized that he assumed she was with Mr. Stafford.

She hastened to correct his error. "Excuse me, but we aren't together."

He halted, tilting his head curiously to the side while a bewildered expression crossed his face, his eyes darting from Andrea to the man next to her. "Do you mean you want two tables for one?"

Out of the corner of her eye she could see Tell Stafford wasn't going to help her out. He seemed to find her telling the host they were not together secretly amusing.

"Yes," she said.

"Two tables for one does sound a bit ridiculous," the man named Stafford said softly. "Would you join me for dinner? It would be a pleasure, I assure you."

Andrea hesitated. The restaurant was crowded and someone might recognize her eventually. But no matter what anyone might say, there was nothing wrong about sharing a table with this man.

"Yes, thank you." She smiled faintly.

Their host's smile mirrored an inner satisfaction as he led them to the table. He held the chair out for Andrea while Tell Stafford took the one opposite.

"I'm sorry," her dinner companion said after they had been left to study the menus. His hand reached across the table to her. "I neglected to introduce myself. Tell Stafford is the name, from San Francisco."

"Andrea Grant." The firm clasp of his handshake eased the tension she hadn't been aware existed until it left.

"From California?"

"No, Oregon, originally," she answered. "Everyone here seems to know you. You must come to Squaw Valley quite often, Mr. Stafford."

"Tell," he corrected, adding with persuasive insistence, "please. Actually, it's Tellman but everyone calls me Tell. May I call you Andrea?" At her nod of agreement, he continued, "I come to Squaw Valley as often as I can. But lately, not as often as I'd like to. I've just been too busy."

"Oh. What do you do?" she asked.

"My family owns a small chain of department stores in the Bay Area," Tell Stafford answered easily, but there was a faint narrowing of his eyes that suggested he was judging her reaction. "And what about you?"

Okay, he was related to a family that was probably wealthy but that didn't mean he was. She didn't have to be impressed. "I've been doing research on a novel, and typing it, too. The author is hopeless when it comes to computers. He writes everything in longhand." Why in the world had she told Tell that, Andrea asked herself. It was too late to retract it now. She had to let it stand.

"Who's the writer?"

Best to talk around that question. She didn't have to tell him everything. "The book hasn't actually been accepted yet. It's his first attempt at that length, but he does have a publisher interested in it," Andrea explained.

To her relief the waiter arrived to take their order.

She had barely had time to look at the menu, so she allowed Tell Stafford to make his recommendations.

"Wine?" he questioned after inquiring how she liked her steak.

"Nothing alcoholic, thank you. Milk, please," she told the waiter.

During the meal, the conversation shifted to general topics. Tell Stafford was very adept at what might be described as table talk, Andrea learned. He answered each question she put to him, yet when their coffee was served, she felt no nearer to discovering what there was about him that fascinated her. She would have been less than honest if she hadn't admitted that she found his dark looks attractive.

All in all, she'd picked up the basics about him yet knew nothing of substance. He was in his early thirties, unmarried, intelligent and possessed a keen sense of humor. His confidence seemed unshakable. They traded the basics of their life stories, and she noticed that he tended to mention his mother more than his father, when he mentioned them at all. She couldn't ignore the feeling that he had learned more about her than she had about him.

Oh, well. She could always look him up online. Tell—or Tellman—Stafford wasn't a common name. Whatever hits came up on Google would be about him. But . . . she hadn't brought her laptop, because she wasn't even going to pretend to work. She could use one of the computers in the hotel business center but what if he walked in?

"What's troubling you, Andrea?" He was leaning back in his chair.

Guiltily, her hazel eyes moved away from him,

aware that her thoughtful silence had stretched longer than she had realized. She started to deny that there was any basis for his question, then laughed and answered honestly. "We've been talking for almost an hour, yet I have the feeling that I don't know you at all."

"That makes two of us." Tell smiled and Andrea liked the way his eyes crinkled at the corners. "Since the first time I saw you in the lobby, I thought there was something different about you. I've finally come to the conclusion that you're not on the prowl."

"Uh, excuse me?" Andrea frowned with amusement.

"Maybe that was the wrong word. Sorry. I didn't mean to be rude to you." His dark eyes lit up when he looked at her, and she understood what he hadn't said. She'd noticed women glancing his way in the restaurant—it stood to reason that some would try to hit on him in the uninhibited atmosphere of a ski lodge. And the attention would ratchet up a lot higher as soon as they found out his family owned a few department stores.

"What I meant, Andrea, is that I like to do the hunting."

"I see." His explanation disconcerted her. It was one thing to view him as a man who aroused her curiosity. Only in a most abstract way did she want to look on him as a potential lover. "Well, whatever." She wanted to steer the conversation back to safer ground. "Let's talk about—what were we talking about?"

"Families. Yours and mine."

"Right. I noticed that you rarely mention your father. Is he alive?"

The corners of his mouth twisted upward, but it wasn't really a smile because it didn't reach his eyes.

"That's an astute observation. And the answer is no. My father was killed in a car accident when I was about ten. My mother has since remarried to a very understanding man. He and I are good friends."

"That's good." Andrea smiled brightly. "Sometimes there's resentment when a parent remarries."

"Jump right in. You're not shy, are you?"

Andrea regretted her attempt to analyze him. But he was intriguing, damn it.

Tell observed her for a long, thoughtful moment, studying the wary expression on her face. "Why do I get the impression that you're determined to keep a certain amount of distance between us? Or is that a nosy question?"

"Actually, yes." The waiter arrived with their check, enabling Andrea to avoid saying more. When she insisted on paying for her own meal, annoyance darkened his lean features.

Then, arching a black brow and managing a smile, Tell relented, accepting the money she handed him. They rose from the table at the same time.

"I'll walk you to the lodge," he stated.

"That isn't necessary," Andrea protested.

But one glance at the resolute line of his jaw told her that he was even more annoyed. She was beginning to sense that he was a man who knew what he wanted to do and did it. Oh, what the heck. She decided to indulge him. As if he had read her mind—or her body language—he took her elbow.

The night sky was still spitting snow, the tiny flakes making a light film on the sidewalk. The touch of his hand through her lined parka made her stiffen ever so slightly. She didn't mind that he was touching her, but she couldn't control her inadvertent response. Their silence seemed out of tune with the laughter and voices of the other skiers traversing the square.

"Were you very much in love with him?" The silence was shattered by his softly spoken question.

"Who?" Andrea stalled, glancing at Tell with false bewilderment. He *had* read her mind. The dark, knowing eyes were intelligent and understanding.

"The man who's made you so afraid of becoming involved again," he answered calmly and confidently.

Staring straight ahead, Andrea neither admitted nor denied his observation. His perception was unnerving. She wished now that she had never accepted his invitation to dine at his table.

"Okay, so you were in love with him," he concluded from her silence. "Was he married?"

There was anger in the glance she darted upward to his face, a resentment that he should want to get into a subject that was so obviously still painful. He met her look and returned it, letting Andrea see that he wouldn't be put off by her silence—he demanded a response.

"No, he wasn't married," she answered tightly. "We were engaged. A month before our wedding he decided he cared for someone else."

"When was this?"

A breeze swirled around the corner of a building, sending a light curl across her cheek. She pushed it from her face with impatient irritation.

"Three years ago," was her curt response.

"That's about the time you told me you lost your father," Tell remarked thoughtfully. "And your mother several months before that. The pain didn't seem to stop, did it?"

Keeping her chin at a defiant angle, Andrea vowed to reject any sympathy or pity from him. But she saw none in his tanned face as he reached past her to open the lodge door.

"It happens that way sometimes," he said, shrugging philosophically. "Got your keycard?"

"Uh-huh." Andrea produced it from her leather purse as his hand again touched her elbow.

"You mentioned that you and your parents came to Squaw Valley quite often in the winter. You must have a lot of happy memories here," he commented.

She almost breathed her relief aloud at the change of subject. It was strange the way the tables had turned. At dinner she had set out to find out about this tall stranger. Instead he was the one who was finding out about her private life.

"Yes, I do," she agreed.

At the door to her room, Tell Stafford took the key and unlocked the door, handing the key back to her after he had pushed the door open. "I haven't thanked you for sharing my table with me. I enjoyed your company."

He offered his hand and Andrea again felt the firm warmth of his grip. There was a dark sparkle in his gaze. She couldn't be certain, but she thought it was from amusement at the vaguely tense smile she gave him in return.

"Yes, thank you, Tell," she said stiffly.

"I'll probably see you somewhere on the slopes tomorrow," was his casual goodbye.

CHAPTER TWO

The end of her second run down Bailey's Beach, Andrea recognized the ski-suited man waiting on the bottom. Sun goggles concealed the direction of Tell Stafford's gaze but he raised a ski pole in greeting as she approached.

In a way, she hadn't expected him to seek her out today, not after their odd encounter last night. Not that it mattered, she told herself. She wasn't interested in him or anyone as a romantic companion for her holiday. But there was a traitorous burst of warmth in her veins at the smile that flashed across the masculine mouth.

"Ready to leave the gentler slopes behind for something more demanding?" he challenged as she stopped beside him.

"What did you have in mind?" The breathy catch to her voice was caused by the high altitude, Andrea told herself.

"Are you up to KT-22?"

"I think so," she said, nodding.

"Let's go." Tell dug his poles into the snow and

pushed off toward the chairlift that would take them to the famous Olympic hill.

It was a test of mettle that required a complete recall of all her former skill to keep up with Tell's slicing skis. She had guessed that he was an expert skier, but she had expected him to consider the years since her last time on skis and choose a route accordingly. He spared neither himself nor her.

The exhilaration that accompanied the successful completion of the run was beyond anything Andrea had experienced. Her senses were vibrantly alive to everything around her. It was like awakening after a long, troubled sleep and finding a fresh new world. She didn't need a second invitation to return up the slopes.

By the end of the afternoon, Andrea was happily exhausted. She had taken a couple of tumbles and knew there would probably be bruises, as well as stiff muscles, making themselves felt by morning but she couldn't remember when she had felt so complete and whole.

"I'll give you an hour in the tub to soak out the soreness and another half an hour to dress," Tell stated with that smile that had added to the bewitching spell of the afternoon, "then I'll expect you in the lobby. No more time than that, because I'm starving."

"I'll be there," she promised as they parted in the hallway, Andrea walking toward her room and Tell to his.

Not until she was lazing in a tubful of soothing bubbles did she realize that she had agreed to dine with him. Ignoring an inner warning that said he was likely to drive her crazy sooner or later, she sighed contentedly. Except for that one moment last night, she had enjoyed his company. Maybe she needed what he so obviously had to offer.

She was beginning to feel alive again and it wasn't as frightening as she had thought. In fact, it was a wonderful feeling, she decided, picking up a handful of bubbles and blowing them into the air.

There was no harm in indulging in a vacation flirtation. Why shouldn't she? Andrea argued silently. True, she hadn't come with that in mind, but where would she ever find a better man for that particular pleasure than Tell Stafford? He was good-looking, fun, maybe too worldly for her, but it would be exciting. She had lived on the fringe of life for three years. It was her turn to enjoy it.

In this faintly euphoric state where nothing could possibly go wrong, Andrea dressed for her date with Tell. A date . . . even that word brought a smile. She hadn't had a date in years. A glow of excitement radiated from within as she hurried to the lobby to meet Tell.

When his dark gaze ran admiringly over her well-toned curves, she felt a surge of satisfaction for getting through all those workouts. Part of the healing process had been her determination to care for herself and it had paid off. Her clothes really fit and the warm tones she'd chosen suited her coloring. Minus the wariness that had held her distant the night before, Andrea found herself willingly following his lead. The lightest touch sent new fires of life through her system.

After eating at one of the more informal spots, Tell didn't take her back to the lodge. "Will your legs take a couple of hours of dancing, or are you too sore?" There was a spark of laughter in his eyes as he looked down at her.

"I don't feel tired," Andrea admitted, "although I can't say how coordinated my legs will be. I can't remember how long it's been since I had as much exercise as I did this afternoon."

His arm slipped around her shoulders as he turned her into one of the lounges. "We probably should have called it a day earlier."

"I'm not complaining." She shook her head firmly and smiled. "I wouldn't have changed anything today. It was all good. The skiing was fantastic."

"I thought it was, too." There was a promise of something else in his low, husky voice.

Somehow, Tell succeeded in finding an empty table in one corner of the crowded lounge. The possessive touch of his hands on her shoulders kept her firmly in front of him, making certain that they weren't accidentally separated in the jostling group of people. A bearded waiter in a ski sweater was at their table within seconds.

"What'll you have?" the waiter asked with a faintly impatient look.

"A Coke," Andrea responded quickly.

"A Coke and what, lady?" the waiter asked, the line of his mouth thinning out. The rude reply earned him a freezing stare from Tell and the other man quickly dropped the attitude.

"A plain Coke. Nothing else," she explained.

With a raised eyebrow he turned to Tell. "And you?"

"Scotch and water." As the waiter departed, Tell let his lazy, contemplative gaze swing to Andrea. "You actually don't drink, do you?"

"It's an acquired taste. I simply haven't acquired it." There was a defensive shrug to her shoulders.

"And I'm not really interested in trying. I'd rather get high on a Sierra sunset."

"There's no need to be embarrassed about it," Tell said gently.

"I'm not . . ." Then Andrea smiled at herself and nodded ruefully at him. "I suppose I am self-conscious about it."

"And defensive." His mouth quirked.

"And defensive," she admitted with a laugh.

The fingers of one hand had been nervously twirling the ashtray in the center of the small round table. Tell leaned forward, stopping the action as he covered her hand with his.

"Then stop it," he commanded softly.

The warmth of his hand traveled up her arm and down her spine, melting the stiffness with which she had been holding herself. His dark eyes held her gaze. At the moment, the pull of his virile attraction was more heady than any drink could have been. Then the waiter arrived with their drinks and her hand was released as Tell sat back in his chair.

The disturbed cadence of her heart refused to return to normal. Andrea was glad for the distraction of having something to drink. It was one thing to respond to his attention and quite another to be carried away by it.

"Hey, Tell, how are you?" A voice broke into the silence as a hand clasped Tell's shoulder in greeting.

There was a scrape of a chair leg and a tall, slim man sat himself down at their table. His face was bronzed to a teak shade by the winter sun and his hair was bleached a wheat gold.

"Hello, Chris." Tell's mouth curved upward, a cynical hardness deepening the grooves in his cheeks. "Why don't you join us?" he mocked.

"You know me, Tell," the man returned, his blue gaze turning to Andrea, "I never wait for an invitation. I haven't seen you around before, have I, beautiful?"

"You're slowing down, Chris. She arrived yesterday." The coolness in Tell's voice surprised Andrea and she returned the stranger's look warily, darting a questioning glance at Tell. "Andrea, this is Chris Christiansen, one of the ski instructors here. Andrea Grant," he introduced.

"Andrea," the man repeated. "I love that name. How about a dance?"

"She's with me," Tell said firmly before Andrea had a chance to answer.

Chris gave Tell a measured look, then directed his admiring blue gaze at Andrea. "Is that right?" Chris asked.

"Yes, that's right," she replied evenly, completely unmoved by his attention, but a warmth radiated through her when Tell's dark gaze burned over her.

"Well—" Chris gave a sighing shrug as he rose to his feet, still gazing down at her "—if you change your mind and decide you want a different teacher, I'm always around. See you, Tell."

As he disappeared into the crowd, Andrea's hand was taken and she was pulled to her feet as Tell rose. "Let's dance," he ordered, a tightness in his brief smile.

They were barely on the small dance floor before he brought her into his arms. There was little room to maneuver in the crowded area. Held closely against him, Andrea didn't object to the crush. She enjoyed his embrace, noticing the broad shoulders on which she could rest her head. But she didn't submit to that pleasure immediately.

Tilting her head back, she gazed at the uncompromising set of his mouth inches above her. "I didn't know you taught skiing," she murmured curiously.

"What?" Tell frowned.

"Chris said if I wanted another teacher . . ." Andrea started to explain.

A low chuckle came from his throat, tiny lines crinkling the corners of his eyes. "He was referring to love, not skiing."

Andrea self-consciously bit her lower lip and stared at the blue cashmere pullover rather than at the face of its wearer. "I didn't understand."

"I'm glad." The arm around her waist tightened as he gently nuzzled the side of her dark blond hair. She didn't feel foolish anymore for not catching the implication of the man's statement.

It was difficult to leave the intoxicating circle of his arms when the song ended. Her awareness of him physically was increasing with each passing minute. Her voice automatically responded to his conversation, but her thoughts were strictly of him, wondering if he too felt the way that she did when he touched her or held her. Probably not, she decided wistfully.

This was only a flirtation—with the possibility of becoming a wonderful fling—but no more than an enjoyable way of passing the time. Tell found her physically attractive, but that was as far as this was going to go.

Andrea had already decided to have no regrets. Under the circumstances, it was the best thing. At the very least, her instant attraction to Tell had shocked her into thinking about how the past was weighing her down. Maybe she would never love again as completely and innocently as she had loved Dale, but she was certain now that she didn't want to keep love out of the rest of her life. John would be so glad to hear that, she thought.

"Are you falling asleep on me?" Tell tipped his head back to gaze into her face.

"No, just thinking," Andrea murmured, smiling lazily at his chiseled, handsome face.

"It's late. You must be exhausted." The song ended and Tell pointed her toward the door. "I'd better take you back to the lodge."

They did not hurry their steps. Reluctantly, Andrea searched for her keycard, unwilling to have the magic day end. As he had the night before, like a perfect gentleman, Tell opened the door and handed the keycard back to her. She couldn't bring herself to say good night. Gazing at him, Andrea wasn't aware of the slight pressure of his hands that drew her into his arms. It seemed that she went of her own volition.

Pliantly, she yielded to his probing kiss. There was hunger in her response. Her fingers curled into the raven smoothness of his hair. Immediately, his mouth became hard and demanding against hers. Then she felt the undertow of desire sweeping away her control.

While she still had the will, Andrea turned her mouth away from his. The fires were not so easily banked as he buried his head in the soft curve of her neck. She moaned softly, really not wanting to protest. What he was doing felt good—very, very good. But even for the zero-to-sixty speed of an honest-to-God fling, this was a little fast.

"Tell, please," she whispered.

"Invite me in for coffee," he demanded hoarsely, nibbling sharply at the lobe of her ear.

"I don't think so," Andrea said, exhaling with shaky slowness.

Taking a deep breath, Tell slowly lifted his head, cupping her face with his hands. The sensually masculine mouth curved into a rueful smile.

"Do I have to accept that no?" he mused rhetorically.

"Yes. But I bet you don't hear it often." She smiled weakly, knowing with a flash of intuition that she was right.

"You're dangerous, Andrea." He didn't look exactly scared.

"Me?" she laughed in disbelief. At this moment she felt completely under his domination.

"Yes. I can't make up my mind if you're slipping away from me or closing in," Tell said evenly. Andrea shot him a puzzled look. "I'm sorry," he sighed, brushing a dark golden curl behind her ear. "A woman like you—well, I can't help being wary."

"Wary of what?" Her tone was annoyed. She was hardly a femme fatale.

"Never mind. What time are you leaving tomorrow?"

"For where?" Her hazel eyes widened in bewilderment.

"For wherever it is that you live in Oregon?" He gave her an oh-so-polite smile.

"I'm not leaving tomorrow; not until Friday morning," she told him, remembering how she had let him believe that first night that she would only be at Squaw Valley for the weekend.

"Why didn't you tell me?" His gaze narrowed a bit.

"At the time," Andrea wavered, not sure what he was getting at. "At the time, it didn't seem important. I didn't even really know you."

"No," Tell agreed. A teasing gleam in his eyes revealed a mercurial change of mood. "I was just some guy you didn't know. You can be cool, Andrea." He tantalizingly brushed his hard male mouth against her lips. "And very warm, too. Have breakfast with me tomorrow? I'll call you around seven."

"Uh—okay." Not a very gracious response, but his invitation had sounded more like an order. Andrea wondered why she'd accepted it anyway. He wished her good night, placed a firm kiss on her mouth and turned away. "Tell?" she called to him hesitantly. He stopped a few steps away but didn't walk back. "When are you leaving?"

"I don't have to be back until Wednesday," he told her. "That doesn't give us very much time, does it?"

He gave her a seriously thoughtful look, then he turned and walked away. This time she didn't call him back.

So Wednesday morning he would go out of her life. So long as she understood that, Andrea told herself, it would be pointless to get depressed about it. This was only a fling. The more she repeated that, the larger her doubts loomed.

The vague depression vanished with the sound of Tell's voice on the phone the next morning. There was no time to feel blue. Blue was the color of the Sierra sky. There was too much perfection in the day for Andrea to worry about the "maybe" of tomorrow.

The sun was a gigantic gold nugget suspended above the Mother Lode country and the granite majesty of the Sierra Nevada range. The sky was a brilliant, cloudless blue, casting pastel shadows on the pure white snow of the mountains and valleys. Near the summit of Squaw Peak, the sapphire blue of Lake Tahoe, the Indians' Lake-in-the-Sky, could be seen ringed by white mountains.

Not even the other skiers on the slopes could disturb the enchanted circle that had drawn Andrea and Tell together. They jointly stretched out each moment, taking their time going down the slopes and eating a late lunch at the restaurant at the top of the chairlift. In the late afternoon, they sat in front of a fireplace and laughed as Tell tried to teach Andrea to play backgammon, ultimately with some success.

But again the precious seconds of the day slipped by. They were in the hallway outside her room, a midnight sky sparkling with stars over the roof of the lodge. There was no mention of coffee or when the other would be leaving. Yet for Andrea, the sense of lost time was there, adding an urgency to the embrace they shared.

When he had left, it was the mirror in her room that brought Andrea crashing back to reality. The soft radiance she saw in her reflection made her catch her breath. Her lips were slightly swollen by the frustrated passion of Tell's kisses, bruising in their mastery. A haunted look replaced the jade sparkle in her hazel eyes.

So you thought you could handle a holiday flirtation. Her mirror image had a mocking look. *You were so confident that it would be fun and exciting and end with no regrets.*

"That's the way it will be," Andrea whispered, choked by the lump in her throat.

Then why was she falling in love with him even though she knew better? And why hadn't she told him the truth about herself? Andrea gave a miserable sigh. She didn't want to think what his opinion of her would be when he found out. Oh, she was a fool. No doubt about it.

Closing her eyes tightly in pain, she turned away from the mirror, knowing that when she opened them nothing would have changed. The truth would be still staring her in the face. *What goes up, must come down,* she laughed bitterly. And she had been feeling so high, foolishly thinking that she still had her feet on the ground.

Tell the truth. Wait. Tell the truth. Wait. The two thoughts hammered in her mind, the pounding dilemma making her sleep fitful and plagued with nightmares. She was no nearer to a decision with the rising of the sun.

Once in Tell's presence, the little courage she had mustered vanished over the breakfast table. She couldn't tell him. Andrea wanted another day of happiness in her grasp. It didn't do any good to tell herself that she was not only a fool but selfish as well. So she waited.

"I've made reservations for one of the dinner shows at the casino tonight," Tell told her as they checked in their skis after an afternoon run. "I hope you brought along something halfway formal to wear. If not, we'll run into town and buy something."

"No, I . . . I have a dress," Andrea assured him quickly. The prospect of Tell helping to pick out a gown was more painful than pleasing. "What time?"

"Six?" He glanced inquiringly at her, a sensual light in his dark eyes as he reached around her to open the lodge door. "Can you be ready by then?"

"Easily," she said, smiling as she walked with him, passing by the desk.

"You have a message, miss," the clerk called, waving a slip of paper at her. "He called about half an hour ago and didn't want to be put through to voicemail."

Without looking at it, Andrea shoved the message in the pocket of her jacket. She glanced at Tell, absently noticing the glistening of the overhead light on the raven sheen of Tell's black hair as he looked her way.

"He? Hmm. Aren't you even going to see who it's from?" he asked curiously.

Self-consciously, she took it from her pocket. She had already guessed it was from John. She had thoughtlessly not called him as she had promised.

"It's . . . it's just from John." She shrugged nervously, trying to indicate that it wasn't important.

"And who is John? A boyfriend you have in Oregon? Is that it?" Tell asked lightly.

"He isn't a boyfriend." Andrea breathed in deeply. The message clutched in her hand could be the means to begin telling him the truth.

A slow smile began to curve his mouth. "He's the writer you've been working for, isn't he?" At her faint nod, he reached out and took the paper from her fingers. "A message from an employer invariably is a call back to work."

"Tell!" she gasped, recovering from her stunned surprise and reaching out to take back the message. But he easily eluded her attempt.

"If you didn't receive the message, then you don't know he called. And you won't have to go back to work." Deliberately, he tore the paper into tiny bits and tossed it into a nearby wastebasket.

"You shouldn't have done that. What if he calls the desk again and gets the same clerk?"

Tell shook his head. "He won't. Not right away. That would be too bossy."

"You're outrageous," Andrea breathed, her gaze swinging from the metal basket to meet his glittering gaze. "But I'm glad you did that."

"If you're going to be ready by six," he glanced at his gold wristwatch, "you'd better get started."

"I'll be ready and waiting," she promised.

Three times in her room, she picked up the telephone to call John, but each time she replaced the receiver. Andrea couldn't understand her own hesitancy. She felt a slight premonition that the next time she heard John's voice, the walls would come crashing down around her. It was a crazy sensation, but she couldn't overcome it. And the knowledge that she was meeting Tell at six easily allowed her to put off calling until the next day.

The road followed the twisting, turning shoreline of Lake Tahoe, its jewel colors hidden by a coat of black satin that matched the night sky. Tall pines stretched upward on the forested slopes of the mountains, their green limbs cloaked in white snow. A smattering of stars winked in the sky waiting for the moon to make its entrance.

The show they were attending was at one of the casinos on the south shore of Lake Tahoe, naturally on the Nevada side. Their circuitous route on the snow-packed, curving road took more time than the miles indicated, but Andrea didn't mind. It was the first time she and Tell had been truly alone and she enjoyed the quiet intimacy they shared as they rode along in the car.

As if by mutual consent, they talked of routine

things: the weather, the scenery, and skiing. Sometimes, they said nothing at all. It was a disappointment to Andrea when the lights of the casinos blinked their neon colors in front of them. She hadn't wanted the drive to end yet.

Inside the plush, garishly decorated gambling casino, the din of the slot machines was neverending, increased by the voices of the players at the tables. It seemed crowded to her, but Tell said it wasn't. The seating had begun for the dinner show, so he promised to take her around the casino afterward since this was her first visit. She enjoyed the name entertainment, but she was more conscious of the arm lying naturally around her shoulders than the songs being sung on the stage.

Afterward, as Tell had promised, he took her around the various gaming tables. Under his tutelage, she placed a bet at the wheel of fortune and won, with the same result at the roulette wheel. At the dice tables, the action was too swift for her to follow, so it was Tell who placed the bet and won. His luck remained the same at the twenty-one tables. This time he let his winnings ride and the stack of chips kept increasing. Finally, when he reached the table limit, he cashed in his chips with a frown.

"What's wrong?" Andrea questioned, studying the uncompromising set of his expression.

Dark eyes bored into her for a moment before his expression softened. "I just discovered I was superstitious," Tell replied, circling her waist with his arm and turning her away from the tables.

"Superstitious about what?" She laughed softly.

"Lucky at cards, unlucky in love."

A blush heated her face and her heart skipped a few beats, but she didn't say anything to that.

"We haven't lost a bet tonight. I would rather have lost it all," Tell murmured thoughtfully. His words brought the haunted look back to her wide hazel eyes. "I didn't mean to frighten you. There's nothing to that old saying anyway," he said in an amused voice. "Now, where would you like to go next? Want to try the slot machines?"

"I'd like to leave," Andrea replied quickly.

"Because of what I said?" There was a flash of regret in the depths of his eyes.

"Partly," she admitted. Her gaze fell away from his tanned face, knowing the other reason was the steadily gnawing fear that had begun the night before. But she tried to make light of it. "And partly because the noise is getting to me—I have an awful headache."

He nodded in understanding and turned toward the exit door. They didn't speak again until they had left behind the lights of the motel and residential district on the south shore. Then Tell reached over and took her hand, clasping it warmly in his.

"You're much too far away," he sighed. "Remind me not to buy another car with bucket seats."

Andrea bit at her lip to keep her emotions under control. "I'll remember," she agreed with pseudo brightness.

"My mother called me before we left tonight about a directors' meeting that had been changed."

"You . . . you don't have to leave sooner, do you?" She held her breath.

"Mother wanted me to come back tomorrow so I could be prepared for the new Wednesday meeting, but I told her that it was out of the question."

There was a sliding smile in her direction before he returned his attention to the road. "She wanted to know if you were very beautiful. Of course, I quickly corrected that statement." The dimple in his cheek deepened with concealed amusement.

"Thanks a lot," Andrea said, laughing, a warm glow spreading through her once more.

"I told her you were the most beautiful woman in the world," Tell informed her in a frighteningly serious voice.

"Tell!" she whispered, stunned by the vibrancy of his statement.

"Are you going to argue with me?" His challenge was issued in a laughing voice.

"I wouldn't dream of it," she said, her voice trembling.

A car came sweeping around the bend in front of them, taking the curve too wide and forcing Tell onto the shoulder to avoid being sideswiped. The snowplows had mounded the snow on the sides of the road. For several yards their car skimmed the side of the snowbanks before the rear tires hit a soft patch and they were stuck.

"Are you all right?" His mouth was forbiddingly grim and anger burned in his eyes.

"I'm fine," Andrea breathed, a weak smile of reassurance curving her full mouth.

Tell nodded thankfully and shifted the car into gear again, but the rear wheels spun, unable to get any traction in the snow. A hard smile lifted one corner of his mouth.

"Thanks to that idiot, we're stuck in the snow!" he snapped, slipping the gear into neutral and reaching for his door handle.

"I wouldn't mind being stuck in a snowbank with

you forever." What had been meant as a flippant remark came out as a throbbing pledge of love.

The dark head jerked around toward her. "You picked a damned awkward time to say something like that," Tell muttered savagely, but despite the harshness of his low voice, she knew it was without anger.

He seemed to release her gaze reluctantly as he opened the car door, cold mountain air rushing in before the door was slammed shut. The rear trunk was opened, followed shortly by sounds of a shovel digging away the snow near the rear tires. The trunk lid was closed and Tell was sliding behind the wheel again. After rocking back and forth a few times, the tires finally gripped and the car pulled onto the road.

Chapter Three

Several miles from the spot where they had been forced off the road, Tell turned the car onto a side road and switched off the engine. Andrea's heart was doing somersaults as she watched him remove his winter coat and toss it into the back seat. With deliberation marking his movements, he turned in the seat toward her and began slowly unbuttoning her winter coat. In a few seconds, her coat had joined his in the rear seat.

Andrea didn't resist the pressure of his hands burning through the black chiffon sleeves of her dress as he pulled her across his lap and cradled her against his chest. The fingers of one hand lightly caressed her cheek.

"Now, tell me again what you said earlier," he commanded.

"I said," she whispered lovingly, "that I would be happy to be stuck in a snowbank with you forever. Sounds kind of goofy, but it's true."

Kissing first the corner of her eye, then her nose and cheek, he finally reached her lips. "Now, tell me what you really meant by that," he ordered.

"No," Andrea moaned softly, pressing her throbbing mouth against the resistance of his. Still he refused to let her feel the fire of his kiss.

"Say it," he growled huskily. "I have to know that you love me as much as I love you."

Breathing in sharply, she was no longer afraid to put her feelings into words. "I love you, Tell. I love you." There. The words rushed out before she had a chance to think about the consequences.

Fiercely possessive, his mouth closed over hers. It was a kiss more wild and glorious than any they had ever shared. The blood pounded through her veins with the wonder of it. His hands were roughly caressing her, crushing her against him, unaware of the strength he was using. With a supreme effort, Tell dragged his mouth away from hers, his lean fingers burying her face against his chest, his heart pounding, his breathing ragged and uneven.

"The first time I saw you registering at the desk, I thought you were a beautiful woman and nothing more," he muttered against the silken curtain of her hair. "When you were there at the restaurant, I thought you'd followed me to attract my attention. The desk clerk who handled my reservation was checking you out, you know. He would have been happy to tell you anything you wanted to know. Anyway, once I saw you I asked you to dine with me more or less for the hell of it."

"How romantic." She didn't believe him. He didn't want to admit to being interested in someone so soon, that was all. Everything she needed to know about him was in his kisses and he put everything he had into those.

He smoothed her hair. "I did want to find out what you were all about. But whenever the conversation got a little personal, you seemed so . . . so vulnerable. There was only one logical conclusion: another man had made you wary. So I told myself that it was self-pity and you would get over the hurt in time."

"I was over it." Her hands caressed the strong column of his neck. "I was simply afraid."

"I didn't intend to catch up with you," he sighed. "Then I saw you coming down Bailey's Beach. You were so damn graceful," his hand stroked the length of her thigh, "with those long legs in that tight ski suit. I don't know if it was the white backdrop of snow or what, but I suddenly pictured you against white sheets lying naked in my arms. I never wanted any woman as much as I wanted you at that moment."

"Wow. I sound fabulous."

"You are, Andrea." His voice was low and serious. "So deciding to seduce you took me about five seconds."

"Determined, hmm?"

"You know I am. And I was stupid enough to think that once I had you, the physical attraction would be enough."

Andrea frowned into his shirt collar. "It's never enough," she whispered. The hand holding the back of her head refused to let her draw away from his chest to look into his face.

He burned a kiss against her temple. "Not with you. When Chris showed up at the bar, everything went haywire. I've never been jealous in my life, but if he'd touched you, however innocently, I would have bashed his face in. He's too freakin' handsome for his own good."

"Was he handsome?" She smiled and nuzzled his throat.

"Like you didn't notice," Tell said, laughing, lifting his head to gaze into her face, soft and radiant. "I still don't know why I let you say no to me that night. I knew I could have persuaded you to change your mind, but I didn't try. Maybe because I wanted it to mean as much to you as it would to me. I think that's when I silently admitted that there was a very good possibility that I was falling in love with you. Boom. Just like that."

She took a deep breath, trying to think of something to say, and ended with a heartfelt sigh that took the place of mere words.

"Andrea—" his expression grew serious "—in the past, I've thought I was on the brink of loving a woman and I've made love to many, but I've never told anyone that I loved them. You do believe me, don't you?"

"I believe you," she murmured with a poignant ache in her heart. "But I still think I shouldn't."

"Hey, we *are* going to give this time," he said huskily. "I'm not that crazy. But you do seem like a dream come true to me."

"Oh God," her voice caught on a sob, "falling in love with you was just too damn easy. Something's got to go wrong."

"Not necessarily. It doesn't always happen that way. Whoever left you was a fool," he spoke against her lips. "But I'm glad he was a fool."

"What I felt for Dale was different—so different. Nothing like what I feel for you, Tell," Andrea declared throatily. "I love—"

His mouth absorbed the rest of her words, bringing an end to the talking. Her lips parted readily under his passionately exploring kiss, and rippling muscles beneath his dark evening suit molded her ever closer to the hardness of his body. The powerful desire that raged through her was just plain awesome.

The expertise and mastery of his touch made simple physical contact incredibly intense. The suddenness of their love made them hungry for each other, as they strained at the physical restrictions that kept them apart. Working quickly, she undid his tie and opened the collar of his shirt. Beneath her hands, his naked chest felt almost burning hot and his heartbeat pounded against her fingers.

"I want you," Tell muttered, claiming her lips again.

Andrea shuddered. "Yes." The answer was an acknowledgment of his need and her own.

"You're trembling." The low pitch of his voice vibrated over her, increasing the tremors.

"I'm afraid," she breathed shakily.

His dark head raised a fraction of an inch, a frown knitting his smooth forehead. "Of me?" he questioned in mocking disbelief.

"I've never been with a man before. I don't want to disappoint you, Tell."

The significance of her whispered statement took a few seconds to sink in. When it did, he became rigidly still, then his fingers curled into the tender flesh of her upper arm and she was lifted and set away, out of his embrace.

"Tell, I do love you." She reached out hesitantly to touch him, balanced and swaying toward him in the passenger seat.

The knuckles of his brown fingers were turning white as he gripped the steering wheel, head bowed. "I know." He breathed in deeply. "Same here, crazy as it is. And I do want you. But not in a car. Damn, what was I thinking . . . just stay there," he ordered crisply, holding up a warning hand as she leaned toward him.

The self-control he was showing kept Andrea in her seat, a glow of happiness shining through her awareness that his concern was first for her pleasure and not his own. He must be for real if he would deny himself what he so obviously wanted. She didn't try to talk him into or out of anything as Tell started the car and returned to the main road. The silence during the rest of the drive to the lodge was emotionally charged, yet infinitely satisfying because of its cause.

When Tell unlocked the door to her room, he held on to the keycard for an instant. Then he suddenly handed it to her. His tense, slightly trembling fingers touched her cheek as Andrea stared at him.

Leaning down, he lightly brushed her lips. "Good night, my love." Then he was striding down the hall away from her.

In a dreamlike state, Andrea changed into her nightclothes. She was filled with the rapturous sensation of shared emotion. As sudden as it all was, she had never felt more loved and wanted in her life. And Tell loved her with an unselfishness that she hadn't believed a man was capable of feeling. It made him all the more precious to her.

When her head touched the pillow, the self-doubt rushed back. She hadn't told him much. How much would he love her when he found out the truth about her?

"I'll tell him in the morning." Andrea whispered her promise aloud. As crazy as this was, he cared for her. He would understand, she knew he would. The feeling was just too intense. It couldn't be any other way. He had said they would give this time, she knew they had to get to know each other, but that incredible feeling wasn't going to go away. It just couldn't.

Love at first sight was as dizzying as a downhill race. But just as when she'd seen him on her first day on the slopes, he was going to be there for her. Tell had declared his love, and whatever happened next . . . she would have to let go and let God, put it that way. Andrea had made a lot of decisions in her life that had seemed oh-so-reasonable at the time. Loving Dale had been one. She'd imagined being secure in that relationship, and, being immature, had expected to find lasting happiness in it. Chalk it up to her own naivete. Then, sledgehammered by the profound grief of losing both her parents, she'd made a few more decisions she regretted just as much.

But hey—wasn't there a statute of limitations on making mistakes that, when all was said and done, hurt only herself? It could be argued that she'd had a partner in that particular crime, but even so . . . John had been insisting lately that she ought to forgive herself and move on, but she hadn't really listened.

Then came Tell. Like a bolt from the blue, he'd shocked her back into full awareness of what it meant to be alive, as opposed to merely existing. His kiss, as real and as highly sensual as it was, had worked like one in a fairytale. His love . . . well, that might lead to a future she couldn't even have imagined a week ago. She hardly dared to dream about it but she drifted off to sleep.

It was late morning before she finally opened her eyes. The heady memory of the night before made her hug her arms around herself to keep the wild joy from bursting her heart.

Since Tell hadn't called, Andrea decided he was

probably waiting in the lobby for her, thoughtfully letting her sleep in. Laying out clothes on the bed, she quickly stepped under the stinging shower spray to wash the sleepiness from her face and body. After the hurried shower, she pulled on a short terry cloth robe, forgoing her regular makeup in favor of moisturizing cream, a little eyeshadow and lipstick.

Running a quick brush over her windblown hairstyle, she noticed the ends of her dark blond hair were tipped with gold from the hours spent in the snow and the sun. It was a nice effect, she decided, and wondered if Tell liked it. The knock on the door sent her floating to answer it. Her heart was already saying that Tell was on the other side.

"Good morning." He was leaning against the door frame, his dark eyes raking her from her brushed hair to her bare toes.

"Good morning," she answered breathlessly.

Then Tell was laughing softly, stepping into the room, closing the door behind him and sweeping her into his arms. With hard, demanding kisses he again staked his ownership of her love and she acknowledged his claim readily.

"You shouldn't have let me sleep late," she protested.

Her senses were filled with the intoxicating aroma from his smoothly shaven cheeks and the heady scent of his maleness.

"I had a lot of very important things to do." His mouth explored the hollow of her throat, sending tingles down her spine where his hands were roughly caressing her back and hips. "And—" He breathed in deeply, dragging his hands from their arousing task to close over her wrists, which were wound tightly around his neck. He pulled them away and forced Andrea to stand free. "If you don't stop trying to seduce me, I'll forget why I came here."

"You didn't come to see me," Andrea teased.

"I didn't intend to see so much of you." His amorous gaze moved over the short terry robe and the length of leg it exposed. "Go get some clothes on while I can still think rationally and I'll tell you what we're going to do."

Andrea started for her bed, pausing near the stairs to smile back at him. "What are we going to do?" she asked. "I mean, I have stuff that I intended to wear, but—"

"Just get some clothes on." His smile thinned slightly as a dark fire leaped into his gaze. "And when you're finished with that, you can start packing."

"Packing?" she repeated, turning all the way around to face him, her back to the stairs.

"That's what I said," Tell answered, walking to her almost with reluctance. He placed his hands lightly on her shoulders as if to keep a safe distance between them. "We're driving back to San Francisco as soon as you're ready. I want you to meet my family and my friends. Mother has invited you to stay with us, so it's all arranged."

"Tell—" Andrea began.

"I don't want you out of my sight," he interrupted firmly. "I wouldn't be able to stand having you in Oregon while I was in San Francisco." He turned her around and pointed her toward the stairs. "So get going."

"Wait." She resisted his efforts, taking two steps up the stairs before pivoting again. "First there's something I have to tell you."

"Whatever it is—" he shook his head patiently "—can wait until we're on our way. The drive takes three hours, more or less. We can do plenty of talking on the way."

"No." Andrea was insistent. She would not put off telling him the truth any longer. "I have to explain to you before we go. I should have told you before. I meant to, but—"

"Let me guess," he said jokingly. "You're a participant in a reality show? You're really a man? No to both questions, right? If it's waited this long, it can wait a little longer."

"Tell, it can't wait. The longer I put it off, the harder it will be to explain so you'll understand."

"Andrea." Eager as he was, his patience was fraying. The ring of the telephone pierced the room, and he pivoted toward it. "I'll answer that while you get ready," he stated crisply. "If it's your employer, can I say that you're quitting and won't be back? Just kidding. I'm not quite that arrogant."

For an instant, Andrea was incapable of reaction; sheer nervousness rooted her to the spot she stood in for several critical seconds. By the time she snapped out of it, Tell had reached the phone.

"Tell, no!" she cried as he picked up the receiver. "Give me the phone, please!"

"I'm going to be charming, trust me." His hand covered the mouthpiece. "Go and get dressed and start packing," he ordered, then removed his hand from the receiver. "Hello."

Biting into her lip, she could barely hear the male voice responding on the other end of the wire. It was John, of course. She knew it even though she could hardly hear the voice well enough to recognize it. He was the only one who would call her. It was too late wishing that she had phoned him yesterday. Her frightened gaze became fixed on Tell's face.

"Yes," he said in answer to a question put to him by the caller. "Who's calling, please?"

There was a fraction of a second's pause before his gaze, darkening to black, swung slowly to Andrea, intent and cold. His lean, handsome features turned to impenetrable granite as he held the receiver to her. "It's your husband." The ice in his voice made her shake.

Her hand clutched the opening of her robe, trying to check her rising nausea. Despair clouded her eyes as her trembling fingers accepted the receiver. Her lashes fluttered tightly down when Tell spun away, rigid strides carrying him to the window of her room.

Twice Andrea opened her mouth before any sound came out. "Hello."

"Andrea? Is that you? Are you all right?" John's anxious, puzzled voice answered her immediately.

"Yes, yes, I'm fine," she responded, wishing the floor would open and swallow her up.

"I phoned yesterday and left a message. When you didn't call I became worried."

"I . . . I was out . . . most of the day," she faltered. Her tongue nervously moistened her lips; her tear-filled gaze turned toward the ceiling as she tried to breathe through the pain in her chest. "It was too late to phone when I came in last night."

"You were out last night?" he repeated.

"Yes."

"With the . . . man who answered the phone?"

"Yes." Her voice broke. She closed her eyes tightly. A tear slipped from her lashes and she roughly brushed it from her cheek.

There was hesitation on the other end before John spoke. "Did you—Andrea, did you tell him about me yet?"

She swallowed hard. "No."

"Oh, honey," John sighed heavily. "What have you done to yourself this time?"

"I don't know." A brittle, soft laugh accompanied her words. It was either that or cry.

"It's my fault. It's all my fault," he murmured.

"Don't—don't say that," she protested.

John breathed in deeply. "Call me when you can. I'm sorry, Andie, I didn't mean to spoil anything."

"Yes, I am, too. Goodbye."

A deadly quiet filled the room after the receiver clicked on the hook.

Wishing she could run rather than face Tell's coldly accusing eyes, Andrea slowly turned to him, or rather to his back. He was staring out of the window. There was no sound but the beating of her heart.

The distance between them was more than just physical, but her hesitant steps tried to bridge it. She stopped herself a foot or so behind him.

"That's what I wanted to explain to you, Tell," she began nervously. "I . . . I know it was a terrible shock for you to find out that way and I know I deceived you by not telling you the truth before, but, Tell, I was going to. I know how it must look, but . . ." Her voice cracked with a sob she couldn't control. "Hey, I really do love you," she pleaded for his understanding. "And—"

He whirled around, the flat of his hand slamming into the wall near him. A framed picture fell off and the glass shattered when it hit the floor. The noise of the impact startled her and sent her reeling backward, the impetus stopped by the hands that reached out to catch her. Remorse flashed instantly across his face before it turned harsh and forbidding. Tell immediately jerked his hands from her shoulders.

"Why did I believe you?" he said fiercely.

He really wasn't talking to her. Andrea knew that. But the intense pain of having him find out by accident what she hadn't been able to prepare him for was hitting her hard.

"I'm incredibly sorry, Tell," she said softly but firmly. "All I can do now is ask that you listen—and listen without judging me. If you can."

His eyes bored into her and she met them unflinchingly. "I want answers and I want the truth. Tell me one thing first," Tell commanded, "was that man on the phone your husband or not?"

"I am legally married to him," Andrea admitted, "but—"

"Are you separated?"

"Tell, please!" Hopelessly, she tried to stop his questions so she could explain in her own way.

"Are you separated?" he repeated forcefully, fury blazing in his eyes, letting her see that his temper was held by a very thin thread.

"No!" she acknowledged in frustration.

"And I don't suppose you love him," Tell jeered.

"I'm very fond of him." Nervously she ran her fingers through the sides of her hair. "But I never have actually loved him."

"Then why did you marry him? Is he rich?"

"That's beside the point," Andrea protested helplessly.

"I take it that he is, then." His mouth curved into a cynical line. "I still don't understand what you meant when you said you'd never known a man. Virgin of the year, huh? So tell me, does he get his kicks knowing you have other men?"

"Stop it!" she cried. "You don't know what you're saying!"

"Maybe I don't," Tell sneered. "But I doubt you're going to tell me the truth. Why would he let you go to a resort by yourself? He had to know every red-blooded male who saw you would try something."

"Stop it, Tell!" She placed her hands over her ears to shut out his sarcasm. Underneath it there was hurt—a hurt she understood only too well.

He grasped her left wrist. "And don't try to make me believe that you always said no!" he growled, holding her hand in front or her face. "You're not even wearing a wedding ring. When did you take it off? After you left his house?"

A sob rasped her throat. "It's being repaired. I lost one of the stones. I swear, it's in the jewelry shop!"

"Right." Anger vibrated through the single clipped word as he abruptly released her wrist.

"Please. Give me a chance to explain." Her chin quivered uncontrollably.

"It wouldn't make any difference," he said coldly. "I don't want you and I don't know what weird game you're playing or who you think you are."

"It's not like that, Tell—"

"Here." He reached into his pocket and removed a ring box. "On a crazy impulse, I bought this for you. You might as well have it as a memento. Or should I say trophy?"

Andrea didn't want to look him in the eye.

"Come on, take a peek," he said sarcastically, "your hunt wasn't totally unsuccessful."

The lid of the tiny box flipped open as he crushed it into her hand. The rainbow colors of a large diamond solitaire shone out. Andrea closed her eyes against the reflecting brilliance of the exquisitely simple and expensive ring. Weakly, she tried to hand it back to him.

"Keep it, I said!" Tell snapped.

Then his long strides were carrying him to the door. On trembling legs, she hurried after him, grabbing the door before he could close it behind him.

"Please, give me a chance to explain," she pleaded.

"Accept that it's over, Andrea. Whatever 'it' was. Nothing you can say is going to change that." A cold smile seemed carved into his face. "Maybe you'll have better luck with your next sucker."

The door was yanked free of her hold and slammed shut.

"Tell!" Her fingers closed over the knob, but she didn't attempt to open the door. Sobbing heavily, she leaned against the door, trying to wash away the intense pain with tears.

Long minutes went by before Andrea regained any degree of control. He had made it very clear that he didn't want to listen to her, but she wanted desperately to try again. Somehow, she had to make him understand. Scrubbing the tears from her cheeks, she forced herself to go to the phone. After taking deep breaths to steady her voice, she contacted the desk instead.

"Mr. Stafford's room, please," she requested.

"I'm sorry, Mr. Stafford isn't in," the clerk replied.

"Do . . . do you know where he is?" She faltered for a second, almost shattered by despair.

"He stopped by the desk a few minutes ago, miss, and asked us to prepare his bill, then he went out."

"I see." She swallowed tightly. "Thank you."

Hanging up the phone, she realized that Tell had probably guessed she would try again to explain and deliberately hadn't returned to his room. He probably also had guessed that she wouldn't want to make a scene in the lobby or any other public place. That left only one alternative.

With shaking fingers, she withdrew several sheets of stationery from the drawer of a small table. Quickly, she began writing the things that she hadn't been given the chance to tell him. Time was critical if she wanted to be sure he received her note before he left, but Andrea was careful not to leave anything out in her haste.

A frightening amount of time passed before the letter was completed and sealed in an envelope. Racing up the stairs to the bedroom, she dressed swiftly and dashed back down the steps and out the door, the precious envelope clutched tightly in her hand.

Near the lobby, Andrea slowed her pace, summoning up a measure of poise before approaching the desk. Unconsciously, she held her breath as she walked in, her eyes automatically searching for Tell. He wasn't among the people in the lobby, which meant he had either not returned or had already left the resort. With fingers crossed, she walked to the front desk.

"Has Mr. Stafford checked out yet?" The brightness of her simple question sounded unnaturally brittle.

The clerk recognized her and answered without suspicion. "Not yet, miss," was the reply.

Trying to seem nonchalant, she placed the envelope on the desk counter, the side with Tell's name on it turned toward the clerk. "When he does, would you see that he gets this note?"

"Be glad to," the man nodded.

The smile on his face indicated that he guessed it was a love letter. He wasn't too far wrong, Andrea thought to herself as she turned away. It did contain her heart. It was all there, unprotected and exposed for Tell's examination.

Leaving the lobby, Andrea didn't return to her room, but found a strategic spot where she could watch the people in the lobby without being seen. The anxiety of waiting got to her: her legs shook and her hands were clasped so hard her knuckles hurt. When the tension had built to an unbearable level, Tell's familiar lean figure walked through the outer doors toward the front desk.

Hardly daring to breathe, Andrea watched him go through the checkout procedure. Fear trembled through her that the clerk would forget her note, but at the very last moment, he handed it to him. The polite smile faded from Tell's face, changing it into lines of uncompromising hardness, which were too severe to be handsome.

She waited; waited for the moment when he would open the envelope and read her note, waited for that instant when the light of understanding would melt the coldness of his expression. Then, she would let herself be seen.

None of that happened. Instead, he tore it in two. With freezing indifference on his face, he tore those pieces into halves again and discarded them all in a wastebasket.

Her hand automatically suppressed her cry. The whole world didn't have to be an audience to this drama. Andrea stumbled down the hall to her room. If she wanted to be melodramatic, she would say that she'd handed Tell her heart and he had torn it into pieces and thrown it away. But it wasn't just that. The loneliness of the last three years had caught up with her at last. Andrea cried long and hard until only dry, heaving sobs racked her body. Finally, even those stopped.

Step by step, she went downstairs to the phone. Staring into space, she waited for the front desk to answer.

"Concierge, please." They connected her. "Hello, this is Andrea Grant." The identification was made in a hoarse voice. "Please call the airport and make arrangements for me for a chartered flight to Medford, Oregon, this afternoon. I don't care how much it costs." She gave him the particulars of her credit card information and then asked to be transferred back to the front desk to finalize her bill.

"Certainly. We'll take care of it right away, Miss Grant."

"It's Mrs. Grant," she corrected coldly. "Mrs. John Grant."

"Yes, Mrs. Grant," the puzzled voice on the other end acknowledged.

CHAPTER FOUR

"Set the luggage inside the door," Andrea instructed, replacing the house key in her purse and extracting the taxi fare to hand to the driver.

"Thank you, miss."

Hesitating, Andrea let her gaze sweep over the familiar, large white structure with the tower, a bit of Victorian whimsy, on one side. She was home.

But home is where the heart is, she thought bitterly, and her heart wasn't here. Inhaling deeply, she reminded herself that she was the only one to blame for that. If she had been honest with Tell in the beginning, he might have understood. As explanations went, hers was one hell of a story but he still should have listened.

He hadn't. She got to go on living and breathing . . . and remembering what might have been. The sound of the taxi pulling out of the driveway into the rural countryside made her aware that she was still standing outside the door in the brisk December air. She shook her head to clear it.

There was another gauntlet to get through, a loving one, but she would have to get through it without faltering just the same. She pushed open the front door and stepped onto the figured rug that protected the hardwood floor. Large, antique hanging lamps, converted long ago from gas to electricity, lighted the foyer. Mrs. Davison, the housekeeper, appeared at the entrance of the hall-way leading to the kitchen, hastily wiping floured hands on her apron. Her mouth opened in aston-ishment at the sight of Andrea, before the thin face changed into a smile.

"Andrea, we didn't expect you back until the end of the week," she announced, bustling forward. "Not that I can say that I'm not glad you're back, because I am. Why didn't you let us know you were coming today? Frank could have met you at the air-port instead of your paying a taxi to come all this way. Mr. Grant has been brooding all day. He didn't touch a speck of lunch, and I'd fixed a really nice fish fry. Steelhead trout, his favorite. Here, let me take your coat."

Slipping it from her shoulders, Andrea handed it to the housekeeper. "Where is John now, Mrs. Davison?"

The older woman pursed her lips together in dis-approval. "Sitting in his study staring at the fire just like he's been doing ever since that attorney, Frank Graham, left."

"I'll let him know I'm back," Andrea said quietly.

The housekeeper cocked her head to one side in a listening attitude. "I don't think you'll need to."

At almost the same moment, Andrea heard the galloping sound. She had a half a second to brace herself before an Irish setter came careening around the corner and launched himself at her. The dog danced madly around her, winding around her legs and shoving his flame-colored head against her hands, only to be overcome by joy and spin wildly away, whining his ecstatic happiness at her return.

"Settle down, Shawn," a male voice admonished the dog gently.

The setter dashed toward his master, circling the wheelchair to sit on the left side, a quivering mass of excitement. Wherever Shawn was, Andrea knew John would not be far. The two were inseparable. The only times the setter left his side were when she took him for an exercising walk.

"Andie." A faint smile tenderly lifted his mouth as John greeted her, his warm gray eyes examining the tautness of her answering smile and the sharp edges of partially concealed pain in her eyes.

"Hello, John." She walked quickly to his side before he could see too much, lightly clasping his hands and bending to brush his check with an affectionate kiss.

"Got tired of all that skiing, did you?" Both of them knew the comment was made for the housekeeper's benefit.

"Something like that," Andrea said, nodding.

"Would you fix us some cocoa, Mrs. Davison? You can bring it into the study for us." John's orders always sounded like a request, but he expected them to be obeyed just the same.

Releasing her hands, he flicked the lever to turn his wheelchair around, the quiet motor providing the power to operate the chair without anyone's assistance. The wheelchair gave him the mobility that a logging accident had deprived him of. He had never truly lost his independence—or the dignity that was so much a part of him. Andrea followed him quietly.

Flames licked greedily over partially burned logs, their yellow tongues bright against a hearth blackened with many years of use. Tan stone blended with richly paneled walls and the leatherbound books on the shelves. The furniture, mostly antique and all of it old, had been in the room for years, adding to the comfortable atmosphere.

Despite the early evening hour, the firelight was the only source of light, flickering on the smooth walls. The dimness of the study increased its air of cocoon comfort.

Andrea walked past the large, leather wing chair and ottoman to the side of the fireplace, and proceeded instead to stand on the brick area directly in front of the fire. Pretending to ward off an imaginary chill, she held out her hands to the flame.

"Well, did you break anything while you were on your holiday?" John asked lightly, rolling his wheelchair to a stop on the alpaca rug.

The offer to accept part of her pain had been made. Without turning around, Andrea pictured the man who had made it: his strong, gentle face, distinguished and handsome, wearing his fifty-plus years well; the broad shoulders and powerful arms, and the paralysis from the waist down that kept him confined to that wheelchair. Never had she heard him complain or express self-pity.

For more than three years she had accepted every offer of help John made, transferring her pain, her grief, her sorrow to his shoulders. She knew being able to help her made him feel needed and necessary. As he said himself, John Grant was of an age where love had many meanings.

She had known him for what seemed like forever. They weren't lovers and never had been—that would have been impossible, for more reasons than she could count. But they were husband and wife.

All she wanted to do was tell him what had happened, explain how suddenly and completely she had fallen in love with Tell. But ever since that moment, it had begun to dawn on Andrea that she was an adult at last. She couldn't tell John everything anymore. It was time she stopped turning to him in lieu of the parents she no longer had, and the man who'd left her, and began to accept the responsibility and the results of all the things that she said and did.

Taking a deep breath, she glanced over her shoulder, tossing her dark blond hair in a deliberately careless gesture and smiling ruefully. "I came out with a few bruises, but nothing that won't heal in time." He knew her too well and for too long to believe that casual lie.

"Are you sure, Andrea?" he asked in a doubting voice.

A lump rose in her throat and unshed tears burned in her eyes. "I never said that the bruises didn't hurt, John," she said tightly.

Nervously, she turned away from the fire and walked to the smoke stand between the wing chair and John. Carefully, she filled and packed tobacco in his favorite pipe and carried it to him, lighting it as he drew on it slowly. Blinking to keep the tears at bay, she knelt on the floor, curling her legs on the alpaca rug and leaning against him. Okay, no one should smoke, but he was entitled to a few pleasures. She didn't choose to nag him about it. The aroma of the pipe tobacco was pleasant enough.

"It was only a holiday thing." Andrea stared into

the fire. "Love sure can go downhill fast," she added with wry flippancy.

"And it came to an abrupt end when I called," he sighed. "My first thought when your friend answered the phone was that he was a doctor and you'd been injured. I suppose that's why I was so hasty in claiming my relationship. Was he very angry when he found out?"

"I suppose so," she hedged. Her cheek rubbed the woolen plaid coverlet on his legs, the same cheek that had felt the touch of Tell's hand before he'd slammed it into a wall rather than hurt her. How much anger there had been in his bitter words.

"Why didn't you tell him, Andie?"

"I didn't want him to get the wrong impression." She sighed this time. "You know what I mean, John—that I was a married woman looking for an affair. I thought he would be good company and fun. He was."

His large hand began to gently stroke her hair. "It's my fault, Andie. When I suggested you marry me, it was with the best of intentions. I was older. I should have known better."

"You're forgetting the vicious rumors that went around when I moved into this house after Daddy died and Dale and I broke up." She grimaced in memory.

"Rather flattering they were to me, considering my circumstances," John said dryly, "but the damage was done. My money-grubbing relatives didn't want my estate to pass to you. They seem to think they're entitled to money they didn't earn and aren't going to get."

"Oh, John, you're a long way from dying. And it

was never about the money." Wistfully she turned, laying her head back against his leg and gazing up at him. "I needed your strength and your comfort and, in a way, you needed me."

"One always needs the affection of the people one cares about," he smiled in reassurance. "Still, I should have found some other way than marriage. There are some people who would question the truth of our motives. You've been exposed to so much pain in such a short time, I would never forgive myself if our arrangement stood in the way of your happiness."

"John, please, don't blame yourself." There was no way now that Andrea could ever confide in him that his worst fear had come true. "If a man really loves me, he'll understand. And if he doesn't—" her voice cracked with pain "—then he isn't really the one who can make me happy, is he?"

The words sounded very wise and profound, yet Andrea couldn't truly believe them. She did love Tell, sudden as it had been. All they had needed was time and he'd known that as well as she did. They could have made each other happy, very happy.

"I wanted to protect you from any more pain, Andie." There was a poignant note of regret in his voice that was heartbreaking. "But I never wanted to keep you from having a life."

"You didn't, John." She fell silent. He might not have meant to, and she had not expected to love again, but what was that old saying about the road to hell being paved with good intentions? It applied in this case. Things would have to change . . . somehow, some way. Andrea had no idea where to even begin, but she had Tell to thank for making her see the light. Inadvertently.

John sighed and seemed to be collecting his thoughts. "Andie—" A tap on the study door stopped him.

The brass knob turned and the housekeeper walked in, carrying a tray with two mugs of cocoa and a plate of sugar cookies. The aroma had the Irish setter dancing a jig behind the housekeeper. Andrea rose to her feet to take the tray. Mrs. Davison's brief appearance ended the mood of intimacy, and John didn't attempt to bring about its return.

The mating call of a bird trilled through the window, but Andrea's pounding head didn't appreciate its song. Rolling onto her side, she pulled the sheets up to cover her ears, but the bright notes couldn't be blocked out. The breeze carried the fragrant scent of pear blossoms. Through closed eyes, she could still see the light of the morning sun.

Groaning a protest, she reverted to her former position on her back, pressing a hand to her forehead behind which a dull ache pounded. Her eyelids felt weighted with lead. Tiredness tightened every muscle.

"Why do I take those sleeping pills?" Andrea murmured thickly.

The answer was obvious. There had been too many sleepless nights without them, and too many nights when exhausted sleep had been punctuated by unwelcome dreams of Tell. Almost six months had passed since her vacation at Squaw Valley, and his image was as vividly sharp as her memories of the brief time they had spent together.

Looking back, Andrea knew she had never really fooled John when she had tried to convince him that first night home that she hadn't fallen in love. Perhaps she had for a short time, but her actions had given away the true state of her feelings. He seemed to respect the fact that she wanted to get through this on her own and made no attempt to encourage a confidence that she was reluctant to give.

When Dale had deserted her, the pain had eased to a dull ache within a few short weeks. This time, the hurt was as tormentingly real as it was that morning Tell had hurled his sarcastic rejection at her. Aching misery was her constant companion, easy enough to see in her haunted eyes.

Raking her fingernails through her hair and lifting the dark blond strands away from her face, Andrea glanced wearily toward the gold antique clock on her night table. Blinking, she looked at it again, unable to believe that it actually was eleven.

"Oh, no!" she groaned, throwing back the covers and sliding quickly out of the brass bed.

With tired haste, she stumbled to the bathroom, and splashed cold water on her drowsy face. A lethargy that couldn't be washed away slowed her movements despite her attempts to hurry. Ignoring the time-consuming task of applying makeup, Andrea settled for a quick brush through her hair and a touch of lipstick, then pulled on a pair of denim jeans and a sleeveless top.

The effects of the sleeping pill were still dulling her senses as her barely coordinated reflexes directed her down the stairs. Without pausing, she turned down the corridor leading to the kitchen.

Mrs. Davison was standing at the sink rinsing a head of lettuce when Andrea entered the room.

Glancing at the clock above her head, the housekeeper said dryly, "You got up in time for me to still say good morning."

"Why did you let me sleep so late?" Andrea frowned, obeying the hand that waved her into a chair at the oak table. "I was going to help you get the rooms ready."

"Mr. Grant said for me to let you sleep as late as possible." Wiping her hands on her apron, the woman walked to the refrigerator, poured out a glass of orange juice and set it on the table in front of Andrea. A few seconds later it was followed by a cup of coffee and doughnuts. "And the rooms are all ready, so you needn't worry about that."

"I still would have liked to help." The juice helped wash the cottony taste from her mouth. "I didn't want to sleep this late."

"Seems to me you should be blaming those sleeping pills for that." Mrs. Davison sniffed her disapproval. "A girl your age shouldn't be taking them."

Andrea wrapped her hands around the coffee cup. "The doctor prescribed them for me."

"Those pills may help you sleep, but they don't cure the cause of your not sleeping," the housekeeper observed caustically. "It seems to me the doctor should have recognized it."

"I . . ." Andrea started to protest, then closed her mouth. There was no point in debating the issue. "What time are Mrs. Collins and her daughter supposed to arrive?"

"This afternoon sometime. Mr. Grant told me to plan to have dinner for them, but not lunch. He isn't sure if her husband's coming or not, but I have a room ready just in case. You've met Mrs. Collins before, haven't you?"

"Yes, a year ago. No, two years ago it was," Andrea corrected wearily. "She seemed very nice."

"Oh, there's no doubt, she's a real lady," Mrs. Davison assured her. "She used to spend a couple of weeks here every summer, her and her husband, but that was when her daughter was wearing braces. Once they came off, her visits were less frequent and shorter. Mr. Grant is her daughter's godfather, but I imagine he told you that."

"Yes."

"The last time I saw her, she was such a pretty little thing, so happy and full of life, and kind, like her mother," the housekeeper sighed, shaking the water from the lettuce and placing it on the drainboard. "It's hard to believe that little Nancy is twenty years old and engaged. Oh, it'll be good to see her."

"Yes," Andrea agreed automatically. She hadn't met the girl before, but she remembered Mrs. Collins showing pictures of her daughter.

"It'll be fun to have visitors staying in the house again." The iron-gray head gave an aggressively affirmative nod. "These past months since Christmas, this place has seemed like a mausoleum."

The pallor in Andrea's cheeks intensified. Her cloud of depression had seemed to darken everyone's spirits. She had already guessed that John's invitation to Mrs. Collins had been issued in the hopes of channeling Andrea's attention away from her misery and heartache, and providing a distraction to ease the pain. His thoughtfulness touched her, but Andrea doubted that his plan would have any lasting success.

Finishing one of the doughnuts, she pushed the saucer with the other aside and drained the last of the coffee from her cup. She fixed a bright smile on her face, one that her jangled nerves couldn't endorse, and turned to the housekeeper.

"Can I help you with lunch?" she inquired.

"The casserole is in the oven and everything else is done except this salad," Mrs. Davison replied. "You could cut some flowers from the garden. It'd be nice to have a few spring bouquets scattered about the house."

It was not the kind of task that Andrea had in mind. This was one of those times when she didn't particularly want to be alone with her thoughts, although there were times when she had to be alone. But she had offered to help, and Mrs. Davison had made a suggestion. There was little else she could do but agree.

With an acquiescing nod, Andrea left the house by the rear door, stopping at the small utility shed to collect the garden shears, a small oblong wicker basket and a pair of cotton gloves. Ignoring the dull throb of her head, she vowed to concentrate on her task.

Through the irises, the late tulips, the daisies and the roses, she succeeded. The route of her snipping had taken her to the white board fence separating the house grounds from the orchard. The pear trees were heavy with blossoms, their scent faintly perfuming the May air.

May and December. Once, the coupling of those two months would have reminded her of the snide comments made about her marriage to John. Now she saw things differently. The heartbreak she had felt in December was just as agonizing in May.

Leaning on the board fence, she stared at the beautiful white blossoms, a symbol of spring and the rebirth of life. It seemed as if she had only lived those few short days with Tell. Her life before and after was empty by comparison.

"It isn't fair," she whispered in self-pity. Surely she had been punished enough.

A dispirited look filled her eyes, eyes that were too tired to cry—but the tears were shed within. Wrapped in the torment of lost love, Andrea didn't hear the footsteps approaching as she looked up at the flower-laden trees.

"If it was any other time of year, I would swear you were out here planning to steal some pears," a low voice teased.

Andrea pushed herself away from the fence with a start. Using a gloved hand to brush a dark gold strand of hair from her face, she concealed her broken look, allowing herself the seconds she needed to fake an expression of composure.

"Hey, Adam," she greeted the sandy-haired man evenly.

"Hey yourself." He smiled naturally, a winning smile that added to his all-American look. His gaze turned to the trees. "I don't know which part of the season I like best. When the trees are white with blossoms, or when the first green pears appear, or in the fall when they get big and gold and weigh down the branches."

"It all depends," she answered lightly. "On how you feel, I mean."

He slid her a curious glance. "Okay. Explain. I'm waiting."

"If you want to just look at something beautiful, then the blossom time is the best. But the green pear urge is hard to resist when you're hungry, and you can't ignore the fall greed when you start counting the profits hanging on the trees."

Adam Fitzgerald threw back his head and laughed. "I should have known you would say something like that. Greed, huh? Gee, that sounds cynical."

His comment was accurate, as far as it went. She had become a little cynical. But she didn't want to think about it. Andrea cast about in her mind for something distracting to say. "You work too hard sometimes, Adam. At harvest time Carolyn hardly ever sees you. She couldn't . . . you're always here. And when you aren't here, you're at some logging camp."

"There's a lot of work to be done. John's given me a lot of responsibility. Carolyn understands that," he replied patiently.

"She's much more understanding than I would be," Andrea told him, then sighed ruefully. "I should be saying how grateful I am for the way you take care of everything for John. I know how much he relies on you. Instead, I'm making it sound like you do too much. Just ignore me when I stop making sense, okay?"

"Okay. And by the way—" Adam shrugged "—Carolyn and I will be married next month. In a few years, she'll probably be glad that I'm not around so much."

"Oh, no," Andrea disagreed fervently—a protest that came from her own conviction that if she were married to Tell, she would miss him every minute he was away from her for the rest of her life, regardless of the reason for his absence. Maybe it was unreasonably romantic of her to think that way, but then they had never gotten past the blazing passion of those first hours. If that was all she ever had to remember him by, it was one hell of a glorious memory.

"As long as I'm not gone for very long." Adam qualified his comment with a smile. "You never did tell me what you were daydreaming about while you were staring at the trees."

"Actually—" Andrea stalled, absently glancing at the basket and the velvet softness of the budding pink rose that touched her hand "—I was thinking that these roses would look nice with a spray of blossoms, and I was wondering if I dared to cut one. Will I escape with my life?"

"Looks to me like you already have plenty of flowers in that basket," was his typically male response.

"Mrs. Collins and her daughter are arriving this afternoon. Mrs. Davison thought it would be a good idea to have flowers scattered through the house, and it's a big house."

"I suppose we could spare one small twig of potential pears," Adam surrendered good-naturedly. "Come on, I'll give you a hand."

Holding the flower basket and the shears in one hand, he helped her climb over the fence with the other, then gave them back to her and vaulted over himself. Now that she was committed to adding pear blossoms to her flowers, Andrea decided to select the perfect spray to use as a backdrop for the roses.

With Adam following indulgently behind her, she followed the path between the white yard fence and the rows of trees, searching the limbs for the right branch. Several yards farther, she spotted the one she wanted.

"Do you see that small branch where the blossoms fan out, Adam?" She pointed toward it. "Can you reach it?"

"I think so." Taking the shears from her, he stretched his long arms, clasping the branch and snipping it from the tree. "There you are."

"Thanks." She took the spray from him and placed it in the basket with the rest of the flowers.

"Now that I've assured myself that you aren't going to destroy the orchard, do you suppose we could go to the house?" Adam grinned. "I came to go over the timber leases with John and I was hoping to persuade Mrs. Davison or someone to invite me to lunch."

"I think that can be arranged," Andrea replied lightly.

Their route along the fence had taken them toward the front of the house. As they turned to cross the fence, they were level with the entrance. This time, Adam vaulted the rails ahead of her, turning as she stepped onto the first board. She reached out to hand him the basket of flowers so her hands could be free to climb the fence. Instead of taking the basket, Adam's hands closed around her waist and lifted her right over the fence.

At the same instant, she realized that a car had stopped in the driveway and doors were being opened and closed. As she made her laughing gasp of protest, Andrea glanced toward the driveway. She stared at the man stepping from the car, the sleeves of his shirt rolled up and the buttons partially unbuttoned to reveal the tanned column of his throat.

It couldn't be Tell. Her mind had to be playing tricks on her, especially because she had just been thinking about him. But that was nothing new, she thought about him all the time. The man was staring back at her, cold, angry shock in his expression.

It *was* him.

Her gaze swung to the two women climbing out of the opposite side of the car. Andrea wondered what he was doing with Mrs. Collins and her daughter. Was Tell Stafford the fiancé that John had mentioned? The thought was unbearable.

Then she watched his gaze flicker from her face to the man who had swung her to the ground. Not even on that long-ago morning when Tell had condemned her so bitterly had she seen his handsome face look as coldly arrogant as it did when his black gaze moved over her.

Andrea knew what Tell was thinking at the moment. He was concluding that she and Adam . . . Her stomach turned with a sickening rush as what little color she possessed receded from her face.

"Andrea, what's wrong?" Adam demanded earnestly, his hands clutching her shoulders.

"It's . . ." She almost said it was Tell, but at that moment Adam had shook her gently, making her turn away from Tell's pinning gaze. "It's Mrs. Collins. They've arrived."

He glanced over his shoulder. Mrs. Collins and her daughter were walking to the front door, neither of them having noticed Andrea and Adam. Tell was following them. Then Adam returned his attention to her.

"There's no reason to be so upset because they're early." His reproof was softened with a gentle smile. "You know Mrs. Davison is a genius in the kitchen. With a wave of her magic spatula, she'll make the food stretch for three people to six."

"Yes, of course," Andrea agreed shakily. He had released her shoulder and she ran a trembling palm down the side of her denim jeans.

"There's another reason, isn't there?" He tilted his sandy head to the side.

"What?" She clutched the basket handle tighter, wondering how much he had read into her stunned reaction. Adam didn't miss much.

"It's your clothes, isn't it?" He tucked her hand under his arm and turned her toward the house. "You wanted to be wearing something a little more chic than blue jeans when the redoubtable Mrs. Collins arrived, didn't you? Well, don't worry about that. You would be eye-catching in sackcloth, but don't tell Carolyn I told you that," he teased. "I don't want a jealous fiancée to deal with a month before our wedding!"

"She knows better than that. I'm hardly a hussy," Andrea replied bitterly, remembering the conclusion that had been in Tell's eyes when he had seen her with Adam.

"Hey, Andrea, this is Adam you're talking to," he said, frowning. "When have I ever pointed a finger at your marriage? I know the circumstances surrounding it and what led John to propose the, uh, arrangement. I'm not condemning you for it. I never have."

"I'm sorry." Her mouth moved into a nervous smile of apology. "Maybe I'm getting slightly paranoid."

"Well, hold your head up. There's nothing to be ashamed of."

His gentle, bolstering words were just what she needed as he released her arm and reached around to open the front door. John was in the foyer greeting his guests, the Irish setter grinning happily at his side.

CHAPTER FIVE

Armored with whatever pride she could scrape up, Andrea walked directly to John's wheelchair, taking a position at his side. She was, after all, his wife and therefore the hostess. Her place was beside him, greeting their guests. That one of them was the man she loved was not the point at the moment.

"There you are, Andie." John smiled up at her. "Out picking flowers, I see."

"Yes." Her side vision caught Tell's sardonic look that said it wasn't all she had been doing. Her fragile composure nearly dissolved, her smile cracking for an instant as she turned it toward the two women. She deliberately ignored Tell while she came to her own defense. John had no way of knowing that she was under silent attack. "I wanted to have some spring bouquets set around the house as a way of saying welcome."

"That is thoughtful, Andrea, and the flowers look very beautiful," Mrs. Collins replied.

"You remember Rosemary, don't you, Andie?" John said, introducing the woman who had just spoken.

"Of course I do. It's good to see you again, Mrs. Collins," Andrea acknowledged, switching the flower basket to the other side in order to shake hands.

Rosemary Collins was the same age as John, in her fifties. She had retained her youthful beauty. Her hair was still a dark brown, although a close inspection might detect a few gray hairs. Her eyes were a soft brown and her face relatively unlined and wearing a smile with easy grace. The years had added a few pounds, but she still had a great figure.

"Please, call me Rosemary," she corrected with friendly warmth, then slipped a hand on the young woman's elbow standing at her side and drew her forward. "This is my daughter, Nancy."

Large, expressive blue eyes studied Andrea curiously from a slender oval face framed by silky fine brown hair. Andrea's smile stiffened slightly as she accepted the girl's hand. She doubted that she could shrug off as paranoia the sensation that Nancy Collins was wondering why she had married John.

"Your mother has told me about you. I'm glad I'm finally getting to meet you," was Andrea's polite greeting.

"I've been looking forward to it, too," the girl replied, smiling naturally and with the same kindness as her mother.

As the handclasp of greeting ended, Andrea caught the flash of a diamond solitaire on Nancy's left hand, poignantly reminding her of the one hidden in her dresser drawer. She couldn't say why she had kept it. Perhaps to remind herself of what she had lost—as if she needed any reminder.

John's hand touched her arm and Andrea braced herself for the introduction to Tell. She knew she would never be able to offer sincere congratulations to him on his engagement to Nancy. Wildly she searched her mind for some vague remark that would not make her look like a fool.

"Tell, I don't believe you've met Andrea, either," John began.

But his introduction was abruptly halted by Tell's slicing response. "Yes, I have."

Andrea had been carefully avoiding looking directly at him until it was absolutely necessary, but his words shocked her into staring.

His hard mouth was set and he ignored the pleading look in her eyes. "Actually," he said lazily, "I saw her when we drove in, picking flowers." He placed cutting emphasis on the last words, before he glanced at John. The sardonic expression was replaced by impassive courtesy. "But we haven't been formally introduced. She's your wife?"

John took hold of her hand. It was a touch of warmth that she desperately needed as cold fear raced through her veins. She looked down with gratitude at his reassurance that she was not alone.

"More than that, Tell. She's my secretary, my companion, my supporter and—"

"Your best friend?" Tell's quiet reply held no trace of mockery, but Andrea knew it was there. Concealed from John, but it was there, as if Tell had wanted to confirm that there was no sexual relationship between the Grants. Odd.

Swallowing nervously, she watched the slight narrowing of John's gray eyes as he silently studied Tell. "That, too, I suppose," he admitted after a long moment. "But let me formally introduce you. Andrea, this is Tell Stafford, Rosemary's son. My wife, Andrea."

Her son? Not Nancy's fiancé? Her knees nearly buckled at the announcement. The different surnames had thrown her. In the unexpectedness of seeing him again, Andrea had forgotten that Tell had told her his mother had married again when he was a child. She hadn't realized the additional agony she had felt picturing him in the young woman's arms until it suddenly dissolved.

The discovery made the beautiful smile she gave him warm and natural. But his expression hardened under the glow of her look. Her hand had been automatically extended in greeting. He glanced at it pointedly. Instantly, her joyous relief vanished as she thought for one humiliating moment that he was going to refuse her outstretched hand. Then his lean brown fingers closed over it, releasing her hand almost immediately, almost as if her touch upset him.

"And of course all of you remember Adam Fitzgerald," John continued, allowing a slight pause for Andrea and Tell to acknowledge their introduction before drawing the group's attention to the man standing just inside the door, "my manager and my legs, so to speak."

His openness about his disability was meant to put others at their ease. John had told her how well-meaning people sometimes stopped themselves from using words like "walk" in his presence and he thought it was ridiculous. His relaxed attitude and lack of self-pity did help. As everyone turned to greet Adam, Andrea slipped back to take a less obtrusive position behind John's chair and escape notice for as long as possible. But Tell picked up on her attempt to fade into the background, raising one dark brow that said it all. Andrea felt like slapping him.

He didn't have to make this harder than it already was. She looked away. It was all she could do.

The respite was brief. Much too soon Andrea was pushed to the foreground when John suggested that she show their guests to their rooms while he quickly went over the timber leases with Adam before lunch. Hotly aware of Tell's dark eyes observing her every move, she led them up the stairs, wasting little time directing them to their respective rooms.

"How thoughtful of John to give me my old room!" Rosemary exclaimed as Andrea opened the door to the damask bedroom, a name she'd given it because of the beautiful, old damask bedspread that covered the antique four-poster bed. "He must have remembered how fond I was of the spectacular view of the mountains from this window." She smiled over her shoulder at Andrea. "And Nancy has her same room, too. It's like coming home."

"We expected your husband might accompany you. That's why the adjoining bedroom is prepared for—" Andrea stumbled, unable to speak Tell's name "—your son. I'm sure Mrs. Davison and I could quickly enough get his old room ready. I'm afraid I don't know which one it is."

It was still difficult for her to accept that Tell had spent any time in the house that was her home.

"He used to have the room on the right where the tower is." There was a faraway look in Rosemary Collins's eyes as if she were silently reminiscing about a bygone time. "It's away from the other bedrooms and he always used to like that. If it wouldn't be too much trouble, I'm sure he would like to stay in it."

Andrea's breathing became shallow and uneven as a warm pink flowed into her cheeks. "I'm sorry,

Mrs. Collins," she murmured self-consciously. "That's . . . in use. It's, er, my room."

"Your room? Oh." The startled voice stopped, but Andrea completed the thought by herself. Rosemary Collins had probably thought that she shared the master bedroom suite downstairs with John. "It doesn't matter," the woman said and shrugged quickly. "Men aren't sentimental about things like that the way women are."

"So you have the tower room?" Tell's voice came from the connecting door between the two bedrooms.

"Yes," Andrea breathed, her gaze bouncing away from his. "If you'll excuse me—" the request was made to his mother "—I'll have to get these flowers in some water. Lunch will be in about an hour. Please make yourself at home."

Her dignified retreat carried her to the kitchen. There, her legs nearly dissolved as a long-postponed reaction set in, but she wasn't allowed time to adjust to Tell's arrival and whatever implications it might contain or the unforeseen difficulties that might accompany it.

Mrs. Davison's magic-making required a helping hand, and she enlisted Andrea as she bustled about the kitchen to come up with last-minute items to supplement the original menu. It had been extended from three to six to seven, since Adam had received his hoped-for invitation to join them. When the task was successfully accomplished, Andrea barely had time to slip upstairs to her room and change before lunch was served.

John supervised the seating arrangements, placing his two female guests on either side of him at the head of the table. That left Tell and Adam to sit at Andrea's end of the table. Mrs. Davison chose not to eat with them, insisting that she would rather have her meal by herself after they had lunched when she could eat in peace.

Andrea wished she could have had the same alternative. She would rather eat alone than endure Tell's cold indifference to her presence. He pointedly avoided addressing any comment directly to her, cutting her out of his conversation with Adam as if she weren't there. To try to carry on polite conversation with the women at the other end of the table was impossible, so Andrea sat through the meal in uncomfortable silence. It was a silence that no one seemed to notice, except perhaps Tell, who wanted it that way.

Gladly, she insisted at the end of the meal that the others take their coffee on the cobblestoned patio while she helped Mrs. Davison clear the lunch dishes. She dallied in the kitchen until the housekeeper finally shooed her out. There weren't any more excuses for not joining the others.

But how could she treat Tell as a stranger when her every nerve ending screamed with the knowledge of his touch, his kiss, his embrace and the love they had shared so briefly? When Andrea thought of what might have been—and that they might never kiss again—it seemed like a cruel game of pretense.

For a numbed moment she stood in the corridor, calling up her last reserves of courage and stamina. Then she heard male footsteps descending the stairs—assertive steps that had to be Tell's. A fleeting second later she knew she had to speak to him alone and this was her prime opportunity.

As she reached the end of the corridor, she saw

Tell at the bottom of the open staircase, turning toward the continuing hallway that would lead him to the rear of the house and the patio entrance.

"Tell?" Her unconsciously pleading call halted him and he slowly turned around to face her, his expression unreadable.

Now that Andrea had his attention without anyone listening, she didn't know what to say. She searched his face for the slightest sign that the months apart might have tempered his attitude with compassion. Fat chance. She didn't even know why she dared to hope.

"Did you arrange this little rendezvous, Andrea?" His low-pitched voice was ominously soft.

"I had to talk to you alone," she murmured, trying to accept that this man of stone was the same one who had loved her so passionately. "I heard you coming down the stairs and—"

"Don't play games," he said calmly enough. "You know very well that I'm referring to the invitation to my mother—and that postscript to remind me how long it had been since I accompanied her."

Andrea breathed in sharply. "Tell, I swear I didn't know who you were. I admit that I knew John had invited Rosemary, but it had been a while. I had no idea she was your mother. That's the truth."

He exhaled in a sigh. "The problem with people who don't make a habit of telling the truth, Andrea, is that others seldom believe them when they do."

"It is true!" she repeated forcefully. "I even thought you were Nancy's fiancé until Mrs. Collins said you were her son."

"I see," Tell mocked. "But John knew very well who I was."

"That's what I wanted to talk to you about."

Andrea stared at her tightly clasped hands. "I didn't tell him about you."

"John must be more gullible than I thought. How did you explain what I was doing in your room at the lodge?" he jeered. "Fixing your faucet?"

"No, of course not," she said. "He knows I met someone, but I never told him your name."

"Naturally, he was very understanding and forgave you for straying. What else could he do? He's getting old and he's confined to a wheelchair."

"There was nothing to forgive." Her chin lifted proudly as she met his gaze.

"Wasn't there?" He gave her a look that held a measure of guilt—his, she supposed, for making a move on a woman who he didn't know was married. "Andrea, you and I have two completely and totally different opinions of fidelity."

"You won't even try to understand." Her shoulders sagged with the hopelessness of trying to explain.

"What happened between us is not something I'm liable to brag about, especially to John. Your secret is safe with me." His mouth tightened. "As for you and Adam, I sincerely hope that John doesn't find out."

"You're jumping to conclusions. Adam is engaged. He'll be married next month," Andrea declared angrily.

"That's convenient. Good way to distract John, too. Maybe by that time you can find someone else to gratify your desires," Tell replied immediately without even a fraction of a second's hesitation at her announcement.

Her chest constricted painfully. "How can you believe that?" she murmured.

"It's easy. I've experienced love, Andrea style. I know you."

"You don't know me at all," she protested, even though she understood how he could see things the way he did. "You won't listen to me. You won't let me explain."

But Tell ignored her remarks, studying her face as if there was more truth there than in her words. "Mother and Nancy will be staying for two weeks as planned. I'll make some excuse to leave Sunday afternoon. Don't worry. I'll make sure it's believable." His tone was bland. "John won't realize that it's because I can't stand to be in the same house with his wife."

"Tell?" He was turning away to leave. Despite what he'd said, he still didn't really understand and Andrea didn't want him to go.

"We have nothing more to discuss, Andrea," he said coldly.

Closing her eyes for a second to stave off tears, she breathed in deeply. "Would you tell John and the others that I'll be out in a few minutes?"

"My pleasure." His mouth curved with cynical politeness as he inclined his head before walking away.

She was damned if she'd cry. There wasn't enough time to splash cold water on her face and de-puff if she was going to give in to self-pity and heartache. She took a few minutes to get a grip before walking to the patio.

The conversation halted briefly when she arrived, then began again as she took a seat on the wicker lawn sofa beside Nancy. Tell was sitting in the large wicker chair on the left, for the most part blocked from Andrea's vision by his sister. John and

Rosemary dominated the conversation with reminiscences of past adventures. Andrea inserted a comment occasionally whenever she felt her silence had been too prolonged.

Tell didn't join in at all. If she hadn't been so sensitive to his presence, she might have forgotten he was there.

Later in the afternoon, John pivoted his wheelchair toward the house, announcing that he was going to look for an old photograph album with some early pictures of a party he and Rosemary had attended. Andrea immediately offered her assistance, but John waved her aside, choosing Rosemary to accompany him instead. Uneasily, Andrea leaned back against the sofa cushions. No neutral subject sprang to mind to fill the awkward gap left by John's departure.

"You have a beautiful home here," Nancy Collins said sincerely. "I've always loved this old house. Scott and I will probably never be able to afford anything like this . . . not that I really mind," she added quickly with a contented and happy smile.

"John mentioned that you were engaged. Is Scott your fiancé?" Andrea seized on a means to keep the conversation going.

"Yes. His name is Scott Hanson." Proudly she held out her hand for Andrea to see her engagement ring, a small diamond solitaire with flanking emerald chips.

"How long have you known him?"

"About two years. Another guy took me to a fraternity dance, and Scott was there. The minute I saw him I knew that was it," Nancy said, beaming. "Of course, Daddy didn't approve of him at first because Scott's background is so different from ours.

We didn't become officially engaged until last January when Scott graduated."

"When's the wedding?" Andrea asked.

"Not until December." The young girl sighed, her large blue eyes revealing her regret at the long wait.

"That's a long courtship," Andrea offered sympathetically.

"Scott's working for an oil company right now. He's on sort of a probationary period. We're waiting until he's sure he has a job." A mischievous twinkle sparkled in her eyes. "And we want to make sure that dear old Dad understands that Scott is not marrying me for the family fortune."

Tell pushed himself out of the chair, his sudden movement choking back the response that Andrea had started to make. With a lazy smile, he walked to stand in front of his sister. Unwillingly, Andrea tilted her head back to gaze up at him, drawn by the flash of his smile, but his gaze was cold when he looked at her.

"Otherwise known as marrying for love, Mrs. Grant," he said with cutting softness. "Ever heard of it?"

Andrea heard Nancy's quickly indrawn breath of shock at his rudeness. Wounded, Andrea tensed to keep the hurt from being shown too clearly in her expression.

"Have you, Tell?" she countered.

"Oh, I believe in it," Tell answered dryly. "But there's something I'm curious about. Can a man buy his wife's fidelity—" his hand reached out to touch the pearl choker, burning her neck, the flames reflected in her cheeks "—with expensive jewelry?"

"Tell!" Nancy's horrified whisper begged him to stop. "What's gotten into you?"

"I wouldn't know." Pride quivered in Andrea's voice. "John hasn't tried to buy mine."

"Then maybe you can't be tempted," he said with amusement, towering above her for an instant longer before he walked away, leaving the cobblestoned patio for the landscaped lawn without another word.

At his departure, Andrea pressed her lips tightly together, refusing to let him get to her. After all, Nancy didn't know what he was alluding to and she probably thought he'd had too much to drink or something.

"I'm sorry, Andrea," Nancy murmured.

She darted a glance at the frown of concern on the girl's face, smiling faintly before she looked away. "It's all right, Nancy," she sighed. "Some people like to talk, so I just let them talk. Doesn't bother me."

That was a lie. Even comments from a total stranger about her marriage to John had the ability to hurt. Tell's reaction was worse, but not all that surprising. Both of them were still in shock at their unexpected meeting. *Stop making excuses for him,* she told herself. He was being an—an unspeakable something.

"It was unforgivable for him to speak to you that way!" Nancy's angry declaration was accompanied by a glowering look at her brother, now some distance away.

"My father once told me—" Andrea breathed in deeply "—that what you can't forgive, you must forget, and what you can't forget, you must forgive."

"Do you believe that?"

"Yes, I do." But her smile had a bitter edge. "I just don't know how to apply it." Brushing an imaginary strand of hair from her face, Andrea rose to her feet. "Would you excuse me, Nancy? I think I should see if Mrs. Davison needs any help in the kitchen."

"Of course. I understand."

Andrea didn't see Tell again until they all met in the living room before dinner. A glance at his granite face told her nothing. She couldn't guess what he would do or say in front of others. The strain of not knowing what to anticipate showed in the taut lines around her mouth.

"I see you've had the tennis court resurfaced, John," Tell commented.

"Yes, a couple of years ago," he acknowledged. "Andrea enjoys playing and the court was in bad shape from lack of use."

Tell's mocking gaze slid complacently to her. "Where do you find your partners? I somehow can't picture Mrs. Davison out there swinging a racket."

Her mouth tightened as she saw the quizzical look John gave him. "I have friends," she replied noncommittally.

"Adam and his fiancé come out occasionally," John explained, "but mostly it's her tennis instructor from Medford, Leslie Towers. Andrea's quite good, Tell," he added with a touch of pride. "Maybe tomorrow if the weather holds, you and Nancy and Andrea can play a set."

"Maybe," Tell agreed affably. "It might be interesting to find out what kind of game she plays."

John missed the innuendo, but Andrea didn't. Judging by the dark blue fire that leaped into Nancy's eyes, she got at least some of it.

"I hope she's good enough to beat you, Tell." It was small consolation to have his sister rushing to her defense.

"She's good, sis, but not that good," he said.

"Don't start bickering, you two," Rosemary Collins interrupted with a light laugh that revealed her ignorance of the undercurrents flowing between Andrea and Tell and intercepted by Nancy. "Why don't you get us a drink, Tell?"

"That's a good idea," John agreed. "I'll have a vodka martini."

"Is the bar still in the same place?" Tell inquired, allowing his mother to divert his attention from Andrea.

"It certainly is," John said, smiling.

Walking to the narrow side of the living room, Tell stopped in front of an ornately carved series of shelves, on which books and figurines were scattered. A series of pear blossoms had been carved on either side of the frame. He turned one of them and the shelves swung out to reveal cut-glass goblets of varying sizes and a supply of liquor.

"I didn't know that was there!" Nancy exclaimed.

"I'm not surprised," her mother said. "The last time you were here, you weren't old enough to drink."

"I still never guessed it was there," she replied. "It's so artfully concealed."

"It used to be a cupboard," John explained. "My father had it converted into a bar complete with an icebox and a small mixing counter during the Prohibition days. He was so proud of it that I think everyone in the county knew it was there," he said with a very satisfied chuckle.

"This house—oh, this entire area—has seen a lot of things," Rosemary Collins commented idly, accepting the iced glass that Tell handed her. "Quite a bit of gracious entertaining was done here. Many young men were sent to Medford in the early nineteen hundreds by their wealthy and strict parents to mend their ways. Most of them stayed to build a new life. My grandparents had a summer home on the Rogue River. Every summer they'd leave San Francisco and spend it here. My mother attended St. Mary's Academy for a while."

"Yes, and in the winter there was a turnabout," John smiled, gazing into the martini Tell had given him. "My family would go to Carmel or Pebble Beach and we'd be entertained by your San Francisco friends. Of course, life wasn't perfect a hundred-some years ago. There was a tent city in Medford for the survivors of the 1906 earthquake in San Francisco."

"But the stories that my grandmother told me of the theater and opera held here more than make up for that," Rosemary smiled, glancing at Nancy and Andrea. "Enrico Caruso performed here."

"That must have been something," Nancy mused.

"Here you are, sis." Tell held out a crystal glass.

She glanced up absently before accepting it. "Thanks."

Andrea held her breath as Tell turned toward her, meeting his hooded look reluctantly. His fingers were gripping the top of the glass, holding it out to her while making sure there would be no accidental contact when she took it from him. It hurt that he didn't want to feel her touch.

"I'm sorry, Tell." John spoke up quickly. "I forgot to mention that Andrea doesn't drink anything stronger than Coke."

She had been staring at the glass as she reached for it, finding it painful to meet his indifferent eyes. But at John's statement, her gaze was jerked to Tell's face. The glass was close enough for her to tell by sight and smell that it contained only Coke. He had remembered her aversion to alcohol and automatically served her an innocuous drink. His expression was grim as he returned her look.

"My mistake," he said curtly, withdrawing the glass from her hand. "I'll get you another."

"It looks like a Coke to me," Nancy observed innocently.

"With a splash of bourbon," Tell stated firmly. "You're not exactly the world's expert on alcohol, little sister."

"I should hope not," Rosemary said, laughing.

The incident was forgotten as John recounted a story of an early party. But it had been a slip that Andrea knew she wouldn't forget and she doubted that Tell would. She hadn't realized how easy it might be to make a mistake and betray the fact that she and Tell had met before. If John found out, she knew he would understand, but she didn't want to suffer the humiliation of having his family learn of it.

CHAPTER SIX

"I'll play the winner," Nancy declared.

Andrea tossed her light yellow jacket onto the fence. The nervous fluttering in her stomach was difficult to ignore as she got her tennis racket out of its case. Tell was standing only a few feet away from her, his tanned legs muscular and long beneath the drill white of his tennis shorts.

"How long has it been since you've played, Mrs. Grant?" he asked.

"Just this week," she answered, adding in a whisper, "and you can stop calling me Mrs. Grant. You're being obnoxious."

He ignored her last comment. "Okay, that should give you an advantage. I haven't played in over a month."

"Don't let him kid you, Andrea," Nancy warned quietly. "He's very good even when he's out of practice."

"I don't doubt it." Andrea touched her hairband, making sure her hair was away from her eyes.

"John told me your instructor usually spends all

afternoon out here. You must get in a lot of practice," Tell commented.

Stiffening, Andrea met his mocking gaze. "Sometimes we just sit and talk."

"About tennis?"

Forget slapping him. She wanted to really let him have it with the tennis racket. "No, about a lot of other things."

"What business is it of yours anyway, Tell?" Nancy challenged.

"Just curious." He smiled at his sister. "Considering the amount of time they spend together, I was just wondering how friendly Andrea was with her instructor—what was his name? Mr. Towers?"

"Leslie Towers and I are pretty good friends, Tell," Andrea retorted. "Not only that, she's female. So if you're through with the trash talk, let's play tennis. Shall I serve first or will you?"

Tell stared at her, hard, black eyes boring into her as if to seek some sign that she was lying. Andrea met his gaze without flinching.

"What's the matter? Are you disappointed to discover that I'm not having an affair with my tennis instructor?"

"Andrea." Nancy touched her arm in a placating gesture.

She sighed and bounced the ball to Tell. "You serve."

"Ladies first," he countered, flipping the ball back to her and walking to the near side of the court. Nancy left, probably needing to use the bathroom. Andrea wouldn't have minded going with her. She felt like throwing up but she steeled herself to face Tell.

With his blazing return of the first serve, Andrea

knew this would be no friendly tennis game. He intended to challenge her skill with every ball over the net. During the first set, she managed to stay close with the help of some well-placed volleys.

By the middle of the second set, as she chased his returns from one end of the court to the other, she knew he intended to run her into the ground. He was in command and on the offensive. Her defense was rapidly crumbling under the onslaught.

Lobbing a return to Tell, Andrea saw him set up for a crosscourt smash. She ordered her tiring muscles to race to meet it. The ball was traveling at such a speed that there was only a slim chance that she could reach it. Stretching, she managed to get her racket on it, but her momentum sent her tumbling onto the court and the ball ricocheted off her racket and out of bounds.

Winded and beaten, she lay for a few precious seconds on the court. Her knee throbbed where she had grazed it in the fall. She pushed herself upright into a sitting position, breathing heavily from the exertion of the game. Overwhelming tiredness pounded through her, a physical and mental weariness that left her drained and vulnerable.

As she brushed the back of her hand over her forehead, her vision was momentarily blurred—whether by sweat or stupid, pointless tears, Andrea didn't know or care. Then Tell was towering above her, his dark gaze not revealing even a glimmer of sympathy.

"Are you all right?" he asked.

Screw you, she thought. Andrea swallowed the lump in her throat. "I bet you're sorry I didn't break my neck. But yes, I'm all right." She brushed at the dust on her pale yellow top.

"Give me your hand. I'll help you up," Tell said.

She stared at the tanned hand extended to her, wanting to feel his strong grip so desperately that it hurt. "No, thank you," she said firmly.

"Give me your hand." It wasn't an offer. It was an order.

Glancing at his tightly clenched jaw, Andrea placed her trembling hand in his. Immediately, his hold tightened, and she felt the strength of his muscles easily pulling her to her feet. Whether it was accidental or deliberate on Andrea's part, the impetus carried her against his chest.

His hands quickly closed over her shoulders, keeping her there. Her head was tilted back to gaze into his face. Her heart raced like rolling thunder when she saw his dark eyes focus on her mouth.

Not seeing anything but the rock wall of his chest, and feeling the pressure of his muscular thighs, the possessive grip of his hands and the nearness of his mouth, Andrea let a sparkle of hope and love shine in her eyes. His expression hardened. In the next instant he had moved a few inches back, keeping only a steadying hand on her shoulder.

She blinked at the ground, humiliated that she had allowed herself to suffer his rejection again. She drew a shaky breath and shrugged free of his hand.

"Oh, Andrea, are you all right?" Nancy asked, running back from wherever she'd disappeared to. Her sneakers squeaked as she came to a breathless halt beside them.

"Of course she is," Tell answered. "She took a tumble. No big deal."

"Okay. Game, set and match to you, Tell." Andrea's chin set with proud anger. "I declare you the winner."

"You've grazed your knee," Nancy observed.

"It's nothing," Andrea responded tautly as Tell accepted her declaration of forfeit without comment. "I'll put some antiseptic on it up at the house and it'll be fine."

"Would you like some help?" The large blue eyes expressed concern and sympathy.

"You don't have to play nurse," Tell cut in. "Andrea can take care of herself."

"One more crack like that and I'll take care of you. Watch it, Tell," Nancy snapped.

"Yes, ma'am."

Frustration and fury at the way he was playing her made Andrea turn abruptly away. Out of the corner of her eye, she saw Nancy's movement to follow her and the hand Tell placed on his sister's shoulder to stop her.

"Let her go, Nancy," he ordered in a low voice.

More words followed, but by then Andrea was too far away for them to be audible. She succeeded in slipping up the stairs to her room without being noticed. John and Rosemary were in the living room visiting, making up for lost years by bringing each other up to date on the happenings of their lives.

In the shower, Andrea didn't attempt to check the welling tears in her eyes, but let them mingle with the water spray. Later, wrapped in her short terry cloth robe, she sat curled in the center of her brass bed, her toweled head bowed, her hands resting listlessly on her crossed legs. She was attempting to meditate. Her conscious mind was relatively blank, but the rest of it was in a whirl.

There was a light rap on her door. "Who is it?" She rubbed any telltale traces of tears from her cheeks.

"It's me, Nancy," was the soft reply. "May I come in?"

"Yes, of course," Andrea replied, blinking several times, hoping there wasn't too much betraying redness in her eyes.

As the door opened, she pulled the towel from around her damp hair and began rubbing the strands in its folds. She managed to smile briefly at the girl who entered the room and closed the door behind her.

"Guess your brother was the winner in your game, too," Andrea murmured dryly at the solemn look on Nancy's face.

"Of course. I . . . I brought your jacket back. You left it on the fence," Nancy replied with a bright and forced nonchalance.

"Thank you. I'd forgotten all about it. Just toss it over the end of the bed. I'll put it away later."

There was a moment of hesitation. "That isn't why I came," Nancy sighed. "I just used your jacket as an excuse."

The drying motion of the towel stopped for a brief second before it started again, more vigorously than before. "What was it you wanted, Nancy?" Unwillingly, a wariness crept into Andrea's voice.

Sitting on the edge of the bed, the attractive young woman stared at her hands, twisting them nervously in her lap. "I wanted to talk to you about Tell."

"Oh yes. Your brother. Well, I'm not going to say what I think of him."

Nancy nodded. "I know how insulting he's been

toward you. I can't begin to apologize for the way he's behaved, but I want you to know that it's not your fault. He's not really picking on you."

"He isn't?" Andrea responded. "With all due respect, what would you call what he's doing? I wanted to break my tennis racket over his head."

"So did I. But what I mean is that he's not specifically singling you out. He seems to be—" Nancy paused, searching for the right word to explain what she meant "—angry at the whole world, not just you. A few months ago he met somebody. I know I probably shouldn't be talking about it, but . . ."

"This sounds very personal." Andrea could see where the conversation was leading. Somehow, she had to stop it. "You probably shouldn't tell me."

"No, I want you to know," Nancy explained, glancing anxiously at Andrea, who slid to the side of the bed and walked to the dresser. "Each December, Tell takes a long skiing weekend during the first part of the month before the Christmas rush. This last time he met a girl at Squaw Valley. Now, my brother is no saint. He's dated a lot of women and probably had affairs with several, but he's never really been seriously interested in any of them."

"Nancy, please. This is definitely too much information." Andrea's fingers curled around a comb, the teeth biting into her palm. Thank goodness her back was to the bed and Nancy couldn't see the feelings that she couldn't hide.

"Let me finish," Nancy insisted. "I want you to understand why he is the way he is. The morning of the day he was coming back, Tell called saying he was bringing this girl home for us to meet. He told Mother to break out the champagne so we all could toast the girl he was going to marry. But when he came home, he was alone."

"Did . . . did he tell you about her?" Andrea had to ask the question, just had to. "Did he say what had happened?"

"He didn't say much about her on the phone except that she was the most beautiful woman in the world. He said we'd find out all about her when we met her. Of course—" Nancy took a deep breath "—he didn't bring her home. Afterward, the only explanation he gave was that he had been lucky enough to discover she wasn't what he'd thought."

Andrea winced. "I see," she murmured.

"He's just been so difficult ever since."

"I noticed."

"He needs to get over himself. I mean, he seems to think he's the only person who was ever disillusioned or something. But that doesn't give him the right to sulk. Not for this long. You know, it seemed like he was getting better, but the second we got here, he was in a bad mood. I don't understand it."

And I can't explain it, Andrea thought unhappily.

"Hey, what if we beat him up together? We'd have a better chance," she concluded.

"Thank you, Nancy." Andrea kept her voice calm. "We probably shouldn't beat him up. I have a feeling he's kind of doing that for himself."

"Hadn't thought of it that way. Maybe you're right. I am sorry, though," Nancy added hesitantly.

There was a moment of silence that Andrea didn't want to break. She had nothing intelligent to say but she did appreciate Nancy's feminine solidarity. It was just too bad if Tell despised her. At least he was giving her a lot of good reasons not to love him. Andrea decided that she was done obsessing over him. Totally done.

"Well," Nancy sighed brightly, "I suppose I should go and shower and change before dinner. I think I have time. When are Mother's friends supposed to arrive?"

"Er—" Andrea breathed in, biting her upper lip as she tried to reply calmly "—around six-thirty. John planned to serve cocktails first and eat around seven-thirty."

"I can hear it now." Nancy walked toward the door, a smile curving her cupid's-bow lips. "'Why, Nancy, how you've grown! I hardly recognize you.'" With a grimace of resignation, she opened the door into the hall.

Andrea wished that Nancy had not reminded her of the small dinner party that John was giving for Rosemary Collins. The only thing she wanted at this minute was to escape. But escape was impossible. A plea of a headache or illness might be accepted by John or Nancy, even Rosemary. But Tell would guess the truth and all of John's friends would draw their own conclusions.

She raised her eyes. If all was fair in love and war, then she was going to get even. But in her own way and on her own time. Clenching her hands, she vowed that she would make it through the evening. Neither Tell's behavior nor the jibes from some of John's friends would make her react. She owed it to John not to make a scene, not to embarrass him in front of others.

Standing beside his wheelchair that evening, a glass of ginger ale getting warm in her hands, Andrea glanced about the room, away from the older couple talking to John and excluding her from their conversation. It was always this way whenever John invited his friends.

Since she had married him, they barely attempted to hide the fact that they thought John had made a fool of himself. In front of him, they treated her with grating politeness; alone, they were sometimes openly rude. The women tended to be worse, giving her the self-righteous glares that older wives reserved for younger wives of men their own age.

That was true of all of his friends except two or three who had known Andrea's father and were more sympathetic to the circumstances surrounding their marriage. It made entertaining difficult. Andrea had tried not to let John see how much his friends upset her because she didn't want to deprive him of their company. After all, he had known most of them for years.

But she was beginning to feel that her patience was wasted on this bunch. With a softly murmured excuse to John that she wanted to check on dinner, Andrea slipped into the dining room. She knew that under Mrs. Davison's expert touch there was no need to be concerned about the meal. But she was glad to escape the suffocating atmosphere of the living room, if only for a few minutes.

Walking to the filmy lace curtains covering the windows where the gold drapes were drawn back, Andrea stared at her reflection in the night-darkened window. She sighed with weariness, knowing that in a few minutes her disappearance would be noted and she would have to return.

"Aren't you enjoying the party?"

That was Tell talking. Damn it. Andrea pivoted swiftly. A minute ago she had seen him in the living room with Judge Simpson. The judge was retired now but still using the title.

Quietly, Tell closed the double doors behind him.

"I . . . I was checking on dinner," she said nervously, stepping toward the table and realigning the already straight silverware.

"Oh, is that what you're doing? You missed a fork. That one there is one-sixteenth of an inch too far to the left." He pointed. "I thought perhaps you were bored. You hardly spoke to anyone in the other room."

"Correction. No one spoke to me." Andrea needed to make that clear. "You see," she explained, lifting her chin proudly, "John's friends have the same low opinion of me that you do."

"Including my mother?"

"No, not your mother and not one or two others who knew my parents," she admitted. "But the others believe that I played on John's sympathy after my father died and tricked him into marrying me."

"Of course your father died penniless, didn't he? A series of bad investments just before his death wiped out the family fortune," Tell mocked. "Isn't that the way those sad tales of the beautiful heroine usually start?"

"You know, I am beginning to hate you."

"Really. Tell me why."

"Because you're right. There wasn't any money when my father died," Andrea said angrily. "I told you all about it before. When I was fifteen, the doctor told us that Mother had cancer. There were operations, chemotherapy, drugs, doctor and hospital expenses and a thousand other things. Despite everything, she died after nearly three years. Less than a year later, my father's heart simply stopped.

But I never regretted one single dime he spent trying to save her."

He looked ashamed of himself. Which was good. He ought to be. "Is that why you married the first wealthy man who came along?"

He wasn't ashamed enough. But she was not, repeat not, she told herself, going to break down and make a scene. "John has more to offer than money." Her fingers nervously gripped the back of the mahogany dining chair.

"Tell me. I'm curious." His tone was neutral.

"He's strong and kind and understanding. He genuinely cares about me, about my happiness and well-being."

"You know, he was actually talking about you being the main beneficiary of his will," Tell said. "He seemed to be proud that he—"

Andrea let out her breath in one quick sigh and wearily bowed her head. "Why am I wasting my time? You don't want to listen. You don't want me to explain," she said dully.

"I'm curious about something else, Andrea. What does John get out of all this? The privilege of having you as his beautiful paid companion?" He met her flashing look of tears and temper. "I took the tour. You sleep upstairs, not with him."

She swung at his face and missed as he dodged her open palm. He caught one wrist, then the other, as Andrea struggled in vain to be free.

"How can you say that?" she hissed.

"Because it's true."

"What of it?" She was no longer fighting his hold. "I don't care what you think of me! John only wanted to take care of me—and in return, I take care of him. Not in the way you're implying, though.

Marrying him may have been a mistake, but I—I can stay or go. He insisted that it be that way!"

A muscle twitched along Tell's jaw, sternly clenched and unyielding. "When you love someone, Andrea—" his gaze narrowed blackly "—there is incredible joy in just knowing her head rests on the pillow next to yours. You would do anything for that person . . . but you couldn't possibly know the feeling I'm trying to describe. You're much too concerned about your own security to take a risk like that."

Gasping back a sob of pain, Andrea knew having Tell next to her was something she wished for every night, but he wouldn't believe her.

"Excuse me, Andrea." Mrs. Davison's hesitant voice came from the doorway of the serving pantry connecting the kitchen and dining room.

Instantly, her wrists were released and Tell was stepping away.

"Yes, Mrs. Davison," Andrea murmured in a choked tone.

"If they don't sit down to dinner pretty soon, that chowder isn't going to be fit to eat," the housekeeper replied.

"Thank you." Andrea smiled tightly. "I'll have the others come in right away."

"Looks like it can't be too soon." And the pantry door closed behind the woman.

Andrea glanced hesitantly at the back of Tell's wide shoulders. "I don't think she was listening."

"And even if she was—" he looked at her fiercely "—you'd be able to come up with some story to convince her nothing is wrong, wouldn't you? This is your safe little world. And I had the bad luck to find you in it."

Andrea spun away. No matter what she said, Tell would not believe her. He was determined to think the worst of her and there seemed to be no way to stop it.

Sleeping pills were a necessity that night. Even then Andrea lay awake for a long time before they took effect and brought that blessed unconsciousness.

The voices in the hall seemed part of a nightmare she was having in which a horde of accusing voices were condemning her for not telling him the truth. She struggled to raise the weighted lids of her eyes, confident that if she could open them, the voices would stop. They didn't. She tried to shut her ears to the sound. Finally the realization that she was hearing actual people penetrated her drugged stupor.

Clumsily, Andrea pulled on her robe and stumbled to the door. Shaking her head to clear her vision, she used the walls of the corridor for support to lead her to the sound. Near the top of the staircase, she saw Tell, his sister and Mrs. Davison. The two women were in nightgowns and robes. Tell was wearing a pair of dark pants with an unbuttoned shirt covering his bare chest, as though he had put it on in a hurry.

"What's wrong?" she asked thickly, trying to push away from the wall and cover the short distance between them. Her legs wouldn't function properly and she had to sway back against the wall for support.

"For God's sake, what's the matter with her?" Tell muttered.

An instant later, Andrea felt his arms sliding

around her, taking her weight against him while his hand closed over her chin and raised her face up for his frowning inspection.

"It's those sleeping pills she takes, I expect," Mrs. Davison answered in her usual low voice of disapproval.

"What does she need sleeping pills for?" Nancy asked curiously.

"To sleep. To sleep and not dream," Andrea responded softly, closing her eyes against Tell's nearness. His arm tightened around her for a second.

"Let's get her back to bed." The harshness of his voice made her wince, then she felt him bodily carrying her back to her room. But it was Mrs. Davison's face she saw as the covers were pulled over her arms and chest.

"Why is everybody up? What's happened?" Andrea asked, trying to sit up, only to have the light pressure of the housekeeper's hand push her back.

"It's nothing for you to worry about, dear," Mrs. Davison said gently. "Mrs. Collins had a slight asthma attack, but she's all right now. You go to sleep. I'll tell you all about it in the morning."

Andrea wanted to protest, but she felt herself slipping away. The bedside lamp was switched off and she remembered nothing else until the sun streamed into her window, heralding the morning.

As usual, her head throbbed dully as she dressed and made her way down the stairs. Her mind had begun to clear, enabling her to separate the dream of last night from the reality of what had actually transpired. In the downstairs hallway, she met Mrs. Davison on her way up with a tray.

"Everyone is in the breakfast room," the housekeeper said, not slackening her step as she hurried by Andrea.

"How's Mrs. Collins?" she inquired anxiously.

"Much better," was the succinct response.

Reluctantly, Andrea turned toward the sunny breakfast area. She had the strange feeling that last night she had allowed Tell to see her in a vulnerable state and she was not all that sure what she'd said or done. However, the first person she saw as she entered the room was John, smiling a greeting and letting her draw strength from his protective presence to meet the guarded look of Tell, seated at the table beside him.

"Good morning." Her greeting was directed to all three and returned by Nancy and John. She avoided Tell's look of concern to smile at Nancy. "How's your mother this morning?"

"She's fine," Nancy answered firmly and with a bright sparkle in her blue eyes that said she was telling the truth. "She gets these attacks every now and then, mostly when she becomes excited or overdoes things."

"I'm sorry I wasn't much help last night." Andrea self-consciously averted her attention to the coffeepot, only to find it in Tell's possession as he poured a cup and handed it to her.

"Tell said that you were a bit out of it," John commented.

"I, er—" she tossed her head back in a nervous gesture, smiling stiffly as she stared at the cup in her hand "—took a couple of sleeping pills before I went to bed last night. You know how they knock me out, John."

"Let me guess. You have insomnia," Tell said.

"Occasionally," she shrugged.

"Quite often in the past few months," John corrected her dryly.

"It can be tough to treat." Tell's remark was bland, but Andrea knew better. "And there are so many reasons for it."

"I had blamed it on spring fever," she countered.

"Thank heaven, I never have any trouble," Nancy sighed contentedly.

"That's because yours is the sleep of the innocent, kitten," Tell said.

"Well, that must be why you work so late at night, Tell," Nancy teased in return. "You're lucky sometimes to have five hours' sleep out of twenty-four."

"Got an answer to that?" Andrea challenged.

"Sure," he answered tautly, meeting her gaze and holding it. "I like my job. I don't mind long hours."

"Well," Nancy folded her napkin and placed it on the flowered tablecloth, "I'll leave you two to argue over the reasons for sleeping or not sleeping while I see how Mother is doing."

"Give her my love," John said, wheeling his chair away from the table, "and tell her how very sorry I am that she wasn't able to join us this morning, but we'll be saving a place for her at noon, and I'm sure we're all hoping she'll be here."

"Knowing Mother, she'll be down," Nancy said, laughing.

"I'll be up later," said Tell. When his sister had left, he glanced at the man in the wheelchair. "Would you like some more coffee, John?"

"No, no, I don't think so." The massive chest rose and fell as the older man took a deep breath. "If you want me, Andie, I'll be in my study."

When the whirr of the wheelchair faded, an awkward silence settled over the room. Tell poured himself another cup of coffee and rose from the table to walk to the window. A pulse hammered in Andrea's temple, not letting her forget he was still in the room. She spread homemade apple jelly over a slice of toast, trying to concentrate on it instead of the virile guy framed in the sunlight.

"This changes things," Tell said quietly, bending his dark head to stare at the cup in his hand. "You realize that, don't you, Andrea?"

"I'm afraid I don't follow you." Her knife was held poised above the toast.

"I'm referring to my mother," he said. "She hasn't fully recovered and I don't really want to leave this afternoon as I'd planned."

"Of course," murmured Andrea, releasing the breath she had unconsciously been holding. Whatever she had been braced for, that wasn't it.

"Only for a couple of days, long enough to be sure she's all right. Believe me, I won't stay any longer than necessary," Tell muttered.

"There's no need to worry," she said stiffly. "I'm not likely to pretend that you're staying for any other reason than your mother."

Glancing over his shoulder, he glared at her coldly. Without another word, his long strides carried him from the room, leaving Andrea shaken and confused. If only she could think of a way to stop this pointless charade—but what concerned her most was that John not be hurt. The thought made her head ache even more.

Chapter Seven

"Are you sure you don't want to come with us, Mother?" Nancy asked again. "We're only driving over to Jacksonville, then into Medford to do some shopping."

"No, you and Andrea go." Rosemary Collins smiled. "I'm sure the two of you will have more fun without me. Besides, John wants me to read the rough draft of his novel so he can have my valued opinion." She glanced laughingly at John as if to say she was hardly a critic to be listened to. "This afternoon will be a good time for that."

"Well, if you're sure." Nancy shrugged and turned to Andrea. "If you're ready, I guess I am."

Touching John's shoulder, Andrea murmured, "We won't be late."

"Have a good time," he winked.

Adding a quick goodbye to Rosemary Collins, Andrea followed Nancy into the hall leading to the foyer. They had just reached the front door when a third pair of footsteps sounded in the hall.

Instinctively, Andrea turned, knowing it was Tell yet unable to prevent herself from looking. She had hardly seen him in the past few days since his mother's asthma attack. It did no good to remind herself that he was deliberately avoiding her.

"Where are you off to, Nancy?" Tell said, frowning.

"Andrea and I are going to do some sightseeing and shopping. Why?" His sister's hand remained poised on the doorknob.

"Do I dare ask you to hold off leaving for an hour?" he asked with faint sarcasm.

"Why?" Nancy repeated, giving him a mulish look.

"I have some spreadsheets to go over that can't wait until I get back to San Francisco. I'd like your opinion on sales trends," answered Tell curtly. "We are running a family business and you are my sister."

"I keep trying to forget that," she said with a grimace. "Spreadsheets, huh?"

"Yes. I'd like your input on the marketing report, too," he said. "I value your expertise and I have to respond to the department head."

"You're just saying that, Tell," Nancy sighed, her hand falling away from the door. "Every time we talk business, you always get so impatient."

His mouth thinned into a grim line as long fingers raked irritatedly though his black hair. "Never mind!"

"See, already you're snapping," his sister pointed out.

"Could I help?" The instant Andrea made the offer she wished that she could take it back. His smoldering dark gaze pinned her with sudden swiftness. "Oh, I guess you think that all I know how to do is ski—or maybe shop. Have you forgotten that I told you I worked for John?"

"Right. Now I remember." Tell responded. "Different area, though. You up for learning something about retail?"

"I'll give it my best." Her reply was clipped. God, he was rude—and so very different from the romantic, sweep-you-off-your-feet guy she'd met at Squaw Valley.

"I didn't know you worked for John, actual office work, I mean." Nancy turned a frowning, curious look to Andrea. "Where was I when you two were talking about that?"

In that stricken instant, Andrea realized that she and Tell, too focused on each other, had made another slip. Her wide hazel eyes pleaded with him to rescue them, to satisfy his sister's curiosity before she became suspicious. His mouth tightened.

"You were there, Nancy," he stated. "Obviously you were daydreaming about Scott again."

"That's possible," she acknowledged, a warm smile curving her mouth. "So, are you going to accept Andrea's offer or are we going to struggle with paperwork for the rest of the afternoon? With me helping, it will take that long."

His narrowed, resentful eyes slid over Andrea's tense face. "I had to stay here longer than I planned and I have to get through everything today, so I don't have much choice. Okay, Andrea, you're on."

She hadn't really imagined he'd take her up on her offer.

"Let's use John's study," Tell said.

She didn't think John would mind. "Uh, sure."

"He already told me to bring my business stuff there, in case you were wondering. Maybe you can just help me draft a preliminary response and we'll let it go at that. I would hate to take up too much of your time, since you're on your way out."

That last remark seemed to hang in the air as

Tell walked down the hall to the study. Feeling as if she were walking into a trap, Andrea hesitantly moved forward and Nancy followed.

"I hope it won't take too long for your sake," his sister offered, glancing toward the door Tell had left ajar. "It was nice of you to offer. Don't let him drive you crazy, Andrea."

"I won't." But her smile was stiff. She wondered what had possessed her to offer to help.

Masochism just wasn't worth it, Andrea thought, hesitating for a split second in front of the partially open door before pushing it open the rest of the way and entering the study. Tell was sitting behind the desk, shifting through a sheaf of notes lying on top.

Hmm. There was an open laptop to one side of the notes and a whole lot of file folders. Looked like he'd been working in here for a while. Aware that he'd deliberately not glanced up since she had entered, Andrea looked around for something to write on and picked up a notepad and pencil. Then she walked to the chair in front of the desk. For several minutes, she sat there, feeling like a secretary in an old movie, waiting for him to begin.

"I'm ready whenever you are," she said finally. If only she'd had black-framed eyeglasses to whip off so he could look at her with surprise and tell her that she was beautiful. The thought was absurd but it served to break the tension in the room, at least for her.

He leaned back in his chair, his brooding gaze centering on her with piercing thoughtfulness. Andrea wished she hadn't called attention to herself. He was deliberately attempting to unsettle her and he was succeeding.

Without any warning, Tell began to dictate a

letter, his low, clipped voice giving her a name and address to which the response was directed. Wow. She really could be in an old movie. Andrea had barely written that down when he began the contents of the letter.

She really tried to keep up with the swift flow of his words, but she slowly kept falling behind, relying on her memory to supply the sentences she had heard a moment ago while trying to concentrate on what he was saying. Finally, she had to acknowledge defeat.

"I'm sorry," she murmured, heat flashing into her cheeks as she refused to look up. "Would you repeat that last part? I'm afraid that I didn't get all of it."

"Oh. Sorry. Not like I usually dictate letters— I guess I was talking too fast," Tell said.

"Not even voice recognition software would get it all," Andrea retorted. "Just slow down. Be considerate. It won't kill you." Even with her head downcast, she could feel his eyes boring into her, delving and examining.

"Okay. Maybe I deserved that. Maybe not. But I really don't think you should be lecturing me about being considerate." It was an effort for him to stay composed. His jaw tightened and his dark brows drew together.

"You know, I get that no one is allowed to tell you what to do. Or to tell you anything you don't want to hear!" Andrea cried, rising to her feet in agitation, knowing that no matter what she said, he was likely to take it the wrong way.

Anger flashed in his eyes and he rose from his chair. "Spare me the righteous indignation, okay?

You were the one who lied to me! Who led me on! Who asked me to believe things that were untrue!"

"Tell, I was going to explain, I swear I was!" Andrea pleaded with him to believe her. "I tried to the morning you came to my room, but you were going on about so many other things that you wouldn't listen. If I'd had the chance, I could have made you understand that things weren't— aren't—at all what you think. Then John happened to call, and you condemned me without hearing my side."

"Does that explain everything? According to you, you didn't even have a boyfriend, let alone a husband," he taunted.

"If I'd told you I was married that first night we dined together, what would you have thought? We were strangers then. I wouldn't have told you the truth about the circumstances surrounding my marriage to John, not to a total stranger. But if you'd known I was married, would you have seen me again?" she demanded.

"No!" Tell snapped. "I'm old-fashioned. I believe the marriage vows between a man and a woman are sacred promises. I don't have a lot of respect for those who don't keep them!"

Andrea didn't miss the strong emotion in his voice. "I haven't broken any promises I made to John," she murmured.

"Really?" he said. "How can you promise to marry one man when you're still married to another? Is that something you promised John you would do?"

"I never promised to marry you!" Her hands trembled visibly as she cast the notepad and pen on the desk. "There isn't any point in continuing this conversation. You don't want to listen. You haven't even had enough courtesy to hear me out before you've judged me. I think I've been punished enough for my mistake without enduring any more of your insults!"

Turning away from the desk, she hurried toward the door. Her vision, already blurring with tears, turned the door into a dark mass and the brass knob into a shapeless, gleaming object. But Andrea wasn't to be granted a reprieve. As her fingers touched the cold knob, her shoulders were gripped and Tell swung her around.

"You don't know what I feel for you, do you?" His voice was raw but oddly tender.

In his hands, Andrea was pulled toward his descending mouth. One quick gasping breath later, the tender force of his kiss was opening her lips. Then his arms circled her, holding her against his chest until the sensual closeness of his body almost overwhelmed her.

Andrea could not bring herself to be afraid. She loved him despite the unlikely circumstances that had brought them together and threatened to keep them apart. There was something in his kiss that gave away the emotions he was so good at controlling as a rule, she suspected. He probably did love her, although she couldn't begin to guess what would happen next as a result. She felt claimed by him in some mysterious way and fighting it was the last thing she wanted to do.

When Tell drew his head away, relaxing his hold, she leaned weakly against his arms, too defenseless to break free now that she had the chance. His gaze moved over her face—she could see his struggle for self-control in their dark depths. Then Tell released her completely and strode back to the desk.

"The hell with this. Being alone with you again just wasn't a good idea," he said evenly. There was something in his calm dismissal that told Andrea that he was serious, that he meant it to mean forever.

Okay. Then the hell with him. *Tough talk*, she told herself. *How come you feel like crying?* Catching back a little sob, she fumbled for the doorknob, opened the door quickly and nearly tripped over the Irish setter whining anxiously on the other side. Andrea's fingers trailed lightly over the dog's head in assurance that she was all right before she bolted for the stairs. In her room, she shed the tears she couldn't hold back.

More than a quarter of an hour later, done with splashing cold water on her face to clear her mind, Andrea walked down the stairs in search of Nancy. She looked at the study door and veered away from it.

"Hey. Finished already?" Nancy exclaimed, quickly bounding from the chair beside her mother to go to Andrea's side. "Well, my brother does know how to get to the point."

True enough, Andrea thought. But she only smiled and asked Nancy if she was ready to leave. She didn't want to explain how disastrously her offer had turned out.

"The last time I was in Jacksonville I was barely thirteen. I hardly remember anything but a lot of old buildings," Nancy chatted easily as Andrea started the car and turned it down the lane past the rows of pear trees. "Of course, the day before we had just taken a float trip over the rapids on the Rogue River. Anything would pale in comparison to that."

"The town has been classified as a National Historical Monument." Andrea was determined to keep the conversation from straying into a personal direction. This was going to be a sightseeing trip and that was all.

Ignoring the entrance ramp onto the fast, divided highway, she chose to take the leisurely and scenic back road from Gold Hill to Jacksonville. As they traveled the road with the pine-covered slopes of the mountains in the background, Andrea talked about the old stagecoach road and pointed out the thickets of blackberry bushes that would be heavy with large, succulent berries in late July.

When they arrived at the frontier town of Jacksonville, Oregon, there was a great deal more to attract Nancy's attention. Parking the car and taking a walking tour of the town, they turned off first down Oregon Street so Nancy could see the Brunner general store that the townspeople had used as a refuge during Indian raids, and the Oddfellows Hall across the street. The two feet of dirt between the roof and the ceiling of the latter structure had been installed to protect the building from fire in the event Indians attempted to burn it with a barrage of flaming arrows.

Other buildings had unique pasts as well. The Beekman Bank handled more than thirty-one million dollars' worth of gold, but never loaned any money in all its years of operation. The gold dust from the dance halls and gambling saloons had helped to fund the construction of churches in the town.

The better part of the afternoon was gone by the time they ended their tour with a walk through the old cemetery.

"Maybe Scott and I will come back in August to hear the Britt Outdoor Music Festival," said Nancy, voicing her thoughts aloud as they returned to their parked car.

"I go every year and I really enjoy it," Andrea responded, unlocking the door and sliding behind the wheel. She reached over to unlock Nancy's door.

"You know, I don't really feel like going shopping. Let's go to Medford another day," Nancy suggested.

"We still have plenty of time and it's not very far." Andrea glanced at her briefly as she started the car.

"Don't you feel too relaxed, though?" Nancy tipped her head inquiringly, a bright sparkle in her sapphire eyes. "I know I do."

"Well, yeah." Which was the truth. She had been able to carry off the day's excursion successfully without Nancy being the wiser about the scene with Tell.

"In that case—" Nancy settled into her seat, watching the scenery ahead as Andrea turned onto the road leading them home "—you can give me the details of the argument you had with Tell just before we left."

"Wh-what?" The startled look she gave his sister nearly made her miss a curve in the road. Andrea had to turn the wheel sharply to keep from driving into the ditch. "What are you talking about?"

"You came out of the study in a great big hurry," Nancy replied calmly. "You didn't have time to do anything—just reading the marketing reports would have taken longer. So my guess is that it was an argument that got you out of there so soon." A faint smile dimpled one cheek. "Am I right?"

Andrea pressed her lips tightly together for a moment, then licked the lower one nervously. "Yes."

"What was it about this time?"

Andrea shrugged. "I'd rather not say."

"He won't either."

There was a moment of silence the rural scenery couldn't make peaceful.

"I'm curious about something," Nancy began.

Defensively, Andrea darted a glance at her. "Go ahead. I actually don't have a lot of secrets."

"How come you married a man who's not only old enough to be my father but is paralyzed as well?"

"Uh—that's pretty blunt."

"Sorry." Nancy paused then said emphatically, "But you're beautiful and really nice and all that. I guess I'd just like to know why you married John, whom I dearly love myself. Would you mind telling me why?"

There was no sarcasm in Nancy's request, nothing that Andrea could pick up but a desire to understand why Andrea had married John. In all that time, no stranger had ever asked to understand. They had either jumped to conclusions or tolerated her presence as his wife, without beginning to think of what she might feel.

In spite of herself, a glimmer of tears welled in her eyes. If only Tell had reacted this way, how very differently things might have turned out. Biting her quivering lower lip, Andrea smiled briefly at her companion in friendship. "Thank you, Nancy," she said tightly. "It means more to me than you'll ever know that you asked me to explain."

A gentleness entered the expressive blue eyes. "Will you tell me?" Nancy prompted in a soft voice.

Staring out the front windshield, Andrea began tentatively to relate the events that had led to her marriage: her mother's long and futile fight against cancer, her father's death several months later, and Dale's leaving her for another woman when she had needed most to know that she still had someone who cared. Nancy listened quietly, not interrupting but allowing Andrea to tell her story in her own way.

"Many people look at John and see an invalid, even some of his friends. When my father died, I saw John's strength and I needed it so badly. He was there, offering sympathy, comfort and compassion. He was understanding and kind. Most of all, he was patient," Andrea explained. "I had nowhere to go and no one to care. My mother did have some relatives in the Midwest, but they were strangers to me. There was only John and, in his own way, he needed me, too."

"Do you love him?" Nancy asked after waiting to be certain Andrea had finished.

"Not the way you love Scott," she acknowledged honestly, "but I do care for him. I would never hurt him."

"I should think not." The light airy note teased away the heavy seriousness that had dominated the last miles. "Now, I have something to tell you," Nancy announced with a smile.

Andrea's answer came naturally, warmed by a new bond of friendship established between them. "What's that?"

"I hadn't really looked forward to coming here. I mean, I love John, as I told you, but I didn't know what I was going to do with myself for two weeks," Nancy explained. "Since I've come to know you, I'm really enjoying myself."

"I'm glad."

"I'm almost sorry that we have to leave—oh my

gosh, we're home already!" Nancy exclaimed as Andrea turned the car into the driveway. "It's about time, too." Laughter lurked in her soft voice. "We were on the verge of establishing a mutual admiration society."

Andrea laughed. The two girls were still chuckling over an extension of the same thought by Nancy as they entered the house. Mrs. Davison was at the base of the stairs, with a huge bundle of freshly laundered towels in her arms.

"Now that's a nice sound." Her thin face nodded approvingly. "I've been waiting to hear that ever since Nancy arrived. Mrs. Collins and Mr. Grant are in the living room. Dinner won't be for another hour and a half."

"My brother's still sulking in the study, huh?" Nancy flashed an amused glance at Andrea, who looked hesitantly at the closed door, unable to smile at the memory of their argument.

"Mr. Stafford? He's gone," the housekeeper replied in a tone that implied she thought they had known.

"Gone?" His sister tilted her head inquiringly to the side. "What do you mean 'gone'? Gone where?"

"Well, back to San Francisco, of course."

Andrea's reawakened happiness was instantly deflated by the housekeeper's words. Tell had left and he wouldn't be back.

Nancy frowned. "Did he say why?"

"Not to me." The housekeeper started up the stairs.

"That's strange," Nancy mused aloud, turning absently toward the living room, conscious that Andrea followed but not noticing the change in her mood. "Tell hasn't even hinted that he might have had to go back without us." She glanced at Andrea. "Did he mention anything about it to you this afternoon?"

His departure hadn't been discussed this afternoon, although she had known he intended to leave as soon as he was convinced his mother was better. That part she ignored.

"He didn't mention it at all," she answered, invisibly crossing her fingers at the near white lie.

"Maybe Mother knows what's going on," Nancy murmured as they walked through the living room.

"There you two are! We didn't expect you back for another hour." Rosemary Collins was sitting on the couch, looking youthful and elegant in a dress of pale yellow. "Did you have a good time?"

"A very good time," Nancy said emphatically.

The Irish setter, keeping his vigil beside John's wheelchair, slapped his tail against the floor in greeting.

"I don't see any packages," John observed. "I thought you two girls were going to buy out the town."

"We spent all of our time in Jacksonville," Andrea explained, hoping the warm gray eyes examining her face wouldn't comment on her pensiveness.

"Yes, we're saving our shopping expedition for another afternoon," Nancy added, sitting on the cushion next to her mother.

Andrea could see the beginnings of the question about Tell forming on his half-sister's lips. She wasn't anxious to be an actual part of the conversation. Not when she wasn't certain she could hide her reactions. "Would any of you like a drink?" she asked quickly before Nancy had a chance to say more.

"A sherry for me," Nancy requested. John and Rosemary stated their preferences.

Andrea was at the concealed bar, separated from the others as Nancy began asking about Tell.

"Andrea and I saw Mrs. Davison in the hall," she said. "She told us Tell left for San Francisco. Kind of sudden, wasn't it?"

"Yes, it was," her mother sighed. "He said some problems had come up that couldn't be handled from here."

"Is he coming back?" Nancy asked.

"He said if he couldn't get back, he'd make arrangements for us."

"Which means he won't be coming back," Nancy concluded.

"That was the impression I had, too," Rosemary agreed.

Andrea closed her eyes briefly against the unwelcome idea, then opened them to measure out the vodka for John's martini. Indirectly, she had driven him away by just being here, she thought. Well, too bad. She lived here. If he couldn't deal with it, then that was his problem.

"It's funny," Nancy said with a frown. "When Daddy called the other night, he said everything was going smoothly. I even teased him about saying that so you and Tell wouldn't worry, but he insisted that it was amazingly true. Now what came up that my father couldn't handle alone?"

"I'm curious about that, too." Rosemary Collins studied the armrest of the sofa, displaying an intense interest in the pattern of the colored threads. "I can't shake the feeling that it has something to do with that girl Tell said he met. I hope my mother's intuition is playing tricks on me. As badly as he was hurt the last time, I hate the thought of Tell seeing her again, no matter what the reason."

The glass nearly slipped from Andrea's hand. Her stomach turned at the thought of Nancy's and Rosemary's reaction should they ever learn she was The Girl.

"Oh, Mother, you don't suppose she had the nerve to contact him again, do you?" Nancy was plainly astounded and outraged by the thought.

"I certainly hope not!" was the emphatic response.

"Now, now," John mildly reproved their harshness. "I don't think anyone could make a fool of Tell twice."

"But he was so very much in love with her," Rosemary sighed.

"People recover from broken hearts," John replied in his wisest voice. "You simply have to be patient."

"Did you recover, John?" Rosemary asked with soft sadness.

"Yes," he breathed in deeply. "I recovered, a bit scarred but as good as new otherwise." He patted the arm of his wheelchair as if wishing the conversation was on another subject. Then he glanced over his shoulder at Andrea. "Do you have the drinks ready yet? She isn't the world's most adept bartender, but I keep her around anyway."

"Coming right up," she replied with brittle brightness.

As Andrea carried the small tray with the drinks to the others, she remembered that time several years earlier when John had confided that he had once lost the woman he loved. He had not explained the circumstances, but Andrea had had the impression that the woman had chosen another.

It had been an admission he had made shortly

after Dale had broken their engagement. Until this minute, she had thought he had said it to make her feel better and more able to face the future. For some reason, she hadn't thought it was actually true. Now she realized from Rosemary's comment that he'd really understood her misery.

Knowing that made her feel much closer to him. She drew new strength from his presence, holding her head up higher when it wanted to bow in defeat. Andrea had a feeling she would never see Tell again.

CHAPTER EIGHT

After dinner that evening, Nancy got a phone call from her fiancé. Nearly a half an hour later, she came gliding out of the study, where she had taken the call in private, seeming to walk on air. Her large blue eyes shimmered with a dewy-eyed rapture that tugged poignantly at Andrea's heart.

"Are you here or floating somewhere above us?" she asked lightly, swallowing her envy.

"Somewhere above," Nancy beamed. Then she hugged her arms tightly around herself. "Oh, Andie, I miss him so much! It's just awful being away from him, even for two weeks," she moaned. "My cell phone won't work up here or I'd be on the phone with him practically all of the time."

"I'll bet the feeling is mutual." There was a wistfulness in her smile.

"He doesn't talk about his feelings very much. He's kind of shy about putting it into words, but I like it that way," Nancy said, smiling, her eyes radiant. "Because when he says he loves me, I know how much he means it."

"I'll take a guess and say that Scott uttered those

three little words not too long ago. Am I right?" she added, laughing hollowly.

The haunting memory of Tell's husky voice, vibrating with deep emotion, and whispering those same precious words, echoed clearly in her mind. She would give anything to hear him say that again, even if all she had was just one more minute of his love.

"Oh, you know he did!" Nancy's smile spread across her face. From the living room where John and Rosemary were, the sound of a strident female voice caught Nancy's attention. "Who's in there with Mother?"

"A Mrs. Van Ryden. She was a friend of your mother's when they were younger. She's visiting locally and heard that Rosemary was staying here, so she dropped over to see her," Andrea explained.

"Do you suppose it would seem terribly rude if we sneaked to my room rather than joined them?" There was a mischievous glint in Nancy's expression.

"I don't think we would be missed." With a toss of her dark gold hair, Andrea turned toward the staircase.

They spent a couple of carefree hours in Nancy's room, indulging in girl talk. Even while she enjoyed it, Andrea discovered a bittersweet pain in hearing Nancy's plans for her wedding, but she talked away, only measuring her words when Tell was mentioned.

As much as she liked and trusted Nancy, she could not trust her with the truth of her previous relationship with Tell. Nancy and Tell were half-brother and sister and the family tie was naturally strong.

* * *

It was after eleven when Andrea slipped from Nancy's room. Rosemary had come up nearly an hour before that. The entire house was quiet. Tiptoeing down the stairs, she whistled softly for Shawn, the setter, to take him for his nightly walk. He padded quietly to her side as if sensing the need for silence in the sleeping house.

Out the veranda doors and into the garden, Andrea walked. The dog trotted at her side for several yards before ambling off to investigate the yard. The air was faintly brisk and cool, the breeze coming down from the mountains bringing the fragrant scent of pines to mingle with the blossoms in the orchard. The sky glittered with stars, a crescent moon suspended in one corner.

There was a lonely peace in the cool night. A promise of romance lay in the shadows, but Andrea was alone. She sighed, telling herself that she might as well get used to the feeling. Nights like this were meant for couples and she was out here walking the dog.

A wry smile pulled up the corners of her mouth as she whistled for Shawn. A few seconds later the setter was trotting out of the dark, moonlight shimmering over his bright coat. He pushed his nose against her hand in greeting, then turned toward the house. As always, he was anxious to get back to John.

In the house, Andrea took the corridor leading to the master bedroom, but the setter didn't follow. She glanced back, surprised. He was looking at her anxiously, then toward the hallway. Andrea frowned, then realized that John had evidently not gone to bed and was somewhere in the house.

"Okay, Shawn," she smiled, retracing her steps. "Where is he?"

With a whine of gladness, the setter whirled quickly around, making straight for the closed study door. Only a flicker of light gleamed beneath it. Andrea tapped once, waiting for John's response before entering.

There were no lights on in the room, but the setter made his way to the wheelchair with unerring accuracy. A fire had been lit in the fireplace some time ago. Red coals were all that remained with an occasional flame springing to life only to fade into the embers.

The faint red glow made the wings of gray in John's hair seem more silvery and white. He was staring into the expiring fire, his strong face heavy with concentration. Andrea walked quietly toward him and stood behind him, placing her hands on his shoulders.

"It's getting late, John," she said gently.

He patted one of her hands, then clasped it and drew her around in front of him. "I'll be turning in shortly," he said and smiled faintly as she settled onto the floor beside him.

"What's wrong?" Andrea asked quietly, her hand still held in his.

"Nothing," he sighed.

"Something is bothering you—I can tell. Now what is it?" Her voice was soft, wanting to reach out to him as he had to her so many times in the past.

"Oh—" he drew his gaze away from the fire with an effort "—I'm afraid I put my foot in it this time."

She looked at him curiously. "What do you mean?"

He gave her a rueful glance. "I finally got up enough nerve this morning to talk to Rosemary about Tell's less than agreeable behavior. She told me about his misfortune with love this year."

This year. Andrea wondered if Rosemary had given him specific dates and places that might enable John to put two and two together and come up with Andrea and Tell. She held her breath, waiting to see if he was going to ask a difficult question.

"She asked me to talk to him. So I did, this afternoon, shortly before he left."

"And?" The darkness of the study hid her tense expression.

"And I'm the one who prompted his sudden departure," John concluded with a heavy sigh. "I shouldn't have interfered."

"Don't say that," Andrea protested.

"Why shouldn't I say it? Tell did."

"What did he say?" She bent her head, apprehension lurking like the darkness of night waiting to rush in when the last glow from the fire died.

"I barely got out what I wanted to talk to him about when he suddenly said that he wasn't about to be lectured by me. I tried to explain, as I did with you, that losing at love should make a person stronger, not harder. That's when he told me that he was leaving and that he doubted he would be back and would I kindly refrain from discussing his personal life in future."

Andrea let out her breath slowly. The last request had been issued as a means to protect both of them from discovery. It was cold comfort.

"You tried, John," Andrea murmured, remembering with an ache the time she had tried to explain to Tell and was turned away. "It isn't your fault he wouldn't listen."

"No, I suppose not. But I could have handled it differently. Things might have ended in a better way." Regret entered his voice.

"It's late." She struggled to her feet. "It's time we both were in bed. Would you like some help?"

"No, you go on. I'll stir out the fire, then push myself off to bed." He waved her offer aside before reaching for the poker and wheeling his chair to the firescreen.

"Good night, John."

"Good night, Andie. Thanks for listening. I only wish Tell had."

"Sometimes people feel that they have to find their own way without any help," she suggested, knowing that she had been unable to turn to John this time as she had done in the past.

"You sound very wise," he said as he smiled.

"You taught me how to stand and walk with my head up," Andrea reminded him. It had been one of the most important lessons she had learned.

"I'm glad. I like to think that I do you some good. Your life is your own, you know. Don't let me make a mess of it."

"You couldn't do that." Telling him to get the rest he needed, Andrea opened the study door and walked into the hallway.

The sleeping pills were slow to work that night. Tell was gone. No matter how she tried to push that fact from her mind, it kept slipping back. The first time they had parted, she had cried with heartbreak. Without quite knowing how much he'd meant to her—everything had happened so fast at Squaw Valley she hadn't had time to reflect or think—she'd cherished the hope that someday they might meet again and rekindle the love they had shared. But that had died with this second meeting.

To live without a dream was a frightening prospect to Andrea.

It was the heavens that cried for her—slow, steady tears of rain gloomily dampening the earth. Melancholy gray clouds blocked out the sun for two straight days. There was a mourning hush to the world outside. The breeze stopped playing in the trees and the mating calls of the birds were silenced. There was only the rhythmic pitter-patter of the rain falling from the clouds.

Nancy was standing at the window, gazing out at the unchanging, steady drizzle. Thrusting her hands in the pockets of her jeans, she turned away.

"I thought the San Francisco fog was depressing sometimes, but it has nothing on this." She waved impatiently toward the window.

"Come over here," her mother suggested. "It's much cheerier by the fire."

Obligingly, Nancy walked over to stand in front of the friendly, crackling flames. She stared into them for long minutes, then sighed again.

"I wish Scott would call," she said.

"Nancy, you're becoming as moody as the weather!" Rosemary smiled and shook her head, barely glancing up from the needlepoint in her lap.

"After two days, I'm not surprised that it's rubbed off on me," she retorted.

"Why don't you find yourself a book in John's study and read? It's a perfect day for it. Mrs. Davison is making some cocoa. She'll be here in a few min-utes," Rosemary Collins replied, then glanced at Andrea. "What are you reading, Andrea?"

She had been aware of the conversation between mother and daughter, but she wasn't paying atten-tion. The sound of her name stopped her wander-ing mind from thinking about Tell and what he might be doing, and forced it to concentrate on the people around her.

"I'm sorry," Andrea murmured self-consciously. "What did you say?"

"That must be a good book." A brow was arched lightly in a teasing look as Rosemary repeated her question. "What are you reading?"

The book had been lying open in her lap at the same page for so long that Andrea couldn't remem-ber which book she had taken from the shelf. Ner-vously she flipped the pages to the front.

"It's a collection of short stories by Hemingway," she answered.

"I don't think she's been reading at all," Nancy said laughingly as Andrea shifted her position on the seat cushions of the bay window. "I think she's been staring out the window, daydreaming."

"Mostly," Andrea admitted with a slightly embar-rassed smile.

"I'm not in the mood to read myself," Nancy stated emphatically. "And after playing solitaire nearly all of yesterday afternoon and discovering on the last game that there were only fifty-one cards in the deck, I'm not in the mood to play cards, either. Do you know how impossible it is to win with the ten of spades missing?" she asked with a rueful laugh.

Closing the book in her lap, Andrea set it on the

cushion beside her, swinging her stockinged feet to the floor. Now that she had been drawn into the conversation, it was impossible to ignore her duties as hostess despite the private sorrows of her heart. The rest of her life was ahead of her. She would get over Tell. It had been an intense experience, despite its briefness. Too intense to last.

Mrs. Davison walked into the living room with a tray. Marshmallows bobbed in the rich, steaming mugs of cocoa.

"Would you be wanting any cookies or cake?" she asked as she set the tray on the rectangular marble table in front of the sofa.

"All I've done since it started raining is eat," Nancy sighed. "Please don't bring any food or I'll have to spend the next month dieting to lose the weight I've gained." A mischievous twinkle entered her eyes. "There are only three times that I overeat, as Mother will tell you. One is when it's raining. Two is when I have nothing to do and the last is when I'm missing Scott. So you see, I'm in real trouble."

"Please, Mrs. Davison, no snacks," her mother agreed. "It's bad enough hearing her complain that she has nothing to wear without hearing her moan that her clothes don't fit!"

"Very well," the housekeeper smiled faintly. "The weather report said there'd be a chance of showers tomorrow, though, so there'll be no immediate hope for two of her problems."

Nancy gave an expressive groan of dismay.

"What about a game of backgammon?" Andrea suggested. "Do you play?"

"Sounds great!" Nancy endorsed the suggestion, pushing the silky fine hair from her face.

"I'll go and get the board." Andrea set her mug

of cocoa on a coaster and went in search of the backgammon set.

They were in the thick of the first game, sitting on the floor in front of the fireplace with the board balanced on their laps, when Andrea spied Shawn out of the corner of her eye as he investigated her mug of cocoa. Quickly she pushed it out of reach of the setter's questing nose.

"Be sure your cup is out of reach," she warned Nancy. "He's crazy about marshmallows, especially if they're half-melted in hot chocolate."

"His one major fault," said John, entering the room after the setter. "He knows he's not supposed to, but he'll knock over a cup of cocoa just to get the marshmallows. Won't you, feller?" he asked the dog, which was gazing adoringly back at him, wagging its tail slightly as if in apology for the weakness in its character.

"Everybody has their faults, even dogs," Nancy observed. "Mine is my inability to beat anyone at backgammon."

John wheeled his chair closer. "Is that what you're playing?"

"Yes, and naturally Andrea is winning." The dice dropped from the girl's hand and rattled across the board.

"I'm not much good at games," he commented after watching them play for a few more minutes. "Andrea has been trying to teach me backgammon ever since she learned it last winter."

"She certainly had a good teacher," Nancy sighed, studying the board with a frown. "Who was it? I'd like to sign up for a few lessons about now."

Swallowing nervously, Andrea smiled and pretended that the question had been asked in jest and didn't require an answer. She couldn't very well tell Nancy that her own half-brother had taught her the game.

"It was somebody you met at Squaw Valley who taught you, wasn't it, Andie?" John asked curiously.

"At Squaw Valley?" Rosemary glanced up from her needlework with a frown. "John, you surely didn't make the trip to Squaw Valley last winter, did you? They have six to eight feet of snow there and more. How could you possibly get around?"

"I didn't go. Andrea went on a skiing holiday," he explained.

"Alone? Without you, John?" The older woman's frown deepened.

The thinly veiled disapproval in her voice brought a hint of embarrassed pink to Andrea's cheeks. She kept her gaze downcast, but she felt Nancy's eyes inspecting her face.

"Oh, Mother," Nancy defended, "there's nothing wrong with wives going somewhere without their husbands. Look at you. Right now you're here without Daddy."

"Well, yes . . ." But the unfinished comment indicated that Rosemary thought the circumstances were entirely different.

"Our whole family used to go quite often." Nancy began to talk lightly to ease the tension in the air. "Were you there during the Christmas holidays? We spent one Christmas there. It was so crowded that skiers were nearly bumping into each other on the slopes."

"No, I don't like to be away from home on Christmas," Andrea hedged, not admitting when she was there.

"I suggested," John spoke up, "that she go over

the New Year's weekend so she could celebrate with some young people instead of staying home with me, but she insisted on taking her trip on the first of December."

"The first of December?" Nancy repeated, astonishment parting her lips. "Andrea, that's when Tell was there!"

"Hmm? Was where?" Andrea asked blankly.

"At Tahoe. At Squaw Valley, to be exact. He took a vacation there the same time as you. Isn't that a coincidence?"

"Yes, it is." Andrea passed Nancy the dice, hoping to distract her attention back to the game.

But Nancy clutched the dice in her hand, her expressive face reflecting the thought that had flashed across her mind, expectant and anxiously excited. "Did you see him?" she whispered.

For a minute Andrea wanted to pretend that she didn't know who Nancy meant, but she didn't think she would be believed. "No, I didn't." She shook her head. "It's your turn."

Nancy rolled the dice around in her hands, a thoughtfulness invading her eyes. "Well, there are tons of people who go there."

"Your brother isn't someone I'd forget, believe me," Andrea lied. Her heart seemed to stop and start a hundred times, especially when the light in Nancy's eyes became a little suspicious.

"Where were you staying?"

"I rented an apartment for a week." That was a half-truth anyway, but she needed something more to convince Nancy. "Considering the crowds at the time, it was tough just to get a table for one at the restaurants." *Oh, no, don't go there,* Andrea told herself. "Anyway, it's really not surprising that I didn't meet him. Besides, I kept to myself—I didn't go out and socialize."

"No, I suppose not." The agreement was made with reluctance. "I was just thinking that Tell really enjoys playing backgammon. Like everything else, he's very good at it," Nancy commented.

The very fact that she didn't glance at Andrea seemed to say that she hadn't completely given up the notion that Andrea and Tell might have met. Outwardly, Andrea appeared composed and interested only in the game they were playing. Inside, she was quaking like an aspen leaf in a storm.

"It's getting to be a very popular game," was Andrea's smiling response. "And it's still your turn."

"It's no wonder you hardly ever win, Nan," her mother teased. "You start talking and your mind gets off on another track. You have to learn to concentrate on what you're doing."

There was a brief moment when Andrea thought Nancy wasn't going to let the subject drop and a cold chill raced down her spine. But it wasn't brought up again. Still, there was a wary curiosity in Nancy's expression each time she glanced at Andrea, as if she guessed that Andrea had not told her the truth. Andrea realized there was a stubborn streak in Nancy just as there was in Tell. She doubted very much if she had heard the last of Nancy's questions.

With that on her mind, Andrea stayed close to John and Rosemary for the rest of the afternoon, not allowing Nancy any opportunity to maneuver her into a private talk. It was hard to do because she liked Nancy very much. She just couldn't take the chance of arousing the girl's suspicions again, since Nancy was so clever.

At half past four, Adam Fitzgerald called at the house to see John on business. Andrea answered the doorbell, smiling a relieved welcome at the sight of his familiar face. He handed her a small paper bag as he walked in the door.

"What's this?" Andrea frowned curiously.

"I stopped by the drugstore and Sam, the pharmacist, sent it with me. He said you'd asked to have it delivered," Adam replied.

In the confusion of the near discovery by Nancy, Andrea had forgotten that she'd phoned the pharmacy that morning to have her prescription for the sleeping pills refilled. Making a wry face at her forgetfulness, she took the package and set it on the foyer table for the time being. She was glad they were out of earshot of the guests in the living room.

"Oh, of course," she said. "I guess I didn't expect you to be bringing it."

Adam gave her a quizzical glance. "You look pale. Aren't you feeling well?"

"I'm fine," Andrea said hurriedly. "I just haven't been getting much sleep lately, that's all."

"Are you still having that problem?" he said, frowning in concern.

She forced the tense muscles in her face into a smile. "It's more of an inconvenience than a problem."

"Does John know you take them?"

"Of course he does. I don't keep it a secret."

Adam arched a sandy brow slightly at her defensive tone, but he let the subject drop as Andrea turned toward the living room. "Is John in there?" he asked.

"Yes."

"Would you have him meet me in the study?" he

requested, turning toward the corridor that led to the paneled room.

"Adam," Andrea spoke hesitantly, "if you don't have anything planned would you join us for dinner this evening?" The longer she could keep a barrier between herself and Nancy, the better her chances would be that Nancy might not ask a lot of pesky questions and Andrea would be safe again.

"As a matter of fact, I'm at loose ends this evening." His cheeks dimpled in a regretful smile. "Carolyn is babysitting her sister's children tonight."

"Good." Andrea breathed a silent sigh of relief. "I'll tell John you're in the study and have Mrs. Davison put a couple of extra potatoes in the pot. After almost three days of being trapped in the house by this rain, we need someone new at the dinner table tonight."

"There's supposed to be more of the same to-morrow," he grinned.

"Don't remind me," she laughingly said over her shoulder as she started into the living room.

With the message given to John, Andrea excused herself immediately to go to the kitchen to inform Mrs. Davison of the extra person for dinner.

"So Adam's invited himself to dinner, has he?" was the housekeeper's gruff response to Andrea's announcement. "I don't think that young man cares much for his own cooking. I'll be glad when he gets married and I won't have to keep juggling the portions."

"I invited him," Andrea explained. "I thought it would be a nice break from the routine. Can I help?"

"The way you've been mooning about the house since Mr. Stafford left, you wouldn't be of much help to me in the kitchen," Mrs. Davison retorted. "You'd be in the middle of something and forget what you were doing."

The last of the housekeeper's words didn't penetrate. Mrs. Davison glanced at Andrea, her shrewd eyes taking in the younger woman's pale face and shocked expression.

"Housekeepers sometimes see and hear things they're probably not supposed to, Andrea," Mrs. Davison said quietly, maintaining the rhythmic stroke of the vegetable brush over a carrot.

"The night of the dinner party . . . did you hear us talking in the dining room?" Andrea swallowed tightly, hoping the woman would deny it.

"I heard enough to guess that you hadn't met him for the first time in this house," she answered.

"I see." Andrea stared at her hands, twisting them nervously in front of her. "And what do you propose to do about it?"

"Me?" The housekeeper shrugged. "I don't plan to do anything about it, or the expensive ring upstairs in your drawer, I'm just wondering what *you're* going to do about it."

"You . . . you know about the ring, too?" Andrea asked in a stricken voice.

"I found it by accident." The thin face was softened by a sympathetic smile. "Haven't you told Mr. Grant?"

"You must have realized that it wouldn't make any difference, Mrs. Davison." With a supreme effort to gain control, Andrea tossed her hair, lifting her chin proudly. "And I've already been enough of a burden to John, I think."

"No, no—I wouldn't say that." The housekeeper sighed. "But it's for you to decide. I won't be saying a word. I probably shouldn't have opened my mouth to begin with, but I watched you silently grieving for your parents and that no-good boy you were engaged to. The haunted look was just leaving your eyes when you went on vacation last winter. I've grown fond of you, child." Her eyes anxiously searched Andrea's taut face. "It hurts me to see the pain back."

Andrea was truly touched by the concern and affection expressed by the usually restrained woman. "Thank you, Mrs. Davison, but everything will work out."

"There, I've gone and upset you." The woman looked at her with genuine regret. "Why don't you go upstairs and take a long, hot bath? I'll make sure no one disturbs you."

"I think I will." Andrea knew she was in no condition to return to the living room. Her precarious composure would not stand up under Nancy's scrutiny or any further questions about her holiday in Tahoe.

CHAPTER NINE

Adam's presence at the dinner table that evening was a godsend for Andrea. His easy, outgoing personality kept the conversation on impersonal topics. It had taken little argument to persuade him to stay for part of the evening. When he finally left, a peaceful quiet settled over the house and Andrea knew she didn't need to be afraid that Nancy might bring up the subject of her brother again, at least not that night.

By ten o'clock, everyone had retired to their respective bedrooms. As Andrea creamed the makeup from her face, the carefree air she had worn that evening began to disappear at the same time. Her large, hazel green eyes seemed dull and even the dark gold of her hair seemed less bright. Staring down at the ring that served as her wedding band, she touched the two stones that had been remounted the previous winter, when she hadn't been wearing it. Slowly, she removed the ring from her finger and laid it on the dressing table.

Walking to the dresser, she reached into the corner of one of the drawers and took out the small jeweler's box hiding in the back. Strangely, the gold band was warm as she slipped it on her finger. The rainbow colors of the diamond solitaire sparkled mockingly into her face.

It had been an incredibly generous, impulsive, utterly romantic gift from a man who'd fallen hard for her.

"I'll only wear it again this once," Andrea whispered in a promise to herself. "Only for a little while." Folding her hands together, she carried the ring to her lips, closing her lashes against the dryness of her eyes. "Thank you, Tell," she murmured.

Walking to the curved window on the tower side of her room, she stared into the black drizzle of the night. She imagined a mountain of white snow and Tell leaning on his ski poles, his dark eyes crinkling at the corners to match the warm smile on the masculine mouth, raven black hair glistening with the brilliant blue hues of the Sierra sky.

For long moments, she allowed the vivid memory of him to dominate her mind before turning away from the window with a dejected sigh. The turned-down covers on the brass bed weren't at all inviting to Andrea, but neither was the prospect of remaining awake with longing.

With another sigh, she walked into the adjoining bathroom and opened the medicine cabinet. Then she remembered that her new supply of sleeping pills was still on the table in the foyer. Frowning because she hadn't remembered them before, she reached for the short terry robe on the door hook, pulled it on and tied the sash around her waist.

The upstairs was quiet and Andrea tiptoed along the corridor so as not to disturb Nancy and Rosemary Collins. She didn't want to run the risk of late-night chitchat with Nancy. At the bottom of the stairs was the soft yellow glow from one of the suspended gold lamps always left on in the foyer. As her bare foot touched the rug covering the ground floor, the Irish setter came padding out of the living room, his feathery, red-gold tail wagging slightly in greeting.

Andrea had been positive that John had gone to his room, but the presence of Shawn indicated otherwise. As she peered into the darkened room, there was no discernible shape that she could identify as John. Then the dog ambled down the hallway leading to the master suite. Andrea decided that he must have been wandering through the house and that she had been right in believing John was in bed.

Hurrying slightly, Andrea moved toward the foyer table and the small package from the pharmacy still sitting on its top. As her hand reached to pick up the small paper bag containing the bottle of sleeping pills, she caught a glimpse of an unfamiliar object out of the corner of her eye. A sideways glance of investigation focused on a raincoat hanging on the coat tree, droplets of water still clinging to its waterproof exterior.

Pivoting sharply, she stared toward the living room and into Tell's impassive expression as he stood in the darkened doorway. Her heart stopped completely in an instant of disbelief.

"What are you doing here?" she breathed.

"I came back," Tell answered simply, as if he had intended to all along.

As he stepped farther into the light of the foyer, the yellow glow marked the contrast of the white of his shirt and the teak brown of his tanned skin. A striped tie of gold and brown was draped around his neck, the top buttons of his shirt were undone. His black hair gleamed with dampness, accenting the raven sheen and shading his face.

"Why?" Andrea whispered, wondering if he enjoyed confusing her.

Her hazel eyes widened. At least she understood why the dog had been in the living room. He had obviously heard Tell's late-night arrival and had wandered around the house to investigate.

Tell shrugged, his unrevealing eyes never leaving her face. "What are you doing downstairs?" A hint of impatience at her appearance underlined his question.

Breaking free of his compelling gaze, Andrea picked up the pharmacy bag from the small table, clutching it in her hands in front of her as if it were a shield.

"I left this downstairs," she explained tautly.

"What is it?" Tell demanded.

"It's a prescription . . . I had filled." She stared down at the bag, breathing in deeply to steady her trembling voice.

"For what?"

Tucking a dark blond curl behind her ear, Andrea forced herself to meet his gaze, sensing by the hardness of his tone that he wouldn't allow her to evade his question a second time.

"It's sleeping pills," she answered stiffly.

Long strides eliminated the distance between them before she could take more than one step backward. He took the bag out of her hands and held it out of her reach.

"Give that back to me!" Andrea avoided any direct physical contact with Tell. To touch him would destroy her fragile defenses.

He folded the small bag around the vial of pills and thrust it in his pocket. "You don't need them," he said firmly.

"Why did you come back?" A sudden feeling of anger made her lash out at him. "To make me more miserable than I already am? If that's your plan, you've succeeded."

"Do you think I wanted to come back?" He turned away and stalked into the living room.

Her sense of frustration and the irresistible need to be near him carried Andrea into the room after Tell. "We didn't miss you that much, you know. So why did you come?" she protested. "No one expected you!"

A light was switched on, illuminating his rigid back and squared shoulders. Tell replied without turning to look at her, "I came back because I couldn't stay away—damn, I didn't want to say that aloud," he answered wearily, lowering his head and rubbing the back of his neck tiredly.

Andrea drew a quick, silent breath, her heart leaping at the admission that he was still attracted to her.

"When I didn't know where you were," Tell continued in a low voice, "I counted myself lucky because I wouldn't see you again. Now that I know you're here, I can't seem to stay away from this place."

Slowly, he turned to face her, an unmistakable hunger burning in his eyes at the sight of her, his expression etched by desire. "So I guess the answer is yes, I've come back to make you miserable. At least we'll be equal."

Andrea swayed toward him, wanting to rush into his arms. "I—I think I know what you mean," she said. "I knew it was best that you leave, but I kept wishing you would come back if only for a moment."

"I've been here for hours," he said with a wry curl of his mouth.

"For hours?" That was impossible. He couldn't have been in the house without someone knowing he was there. "Where were you?"

"I was walking, trying to convince myself to leave. I saw Adam's truck in the driveway and—Andrea, you have to tell me if there's anything going on. I want to know."

"Oh, Tell," Andrea murmured in a choked voice. "You don't still believe there's something between Adam and me, do you? He's engaged to a girl that he loves very much. He's nothing more than a friend, more of John's than mine."

"Good."

"He's not important. Forget about him. We have to talk about what happened between us."

"Go ahead."

Andrea took a deep breath and tightened the knot of the sash of her robe, just to have something to do with her hands. "It's the truth that what you and I felt was something very special and rare. It's a feeling that I've never known before or since I met you. I haven't gone in search of anyone to replace it."

"Not even your husband?" Tell retorted harshly. "Or wasn't I supposed to remember he exists?"

"He isn't really my husband." Frustration filled her as she averted her gaze from his face, not certain she could endure another argument with Tell.

"Don't say that, Andrea," he frowned darkly. "You can't deny that you're married to him."

"But what you won't understand or let me explain

is that it isn't really a marriage at all. It's an—an arrangement," she protested.

"That's the way *you* look at it," he interrupted.

"That isn't true." Andrea closed her eyes briefly. "I don't love John in a romantic way and he doesn't love me." Her voice was tired. The strain of the last months had taken away its force, but this time she was going to tell him the truth. She would not allow herself to be sidetracked by his questions. "It was never my intention to marry John, not for his money or any other selfish reason you want to think. It was his idea for us to get married."

"You can't have put up much of a fight or you wouldn't have married him," Tell observed dryly. "John is a big man. I'm sure you can shift all the blame on his shoulders. He's accustomed to carrying heavy burdens."

"Yes, John is a big man." A proud defiance gave Andrea strength to protect the man who had given her so much for so little in return. "And I'm not trying to blame anyone. What I'm trying to do, Tell, is to explain what happened."

"By all means explain." His eyes were shadowed but she caught a glimpse of the fire in them. "That's all you've wanted to do, as if it will make any difference." The pain of longing and love flashed across his face. "As if anything will make any difference."

"Just listen, okay? Shortly after I moved here when my parents died, there was a lot of gossip about John and me."

"People talk. They always do."

"It mattered to me. I was already so traumatized that I—I just wanted to hide away from the world. I didn't want to think, didn't want to work, didn't want to go to college. I'd known John all my life

and he—well, he was afraid for me. It was his idea
that we get married and I went along with it. In retrospect, maybe I shouldn't have but it worked for
us. Don't you see, Tell, it was to give me protection." Andrea pleaded with him to understand.

"And the money?"

Andrea wished he hadn't asked that question. "I
hate that word."

"But maybe not the things it can buy."

"No, I don't hate the things it can buy." She
laughed shortly and bitterly. "And I did feel safe
with John. Until you came along. Not even sleeping
pills keep me from dreaming of you."

"You're not the only one who isn't sleeping well."
In the next instant, she was turned around to face
him, something she really didn't want to do. "How
can you expect me to forget this—that you're wearing another man's ring?"

A frozen stillness held him motionless as Tell
took her wrist to bring her left hand into view and
found himself staring at the engagement ring he
had given her. The lamplight played over the diamond facets, the rainbow hues catching his gaze.

An odd calm softened Andrea's voice. "I often
wear it at night in the privacy of my room," she told
him, "and stare at the empty pillow next to my own.
Does that sound melodramatic?"

"Yeah, kinda."

"It's true, though." Sighing, she glanced from his
handsomely chiseled features to the ring that
claimed his attention. "And I don't expect you to
forget that John's ring belongs on my finger, but I
expect you to understand how it got there."

Slowly, he let her hand return to her side, releasing

his hold on her wrist as he took a step to the side. A frowning, confused look moved wearily over his face.

"I'm trying to understand, Andrea," Tell murmured, but the expressive shrug of his wide shoulders indicated his lack of complete success in the attempt.

Andrea removed the ring and held it out to him. "Here, it's time I gave it back to you," she said tightly. "I should have left it at the lodge desk with the note that you tore up without reading. Instead, I waited in the hall outside the lobby, hoping that when you'd read what I'd written, you might ask me to wear it with the blessing of your love instead of a curse."

His acceptance of the ring seemed automatic, the brilliant colors of the diamond dying in the shadows of his open palm. Andrea didn't say anything more as she turned away to seek the dubious refuge of her lonely room.

"Wait." His pained voice stopped her. "Don't go. Not yet, Andrea."

She couldn't turn around. The tears that had been denied her since his sudden departure now filled her eyes. What little dignity and pride she had left made her not want to let him see her cry.

"There isn't any point in staying," she answered in a low, quivering voice. "What happened at Squaw Valley is over. It seems more and more like a dream to me—like something I wanted so much I believed it was real. But it wasn't. I think we should both just accept that."

"No," Tell's husky voice replied. "It was real. I still want to hold you. It's all I can think about."

He was directly behind her. His hands touched her, drawing her shoulders against the hard muscles of his chest. A shiver of impossible-to-resist sensation quivered through her, the shock waves of physical contact with him undermining her resolve to leave him quickly.

"Don't . . ." Her voice broke for an instant. "Don't make it difficult."

"Huh." He exhaled a short breath. "It's always been difficult to keep my hands off you. Why should now be any different?"

When his hands molded her closer to his body and Andrea felt his warm breath against her hair, she knew that in another minute she would be lost completely to the magic of his embrace.

"No!" Stepping quickly forward, she eluded the light grasp of his hands and turned inadvertently toward him.

He tipped his dark head to the side. "Hey, you're crying." Regret flickered in his dark-lashed eyes. "It hurts me to see it. It hurts me even more to know that you're married to another man when you should belong to me."

Andrea intended to run from him, but Tell's finger touched her cheek and followed the trail of the solitary tear that had slipped out before she could dash it away. His touch felt like the gentlest thing she had ever known.

"Don't," she begged. "It makes things much harder when you're so tender, Tell, so don't."

Tell simply shook his head. "I'm not big enough to understand, and I'm not strong enough to stop loving you."

Her head was swimming dizzily with his nearness. A betraying light of hungry love burned in her hazel eyes, letting him see how susceptible she was to his caress. His hand curled around the back of her neck, pulling her toward him. Weakly, she strained against his arms, struggling to deny the wild, breathtaking beat of her own heart.

But her resistance faded swiftly as Tell kept her close to his lean body. She felt the acceleration of his heart beneath her hand and felt him shudder when she yielded to his embracing arms. Muffled endearments were murmured against her hair, making the world spin crazily until Andrea no longer knew what was right or wrong.

She didn't know how long Tell held her in his arms, crushing her against him as if there was satisfaction in just holding her. And after all the time they had been apart mentally and physically, it was almost enough for her, too.

Then, slowly, his mouth began moving along her hair to her face and she knew the moment had to climax with the searing fire of his kiss. She moaned softly in protest at his slowness. His possessive kiss, when it came, was as glorious as she had known it would be, sensually exploring and masterful and driven by a thirsty passion that Andrea wanted to quench.

She desired him, body and soul. Her hands were locked around his neck to keep him kissing her. His own hands were kindling erotic fires along her back, waist and hips. At last he dragged his mouth from her lips, burying his head in her throat and igniting more sparks of passion that traveled down the sensitive cord in her neck. The collar of her robe got in the way and he pushed the material aside, taking the opportunity to explore her white shoulders and sending more shivers of desire down her spine.

"I love you, Tell," she whispered with aching longing. "I love you."

Drawing his head back, he studied her face with lazy thoroughness, the ardent fire in his half-closed eyes touching each beloved feature.

"And I love you." His deep voice caressed her. "Whenever you're around, I know that all over again. It's like a fever that won't go away or diminish no matter what I do."

A barely stilled gasp split the air, cleaving a space between Andrea and Tell as she pulled guiltily free of his resisting arms. Nancy stood in the living room doorway. Her luminous blue eyes focused accusingly on Andrea. "You're the one!" she gasped, drawing her hand away from her mouth and taking a step forward. "You're the one Tell met at Squaw Valley!"

Tell's arm reached out to circle Andrea's shoulder protectively, but she moved away from it into the shadows where she could hide her humiliation in the darkness until she could regain her composure.

"Nancy, this is personal," Tell spoke quietly but firmly, "between Andrea and myself."

"How can you say that?" his half-sister demanded. "You know, I was beginning to suspect something, but she managed to convince me that she hadn't seen you before. I was even beginning to think she was my friend." She stared at Andrea with hurt scorn. "And all the while, she was using me to get to you!"

"That's not true," Andrea protested, checking the tiny sob that tried to slip through with the last word.

"I believed that story you told me about why you married John. It was all lies, wasn't it?" Nancy accused, running a hand through her silky hair as if unable to believe all of this was happening. She turned to Tell. "How could you have fallen in love with her when she was already married to John? You must have been insane!"

"If it's any of your business, I didn't know!" Tell snapped.

"You're my brother and it is my business!" Nancy retorted.

"You're only making matters worse. Why don't you leave us alone?" Tell shot her an impatient look.

"I just heard you say not two minutes ago that you loved her. You're in love with the wife of our mother's best friend. How could anything be worse?"

"Nancy, please." Andrea extended her hand in a beseeching gesture. "He didn't know who I was or even that I was married. It just sort of happened— and it happened awfully fast."

"I bet it did. You let him fall in love with you and didn't bother to let him know that somebody had a prior claim?" Nancy's tone was incredulous.

"I know it sounds unforgivable . . ." Andrea began.

"That's an understatement," Nancy observed dryly.

Andrea spun away, clasping her hands to control their shaking. "I meant to explain to him," she continued, "but he found out before I even had a chance to begin."

"I'm surprised he didn't just tell you to go to hell!" Plainly indicating that if Nancy had been Tell, she would have.

"That's enough!" Tell ordered, flashing his sister a silencing look.

This time Andrea wasn't able to elude the arms that firmly encircled her. She held herself stiffly, unable to accept his protection from Nancy's barbed remarks.

"Wait a minute," Nancy said suddenly as a thought occurred to her. "A second ago you said Tell didn't know who you were. Are you saying that he didn't know you were John's wife even when he came here?"

"No, I didn't know," Tell answered for Andrea, tenderly wiping a tear from her cheek and gazing anxiously into her face, "any more than she knew I was Rosemary Collins's son."

"At least now I understand why you were in such a foul mood from the second we got here. And to think I felt sorry for her," Nancy sighed. "Would you mind telling me why you're protecting her now?"

"Because, in spite of everything, I still love her." His voice was grim, but filled with conviction.

"But Andrea is married," she protested.

"True enough," Andrea spoke softly, heartbreak in her voice. "Yet neither of you seem to understand that it's only an arrangement. You both seem to think it's wrong that I fell in love when I'm already married, but it's what John wanted . . . for me to find someone to love. He wouldn't call it being unfaithful."

"Andrea—" Tell tried to interrupt, but she wouldn't let him. She was determined to finish her story.

"And you just said that you loved me in spite of everything. That means a lot to me." Her chin quivered as she searched his face. "But there has to be more than that. Trust. Respect."

Nancy snorted disrespectfully.

"Tell, I love you completely and totally. The only

regret I feel is that we've been pretending in front of everyone else that we're strangers." She turned her tear-filled eyes to Nancy. "I apologize for deceiving you, but we'd both taken the lie so far that I had no choice."

Nancy was silent, a shadow of doubt flashing across her expressive eyes, revealing the thought that she might have been too hasty to condemn Andrea for her brother's sake.

"Please, Tell, let me go," Andrea begged. "I'm very tired."

In truth, she felt torn into a thousand tiny pieces. She barely had the strength to make the protesting twist that freed her from his reluctant arms. She wasn't certain that she could put all the pieces together again, or that she even wanted to try. Keeping her gaze averted from both of them, she moved toward the door.

"Andrea, please, we have to talk," said Tell. "We can't leave it like this."

She paused, her eyes downcast, her head slightly turned in the direction of his voice. "There isn't any more to say, besides that we probably got a little carried away. Love is great but it isn't everything— and it doesn't work when lovers lie. We have to be truthful to each other and to everyone else. Without that, I'm better off with nothing. So are you."

Tell followed her to the foot of the staircase, but he made no further attempt to stop her. Every step away from him was an effort. The joy of loving they had shared only a short time before was something she never wanted to let go.

She could feel his silent demand for her to return to his arms where she belonged, yet didn't belong. But this was one time she was sure that she had done the right thing and not responded purely out of instinct—or worse, her own loneliness. At least she had told him the truth, not as succinctly as she would have liked, but it had been the truth.

Without the sleeping pills, now in Tell's possession, Andrea lay awake in her bed, staring blankly at the ceiling, feeling the dampness on her cheeks moistening the pillow under her head. Half an hour later, she heard light, feminine footsteps coming up the stairs; whatever discussion Nancy and Tell had been having was obviously concluded.

It hurt to know that she had alienated Nancy. She had guessed all along that Tell's sister would feel badly toward her if she ever found out that Andrea had been the girl at Squaw Valley. But it was perfectly natural. She could hardly blame Nancy for turning against her considering what she'd put Tell through, but it was painful just the same.

Much, much, later, Tell's even tread sounded on the stairs. Without even trying, she could picture the weariness and defeat in his face. His footsteps halted at the top of the stairs. Andrea held her breath, waiting for them to continue to his room.

Her shaking sigh when they started again was caught sharply back the instant she realized they were coming toward her room. She couldn't bear another confrontation with Tell tonight. Her love for him was new and raw—when it came right down to it, they were right back where they'd started six months ago—and no matter what she'd said, she was just plain terrified of losing him a second time.

When Tell hesitated outside her door, her heart pounded so heavily she fought the irrational thought that Tell could hear it in the hall. She held still and remained silent. If he believed she was sleeping, he might go away.

Sleep. How could Tell possibly believe she could sleep after denying the only man she had ever loved? Her teeth bit into her lip, drawing blood. When she felt she could endure the waiting no longer, his footsteps started again, this time away from her door. Seconds later she heard the quiet closing of the door to his own room and sighed with relief.

Chapter Ten

At first the knock on her door seemed to come from a great distance. The longer Andrea ignored it, the louder it became. Wearily, she opened her eyes, focusing them on the sunlight streaming through her window. It couldn't possibly be morning already, she thought. She had only just fallen asleep. Her exhausted brain couldn't even remember what day of the week it was.

There was another persistent knock at her door. Andrea rolled on to her back, letting her eyelids relax to cover her tired eyes. "Who is it?" she asked in irritation.

The only answer she got was the opening of the door. She frowned, opening her eyes listlessly to identify the culprit who had interrupted her sleep so early in the morning. All thought of sleep vanished completely. Was she dreaming, or was Tell standing beside her bed?

"Good morning." The vision spoke, proving he wasn't really a vision.

"What are you doing here?" she breathed her astonishment.

The expression carved on his leanly handsome features was resolute and hard but his dark eyes were gentle as they moved over her face. The memory of last night came flooding back and Andrea turned her head quickly aside, pulling the covers around her chest, wanting only to hide.

"Please leave, Tell," Andrea whispered.

"No," was his firm and unequivocal reply. The edge of the bed took his weight and Andrea closed her eyes tightly against the intoxicating sight of him. "I love you, Andrea, and I can't accept your decision last night as being final."

"It has to be."

"I don't see it that way, unless—" Tell paused "—unless you never were in love with me and are looking for an excuse to end things."

"How can you say . . ." Andrea jerked her head around, her eyes wide, denying immediately that there was any truth to his words.

Then she saw the complacent smile curving his masculine mouth and crinkling the corners of his eyes in the way she adored. Her heart somersaulted. He had been teasing, not accusing or mocking.

"You see, Andrea," the loving light remained in his gaze as he studied her face as if he would never grow tired of looking at it, "neither one of us can deny how much we love each other. That's a pretty good foundation to build on, isn't it?"

"No." Andrea wasn't sure what she was saying no to, but it was imperative that she not yield to his persuasion.

His smile deepened at her puny attempt to argue. She started to turn her head away, but he captured her chin in his fingers and refused to let her avoid him.

"I walked away from you twice," Tell said. "I won't do it again and I won't let you go away from me."

"No," Andrea protested automatically.

He tipped his head to one side, a hint of determination in his smile. "You're going to have to stop saying that word."

"No," she repeated.

"Yes," he said firmly.

His mouth descended onto hers, taking her lips in a sweetly possessive kiss that was tender and firm. Andrea was unable to check her response, letting her lips move lovingly against his. She had neither the strength nor the will to deny the power of his touch.

"How can you possibly deny this, let alone forget it?" Tell asked as his mouth followed the curve of her cheek to her ear.

His sensuous caress made her skin tingle with longing. Her hands touched his chest, knowing they had been ordered to push him away and unable to obey.

"I can't," she murmured, "but—"

He kissed her hard and long, shutting off the protest she would have made against her own admission. Her breath came in shaking gasps when he finally lifted his head to gaze into her love-soft eyes with satisfaction.

"Are you going to keep fighting with me?" he asked with gentle mockery. "Because if you are, I feel I should warn you that your defenses are in pretty sad shape."

"You're not being logical," Andrea murmured

quietly into the warm wall of his chest, as her heart finally stopped racing.

"Now it's logic you want." He smiled with amusement. "Last night you asked me to have trust and respect. That's a given, loving you. Hey, no matter what you say, I have faith."

"Blind faith?" There wasn't much hope in her questioning voice.

"Is there any other kind?" he countered lightly.

"Yes," she nodded slowly. "There's the faith that comes from understanding."

The amusement faded from his eyes as he held her gaze, his jaw tightening. For what seemed like a long time, the only sound she heard was that of her own heartbeat.

"Tell?" Rosemary Collins's voice called from the hallway.

"Mother, wait a minute!" Andrea recognized the anxious voice giving the command as Nancy's.

The door to her bedroom was open. Tell hadn't closed it when he came in. Her hands found the strength to try to push him away, but he simply clasped them in his own, holding them tightly so she couldn't pull free.

"I love you, Andrea," he said, "I'm not ashamed to be seen with you."

"But your mother . . ."

The quick footsteps of the older woman had nearly reached her door. An instant later she appeared, a smile of surprise and welcome spreading across her face at the sight of her son.

"Nancy told me you'd come back," she began, then suddenly seemed to realize that Tell was in Andrea's bedroom. "Is something wrong? Is Andrea . . . is she ill? What's wrong?"

There was a long pause before the word "wrong" was weakly murmured at the end of Rosemary's question. Tell had carried Andrea's hands to his lips, pressing an intimate kiss on the inner wrist of each in full view of his mother's gaze. The dazed look of shock that halted Rosemary's movement into the room made Andrea feel even more awkward and embarrassed.

"Other than a case of supreme stubbornness, Andrea is in the pink of health," Tell answered.

"I'm sorry." Nancy entered the room behind her mother, apology clouding her sad eyes as she sought Andrea's forgiveness. "I wanted to explain to Mother first, but she didn't give me a chance."

"It's all right, Nancy," Tell assured her instead, releasing one of Andrea's hands and turning slightly on the bed to face his female relatives. "Come here, Mother. I want you to know that Andrea Grant just happens to be the woman I love," he said in a matter-of-fact voice.

"But she's John's wife," Rosemary protested as if for a moment she believed that Tell might have forgotten that fact.

"Mrs. Collins," Andrea's voice was as icy cold as her heart had become at Tell's attempt to use his mother to trap her, "would you please ask your son to leave my bedroom? I've asked him to go, but he just ignores me."

A frown of confusion drew Rosemary Collins's eyebrows together as she glanced bewilderedly at her son.

"Andrea, don't do this," Nancy pleaded. "The things I said last night were wrong—I didn't know it then but I realize that now."

"It's okay, Nancy," said Tell, looking almost

surprised by his sister's protest in his behalf. "It's all out in the open now. I'll leave the room if that's what you want, Andrea, but I have no intention of getting out of your life. I think you should understand that."

"Come on, Mother." Nancy quietly guided Mrs. Collins from the room.

Tell released Andrea's hand and walked as far as the door before turning around, a hard glint in his eyes. She knew by the look on his face that the battle of wills wasn't over.

"Are you coming down for breakfast, or should I explain to John why you're hiding in your room?" A dark brow was arched arrogantly in her direction.

"No," she answered swiftly. "I'll be down, Tell, in a little while."

He knew, as Andrea did, that she wanted to be the one to explain the situation to John; to try to make him see just what had happened. He gave her a brief nod. "I'll see you downstairs."

Was it a warning or a threat? Andrea couldn't decide as Tell closed the door behind him and she heard his footsteps receding along the outer corridor. Perhaps it was both.

Andrea took her time dressing, not just to prolong the moment when she had to go down. She remembered the male vigor that had surrounded Tell, the vitally refreshed air. Only a feminine version of the same could hope to stand up under the incredible onslaught of his masculinity.

The mirror's reflection was satisfying when she was through. The simply styled linen shift with its scalloped neckline, the color of a milky sky, brought out the golden highlights in her dark blond hair and the jade green flecks in her hazel eyes—eyes that revealed her mixed emotions. They, and her heart, were the weakness in her armor.

After slowly descending the stairs, she walked to the breakfast room, taking deep steadying breaths to control the nervousness that had settled in her stomach. All three—Tell, Nancy and their mother— were seated around the table. Tell was calmly sipping a cup of coffee, not even glancing up when Andrea appeared in the doorway. Nancy's troubled expression seemed to echo her own feelings. Mrs. Collins appeared composed until Andrea noticed the way she was fiddling with her napkin.

"Hasn't John come in yet?" Andrea murmured.

"Not yet," Nancy answered, glancing anxiously at her half-brother, who had leveled his gaze at Andrea but hadn't bothered to respond to her question. "Mrs. Davison said he would be here in a few minutes."

Reluctantly, Andrea came the rest of the way into the room. There was a chair vacant next to Nancy on the opposite end of the table from Tell. Ignoring the warming dishes that contained eggs and meat, Andrea poured a glass of orange juice and selected a sweet roll. Her rolling stomach didn't really want anything to eat, but she felt that she had to make the pretense if only for pride's sake.

"I'm sorry about last night," Nancy offered hesitantly in a low voice.

"I understand," Andrea answered self-consciously. "I don't blame you for jumping to conclusions after the way I deceived all of you."

"If you feel that way," Nancy began earnestly, still keeping her voice lowered in an attempt at privacy, "then why can't you understand what Tell is going through? He really loves you, Andie."

"Nancy, let her be for now," Tell broke in.

Andrea stiffened, her gaze moving away from the directness of his. "Are you letting the condemned eat a hearty meal?" It was a strange question, but then it had been a strange morning.

"Uh-oh," he said. "Condemned, huh? Is that the word you would use to describe a life with me?"

"Of course not," she murmured with a sigh. In her nervousness the butter knife clattered against the saucer.

"Thank you." His voice held a trace of mockery. "May I pour you a cup of coffee?"

"Please."

The whirr of the wheelchair sounded in the hallway outside the breakfast room. Tell held Andrea's gaze for a long moment, letting her look away when the flame-colored dog appeared in the doorway. The setter surveyed the room, wagging his tail briefly at Andrea before looking back at his master.

"Good morning, everyone." John's cheerful voice sounded out of place. The room had become permeated with tension.

There were stilted echoes of his greeting by all except Tell, who responded naturally enough. John positioned his chair at the head of the table. Andrea quickly offered to dish his breakfast.

"I must admit, Tell," John said after Andrea had set his plate in front of him, "I was a little surprised when Mrs. Davison told me you'd returned."

"I don't know why you should be," Tell responded easily. "I did say I'd be back if I could straighten out the problems that came up."

"Yes, you did," John agreed as he spooned honey on his biscuit, "but I had the impression that maybe you didn't want to come back, from the last of the talks that we had."

"Where would you get an idea like that?" Despite his relaxed pose, Andrea noticed the watchfulness in his dark eyes as he returned John's glance.

"As I said, it was just an impression," John said, shrugging. "Impressions can be misleading, but perhaps you've discovered that."

Andrea's gaze darted quickly to John. Had there been a hidden meaning to his statement?

"We're all certainly glad you were able to come back, Tell. Isn't that right, Andie?" His warm gray eyes met her troubled look.

The taut muscles around her mouth could only manage a fleeting and somewhat tense smile. "Of course," she agreed quickly.

An uneasy silence followed. While John ate, the others displayed an unnatural interest in their coffee, staring at the dark liquid as if it were a crystal ball that could predict the future. As the silence stretched out, Andrea felt her edginess increase.

"By the way, Tell, thanks—you brought some of that California sunshine back with you," John said, glancing out the window where the sun was trying to peek through the broken cloud cover. "It's been rainy and gloomy around here for the past few days ever since you left."

"I don't think I can take the credit for the sunshine," Tell replied, draining his cup and placing it on the saucer. "There was only fog and gloom in San Francisco while I was there."

"Andrea," John sighed, pushing his partially clean plate away from him, "I think you were too generous with your portions." A strip of bacon remained on the plate. He took it and gave it to the dog lying beside his chair, unaware of any tension in the room.

"Mr. Grant," the housekeeper's disapproving voice came from the doorway into the kitchen, "how many times have I told you that you shouldn't be feeding that dog at the table? He gets crumbs all over the floor and grease, too. Do you have any idea how hard that is to clean up?"

"I'm sorry, Mrs. Davison." John smiled broadly, a mischievous light in his eyes. "I'll remember the next time. I think we're all finished." He glanced around the table to see if there were any objections to his statement. There were none. "Why don't you bring us some coffee in the living room?" Wiping his hands on the napkin and setting it on the table, he turned the chair away from the table. The dog immediately rose to his feet. "Shall we?"

John looked back at the others around the table, plainly indicating that he expected them to follow. Reluctantly, Andrea became a part of the general exodus from the room. She wanted to ask to see John alone, but she was too self-conscious about her reason to make the request in front of the others. She chose a chair in the living room that set her apart from the others, hoping to be left out of the conversation so she could have time to straighten out her thoughts.

"I have a little story I'd like to tell you," John announced when everyone was settled as comfortably as the lingering tension would permit. The housekeeper had brought in the coffee tray, so that was taken care of. "Andrea knows it. Perhaps some of you know part of it, but I think that all of you will probably find the whole story interesting and enlightening."

She wondered which of the stories of bygone days he had compiled for his book John intended to relate. He and Rosemary had reminisced so often in the past few days that she thought nothing of his statement.

"It concerns a friend of mine," John began. "We went to school together, but as often happens, life led us down separate paths once we graduated. We did keep in touch, though, and I was best man at his wedding. After I became confined to this—" he patted the arm of his wheelchair "—we didn't see each other quite so often. He and his wife had a little girl, a real charmer, with her mother's looks and her father's remarkable gift of giving unselfishly."

Andrea slowly raised her eyes to John's face, unable to accept that he was actually talking about her. His eyes were gentle as they met her wary look.

"Several years ago," John went on quietly, "my friend discovered that his wife had cancer. I saw him often during that time, but never once did he ask for pity. I'm not going to get into the details by relating the whole tragedy of that time. It'll suffice to say that even though my friend spent every cent he had, sold everything he owned, borrowed against his insurance, researched medical knowledge and found the best doctors available, in the end, cancer won. When he lost his wife, my friend seemed to lose his own battle with life. One morning he simply didn't wake up. You can imagine the grief his daughter must have felt at losing both her beloved parents within the span of a few short and disastrous months."

Andrea bowed her head, aware of Mrs. Collins's shifting uncomfortably on the sofa and Nancy's sympathetic look directed toward her. Through the screen of her lashes, she saw Tell intently studying John.

"At the time of her father's death, the girl was engaged, to a rather feckless young man, as it turned out. After the funeral, I invited her to spend a few weeks here. It wasn't too great a distance for her fiancé to drive and she had no place to live. I didn't think she'd recovered sufficiently to get on with the business of making a living. Unfortunately, the separation from her boyfriend was not a case of absence making the heart grow fonder. He found someone else more available and more eager to have a good time, so he broke off their engagement less than a month after the funeral."

John paused, letting his audience think that over for a little while. "I don't imagine you can appreciate how traumatic such a series of experiences can be, followed one after the other, unless you'd lived through it yourself."

"Please, John," Andrea whispered, not wanting him to continue.

"This isn't necessary," Tell added curtly.

"Oh, I believe it's very necessary," John disagreed with a wry twist of his mouth, and continued. "After her boyfriend's desertion, I invited her to stay as long as she wanted. At that point, I don't think she cared very much where she was. Unfortunately, the fact that there was a beautiful young woman staying in my house meant a lot of mean-spirited rumors began to circulate about her. I never exactly understood what they thought I was doing, maybe chasing her around the couch in my wheelchair. I expected the gossip to die, but it kept right on going even though it had nothing to feed on. She never said one word about it to me, but I began to feel responsible for adding to her suffering."

"Is that why you married her, John?" Rosemary asked. Andrea didn't miss the disapproving expression on the older woman's face.

"Not only for that reason, Rosemary," he said. "I felt a lot of concern for the daughter of an old friend, a fatherly affection for her, an anxiety about her future, and the idea that someone needed me was very appealing. Plus—" he scowled "—I was swayed by her assertion that she would never love anyone again; that she had lost the only man she could ever love, the fiancé who had left her for someone else.

"I'd known love like that and, even though she was very young, I felt I had to consider the possibility that what she said was true. Under the circumstances, I suggested that we be married. She didn't accept immediately, but I managed to persuade her of the practicality of my offer."

Tell got to his feet, moving impatiently away from the center of the room. "I don't know what the point of all this is, John," he said, "but if it's a subtle attempt to let us know that you're aware I'm in love with your wife, then—okay, I'll admit it. Can we end this discussion? I have a ring in my pocket that I tried to give Andrea earlier. I'm trying to do the right thing."

"Be patient, Tell." John met his glaring look evenly and calmly. "Your anger and the fact that the ring isn't on Andrea's finger means there's still some misunderstanding. I think your intentions are honorable, if you don't mind the old-fashioned phrase. And I do understand that you're in a very awkward position. But let me finish. You'll probably find the rest of my story very informative."

"Do I have a choice?" Tell sighed.

John merely smiled and glanced toward Andrea's wan face. "As I said, Andrea did consent to marry me, but she made one stipulation that I didn't question. She asked that our wedding be a civil ceremony. Obviously it's as legally binding as any conducted by a minister. Only someone who had a very deep feeling about the permanency of sacred vows exchanged in God's house would appreciate the fine distinction between the two ceremonies. And we had an understanding: if she ever found someone else she loved, I would very readily grant her an annulment."

He reached into the inner pocket of his jacket and withdrew a folded legal-size document.

"Last December, when Andrea took a vacation in Squaw Valley, I called her room. Am I mistaken in believing that you were the one I talked to first, Tell?" John asked.

"No, you're not," was the clipped answer.

"I could tell by Andrea's voice when she subsequently came on the line that she'd found her special someone. Don't ask me how I sensed that—I just did. And don't forget that I've known her all her life."

Tell only nodded in reply.

"It was clear that she'd neglected to mention me to you, but I was positive that if you loved her enough you would accept her explanation eventually. At that time I took the liberty of having the annulment papers drawn up—prematurely, as it turned out, but here they are."

"Were you aware I was the man all along?" Tell asked incredulously.

"No. That was fate, I guess," John said and shrugged. "But I think I began to suspect shortly after you arrived that you and Andrea had known each other before. Last night . . . well, your voices carried fairly clearly down the hall to my room."

He wheeled his chair to Andrea, handing her the document with a tender smile. Her trembling hands accepted it as she said a silent thank-you for his understanding and unshakable affection.

"Now!" John wheeled his chair sharply around to face the others, a broad smile on his strong features. "If I've staged this correctly, Rosemary, this is the moment when you and I and Nancy are supposed to skedaddle and leave these two alone to work the rest of it out for themselves."

Nancy permitted herself a heartfelt sigh and an oh-how-romantic look over her shoulder at her brother and Andrea, before her mother led the way out. John followed.

Aware of the room emptying except for herself and Tell, Andrea stared at the document clasped in her hands. The silence continued for several minutes more with neither she nor Tell moving or speaking. Then the shine of his neatly polished shoes was before her downcast gaze.

"Here," Tell said stiffly.

His right hand was extended toward her. The diamond engagement ring she had returned to him last night was held between his thumb and forefinger. She looked at it blankly, then at his tightly controlled features.

"I knew that day I saw you on the slopes that I wanted to see your eyes shine when I gave you a diamond ring—I wanted the moment to be as perfect as that day."

She remembered every detail: white snow gleaming under a pure blue, cloudless sky, and a man waiting for her at the bottom of a slope with a smile that was brighter than any of it. She hadn't known at that moment what was going to happen, but she'd gone to him as swiftly as she could, instinctively aware that what she'd hoped for most was about to happen.

The misunderstandings and hurt feelings seemed no more than a bad dream. One that was over now, thanks to John's kindness.

"Allow me to ask you one more time—" He broke off, as if he were upset with himself for ever having doubted her. "Will you marry me? I promise never to hurt you and never to leave you . . . only to love you."

A hard lump filled Andrea's throat, keeping her from saying the words that filled her heart. With her eyes fixed on his proud, handsome face, she slowly rose to her feet, ignoring the ring still outstretched toward her. A tear slipped from her lashes, then another, sliding unchecked down her cheeks as Tell frowned at the sight of them.

She took two shaky steps and her arms were around his waist as her head found its resting place against his chest. A shudder trembled through him before his arms folded around her and she was brought against his muscular body.

"Forgive me, Tell," Andrea whispered against his throat.

"What is there to forgive?" he murmured thickly. "I'm the one who made all the mistakes."

"Oh, Tell. I was so busy trying to make you understand me that I didn't try to understand you. But I think I do now."

He pressed a kiss to her forehead. "We still need a lot of time before we make our next move." He chuckled just a little. "We. I really like the sound of that."

"Me, too." Removing the birthstone ring that had served as a wedding band for a marriage in name only, she held out her hand to him. "Would you put it on for me?"

Carefully, he slipped the diamond solitaire onto her fourth finger. His mouth was firm, but the fine lines around his eyes were smiling.

"I would certainly like to turn you into a bigamist, Mrs. Grant," he teased huskily, then sighed, "but our church wedding will wait until you're legally free, which won't be too long, thanks to John."

"Yes, thanks to John," Andrea agreed. The warmth of his ring on her finger carried the fire of his love, and there was an answering fire in her heart.

"We owe him, Andrea, both of us do," Tell said, gazing deeply into her eyes, "but right now . . . I only want to be with you."

Andrea met his lips halfway, sealing their silent promise to trust, respect, and love each other for the rest of their lives on earth. The sun burst from behind a cloud, shining through the lace curtains to bathe the embracing couple in a golden glow. The light flashed over the diamond on her finger, sending a rainbow arc of promise from the circling band of gold.

FOR MIKE'S SAKE

CHAPTER ONE

The compact convertible zipped down the street, trees leafed out into full foliage to shade the lawns on either side.

The car's top was down, wind ruffling the scarlet gold hair of the driver, dressed in snug-fitting jeans and a blue madras blouse with the sleeves rolled up to the elbows. Expertly shifting down to make a running stop at an intersection, Maggie Rafferty saw no traffic approaching and let the little car dart across. Ahead was the ball park and Maggie slowed the car to turn into the small graveled lot near the stands.

When the car came to a full stop, she lifted the smoke gray sunglasses from her nose and perched them on her head. Her green eyes scanned the cluster of young boys as she pressed a hand on the horn.

Instantly one separated himself from the others and ran toward her, a baseball glove in his hand. He paused once to wave at the group, backpedaling toward the car.

"See ya Friday, guys!" When he hopped into the

passenger seat he was almost breathless, his dark eyes glittering with excitement. "Hi!"

"Hi, yourself." Maggie smiled, tiny dimples appearing in her cheeks. "Sorry I'm late. I hope you didn't have to wait too long."

"That's okay." He shrugged away the apology, absently punching a fist into his glove. "I'm getting used to you always being late," he said with the patient indulgence of an adult.

"Thanks a lot, Mike." She laughed and reached over to tug the bill of his baseball cap low on his forehead. Punctuality had never been one of her virtues, but she didn't need her ten-year-old son reminding her of it.

"Hey, come on!" Mike protested, removing his cap and putting it back on at his preferred angle. Under the hat was a head full of coal black hair, a shade darker than his eyes.

Maggie's gaze skimmed his profile, lighting on the sprinkling of freckles across the bridge of his nose. They were the only thing he might have inherited from her.

"I told you not to do that."

"Sorry, I forgot," Maggie said. Which wasn't completely true. Mike thought he was too old for hugging and kissing.

Public displays of affection embarrassed him. Maggie just couldn't smother the urge to touch him, so she hid it under the guise of teasing pokes and gestures.

"Are we going home or not?" he prompted.

"Yes, right now."

As she turned to look over her shoulder for traffic before reversing into the street, Maggie's gaze was caught by the man standing on the driver's side of the jeep parked beside her.

He was very good-looking. Tall, in his thirties, with light brown hair and hazel eyes, as tanned as a lifeguard. The look in his eyes was decidedly admiring of her. His mouth quirked into a smile, accompanied by a slight nod of his head in silent greeting.

Maggie returned the smile and the nod without hesitation. One of Mike's teammates raced around the jeep to climb in the passenger seat, and Maggie breathed out a sigh of regret. Why were the good-looking ones always married? She flipped the sunglasses down on her nose and reversed into the empty street.

"How was your first practice?" The Little League baseball season was just beginning. Maggie didn't want to think about the hectic summer schedule that would be ahead.

"Great. The coach says I'm going to make a good utility man, 'cause I can play any position on the field . . . except pitcher. Maybe I should practice pitching." He considered the idea.

"Instead of being good at every position, you should concentrate on one or two and become the best at those."

"I guess," Mike said. "I've gotta improve on my hitting. I didn't do too well today."

"It's only your first practice," Maggie reminded him.

"Yeah, I know. Coach said he'd give me a few pointers about switch-hitting and all if I'd come earlier than the other guys for practice. Do you suppose you could manage to bring me early?"

"You wouldn't have been late today if Aaron

hadn't called from the office just as we were leaving." Maggie knew he was being sly.

"Yeah, but you always leave everything to the last minute. Then when something comes up, we're always late."

"We'll get an earlier start next time," she promised.

There was a flash of blue at the end of a side street, the shimmer of sunlight off the smooth surface of water. In Seattle there always seemed to be a flash of blue around the corner, whether from a lake or an inlet or Puget Sound itself.

"You don't have to take me. I could always walk."

"We've been through that before, Mike." Her mouth was set in a firm line. She'd made her feelings on the subject known many times before. "It's too far for you to walk."

"It wouldn't be too far if I had a bike, a ten-speed. I saw one the—"

"Your birthday is coming up."

Mike groaned.

"Summer will almost be over by then!"

"If you'd taken better care of your old bike, you wouldn't be without one now."

"I only forgot to lock it that one time. How was I supposed to know someone was going to come along and steal it?"

"I hope it taught you a lesson and you'll be more careful with your next bike."

"If you're going to get me a bike for my birthday, do I have to wait till then? Couldn't I have it early?"

"We'll see."

"Maybe if I wrote Dad, he'd buy me one now," he muttered, not content with her half promise.

Maggie gave him a sidelong look.

"You just about ruined your chances of getting a

bike before your birthday. I've told you that it's not good to play me and your father against each other. If he buys you a bike before your birthday, I'll lock it up until your birthday. Do you understand?"

"Yes, ma'am," Mike grumbled, hanging his head, his mouth thinning into a sulking pout.

Concealing a sigh, Maggie let her green eyes look back to the road. God, how she hated playing the heavy-handed parent!

But she had little choice, really. Mike was only behaving like any child of divorced parents would. If she let him get away with that kind of emotional blackmail, he'd be walking all over her. And nobody walked over her, certainly not her own son.

"It isn't so bad, is it?" she asked, trying to ease the friction between them. "To have me take you to practice?"

"No, it isn't so bad," he agreed glumly.

"From now on, I'll make sure you're there early so the coach can give you some tips on hitting, okay?"

"Okay."

As she glanced at him, Mike gave her a knowing look through thick black lashes. A sudden, impish light glittered in his dark eyes. "I know why you're going to get me there early. It's the coach, isn't it?"

One thing about Mike, he never held a grudge, a trait that was totally his own.

Maggie smiled. "The coach?" She didn't follow his comment.

"Yeah, the coach." There was a knowing grin on his face. "I saw the way he looked at you."

"The way he looked at me?" She laughed in bewilderment. "I don't know what you're talking about. I didn't even see Coach Anderson at the ball park."

"He isn't our coach this year. We've got a new one, Tom Darby."

"Oh," said Maggie and then repeated the sound when she realized who the new coach was. "Oh, he was the one by the jeep, the tall, good-looking man."

"Yeah, do you want me to introduce you?"

His dark eyes were twinkling with awareness beyond his years, but then children seemed to grow up quicker nowadays.

Maggie hid a smile at his matchmaking attempt, but there were telltale dimples in her cheeks despite the straight line of her mouth.

"The coach's wife just might object to that, Mike."

"He isn't married."

His grin deepened.

"The boy who got into the jeep with him . . ."

". . . was Ronnie Schneider. Coach was giving him a ride home. You don't think I'd try to hook you up with a guy who's married and has kids of his own, do you, Mom?"

"You can just forget about that. If there's any hooking up to do, I'll take care of it." As they turned a corner the wind blew her hair across her cheek, flame silk against her ivory complexion. Maggie pushed the tangling strands back.

"From the look he gave you, it won't take much," Mike said. "He liked you—I could tell."

His candor brought a bubble of indignant reproof, but Maggie swallowed back most of it, releasing a tame reprimand.

"You see more than you should."

"It's a fact of life, Mom. A guy can't ignore it." He shrugged, knowing he was bordering on outrageous and enjoying the feeling.

"It's not my fault I have a beautiful mother and that half the guys think you're my older sister."

"Do you mind?" she asked as she turned the car into the driveway of their home.

"Nah, I just tell everybody you had a face-lift and you're really a lot older."

"Mike!"

She didn't know whether to be angry or laugh, and in the confusion became capable of neither.

He laughed, finding her astonishment riotously funny. "I don't tell them that, Mom. But you should have seen the look on your face!"

Maggie stopped the car in front of the garage door. "Wait until you see the look on your face if I ever find out that you have!"

"Seriously, Mom—" he opened the door and hesitated before stepping out of the small car "—I don't mind that you look young and beautiful. And I wouldn't mind a bit if the coach was your boyfriend."

"Oh, you wouldn't?"

Maggie switched off the engine and removed the key from the ignition. "Do you think it might help you to score a few points with the coach?"

"It couldn't hurt. It would be pretty hard for him to bench the son of the girl he's dating, wouldn't it?"

"If you deserve benching, the mother might suggest it to the coach."

"Oh, well," he sighed as he climbed out of the car, "you can't blame a guy for trying to cover all the angles if he can."

With a shake of her head, Maggie stepped onto the concrete driveway. Mike took the short flight of steps to the front door two at a time and waited impatiently at the top while Maggie rummaged through her cloth purse for the house key.

"What's for lunch? I'm starved!"

"Homemade noodles." She handed him the key to unlock the door and reached for the letters in the mailbox.

"Can we eat now?"

He was in the house, tossing his baseball glove on the sofa as he headed for the kitchen.

"The glove belongs in your room and we'll eat in twenty minutes, after you've washed and I've fixed a salad."

"You're trying to turn me into a rabbit. Salad!" Mike declared.

"The glove and wash," Maggie reminded him, catching him before he reached the kitchen and turning him back to the living room. "And you like salad, so I don't know why you're complaining about it now."

"I don't like it for every meal."

As Mike retraced his path to the living room, Maggie had to admit her menus had been lacking in imagination lately. She supposed it was a problem all working mothers faced. Cooking for only two people wasn't easy, either.

Still, Mike's criticism was justified and she should do something about changing it in what was left of her two weeks' vacation.

Maggie set the mail on the counter and began rummaging through the kitchen cupboards. There would be time enough to look over the bills later. Right now, she had a hungry boy to feed.

Boy. Dimples were carved briefly in her cheeks at the word. After that observation about his coach, Mike was fast outgrowing the term of "boy".

And here he was matchmaking. Still, it was better that he had no objections to her dating. It would have been unbearable if he were jealous and resentful of her seeing other men.

But Mike had only been five years old when Maggie had finally obtained her divorce, so his emotional scars were few.

Mike evidently liked his new coach. Tom Darby—Maggie remembered the name. He was good-looking, in a jock sort of way, and she would have been less than honest if she didn't admit that she was attracted to him. He liked children, otherwise he wouldn't be coaching a boys' Little League team.

Most of the eligible men she had met lately had either been too young or too old, but this Tom Darby was . . . Maggie took a firm grip on her imagination. The man hadn't even asked her out yet—if he ever would—and here she was assessing his possibilities!

Mike burst into the kitchen.

"My glove's in my room and my hands are washed. Can we eat now?"

Maggie made a brief inspection of him and nodded. "Set the table while I see what I can fix instead of a salad."

"Can't we just forget the salad? I promise I'll eat two helpings of green vegetables at dinner tonight instead. I'm starved! I really worked up an appetite at the ball field."

She smiled crookedly and gave in.

"All right, set the table and I'll dish up the beef and noodles."

Later when Mike helped himself to another portion of noodles, Maggie carried her empty plate to the sink, picked up the mail from the counter and returned to the table. She sifted through the half-dozen envelopes, a mixture of advertisements and billing statements, until she came to the last.

Even before she saw the Alaskan postmark, she recognized the boldly legible handwriting. Her heart missed a beat, then resumed its normal pace.

"You have a letter from your father, Mike."

Her thumb covered the return address and the name Wade Rafferty as Maggie handed the envelope to her son. In an age of e-mails and phone calls, Mike's dad still wrote his son letters. "Great!" He abandoned his plate to tear open the flap with the eagerness of a child opening a present. Maggie sipped at her glass of milk, trying to ignore her pangs of jealousy.

Mike read the first paragraph and exclaimed, "Oh, boy! He's coming home!"

Her heart missed another beat. "Why is he coming to Seattle?"

She refused to use the word "home".

"To see us, of course." Mike continued to read the contents of the letter.

Not us. He's coming to see you, but not us, Maggie corrected him silently.

Wade had no more interest in seeing her than she had in seeing him.

"Does your father say when he's coming?"

It had been six years since she'd seen him last, shortly after their divorce, before he'd left for Alaska, a transfer Wade had requested from his company. Of course Mike had seen him regularly, flying to Alaska in the summers and during Christmas holidays.

The first time Mike went was awful, and Maggie worried about him every second. But it had been even worse when he came back, every other sentence containing "Daddy." Even today, she still experienced moments of jealousy, although none as intense as that first time.

To say her five-year marriage and year's separation from Wade had been stormy was an understatement. It had been six years of turmoil. They were insanely attracted to each other, but he was older than she was, and Maggie sometimes felt that she was no longer in control of her own life. She was naturally independent. Marrying young had taken its toll. During heated moments, Maggie would demand a divorce, until he finally conceded.

They had been too much of a match for each other, her fiery temper equal to his sometimes black rage. Yet, since their divorce they had managed to be civil to each other for Mike's sake, albeit at long distance.

"He's coming home Sunday the . . ." Mike glanced up at the calendar hanging on the kitchen wall, notes scribbled on various dates. "Wow! He's coming home this Sunday!"

He pointed at a section of the letter. "He says right here, 'I'll see you on Sunday. I'll call you first thing in the morning.' This Sunday. Wow!" Mike repeated with incredulity and delight.

"Does he say why? I mean, didn't you write him in your last letter and tell him how much you were looking forward to coming to Alaska this summer?" Maggie felt uneasy. It was so much better when there were hundreds of miles separating her from Wade.

"I'd much rather have him come here. Dad knows that, 'cause I keep asking him to come home. Mom, do you suppose he could—"

"He is not staying here!" She read the rest of the

question in Mike's expression and immediately rejected the idea. "And I'm sure your father wouldn't want to, anyway."

"It was just a thought." Mike shrugged and tried to hide his disappointment.

There was sudden perception in her green eyes as Maggie studied her son's face.

"Mike," she began hesitantly, "I hope you aren't holding out any hopes that your father and I will get back together again. We both tried very hard to make things work, but we simply couldn't get along." Maggie had no qualms about telling Mike the truth. He was growing up and it didn't make sense to lie or encourage any ideas at this point.

"Yeah, I know." He neither admitted nor denied that he had been hoping. "I remember the way you used to yell at each other. That's about all I can remember."

"I'm sorry, Mike."

He folded the letter and put it back into its envelope. "I hate fighting," he declared with unexpected vehemence.

Maggie's head lifted a fraction as she realized that Mike's unwillingness to argue or remain angry for long was a result of the shouting matches he had overheard. It was amazing how children could be so strongly affected by what they'd seen. "Arguments can sometimes be good, Mike. They can clear the air, bring things out in the open and straighten out misunderstandings. It's normal for two people to argue. In the case of me and your father, we were simply never able to resolve our differences. We weren't able to reach a mutual understanding. Sometimes it happens that way." She tried to explain, but it was difficult.

"Weren't you ever happy with him?"

"Of course. In the beginning," Maggie admitted. "Your father swept me off my feet. It wasn't until after we were married that I realized that maybe we'd jumped into things a little too soon."

Mike impatiently pushed his chair away from the table. "Why do you always have to refer to him as 'your father'? He has a name just like everybody else," he muttered.

"It's a habit, I guess. Something that's carried over from the days when you were younger. I'm sorry that bothers you." That wasn't exactly the truth. It was still difficult for her to say Wade's name. To say "your father" came easier; Maggie couldn't explain why.

"Well, he's coming Sunday anyway, and I'm glad." Mike rose from his chair, ignoring the food on his plate. "I think I'll go see if Denny wants to play catch."

It was his turn to do the dishes, but she didn't bother to remind him of it.

She'd do them this time.

At the next practice session Maggie kept her word and arrived early at the ball park so Mike could get the extra coaching on his hitting game. One of his young teammates was already there, sitting in the bleachers and tossing a ball in the air.

"There's Ronnie!"

Mike hopped from the car before Maggie could shift the gear into park. Closing the car door, he paused a second to ask, "Can you stay for a while to watch me practice?"

Tom Darby's jeep was nowhere to be seen.

Maggie hesitated, then agreed. "I'll stay, at least until your coach gets here."

She didn't like the idea of leaving Mike alone. She took an overly protective attitude toward her only child, but it was to be expected.

There was also the motivation, though, of wanting to see Tom Darby again. First impressions could be misleading. Perhaps on second meeting Maggie would find him less attractive.

"Great!" Mike responded and raced off to greet his teammate.

Maggie followed at a more sedate pace.

By the time she reached the tall wire fence protecting spectators from the batting area of the diamond, Mike had persuaded the second boy to join him on the field. Maggie leaned a shoulder against a supporting post and watched them tossing the ball back and forth.

A car door slammed and she glanced over her shoulder at the sound. An iridescent shimmer brightened her eyes as casual, effortless strides carried Mike's coach toward her.

He was good-looking, almost too good-looking, she decided, letting her attention shift back to the boys on the playing field.

"Good morning." His voice was pleasantly low as he stopped beside her.

With the greeting, Maggie let her gaze swing toward him. The hazel eyes regarding her so admiringly had definite gold flecks. Now that he was up close, she found herself even more attracted to him. "Good morning," she replied. "It's a beautiful day, isn't it?" *Is that the best you could think of?* she silently asked herself.

He nodded and added, "The kind of day Seattle people always brag about, but seldom see."

She let her smile widen and asked, "You aren't from around here, then?"

"No, not originally, I'm a native Southern Californian." It fitted. With that deep golden tan, he looked as if he had walked straight off the beach. "But I'm beginning to enjoy the change of scenery."

The lazily explicit way he was eyeing her plainly said he wasn't referring to the landscape of mountains and sea. No woman with an ounce of femininity would be immune to that look.

That look was meant to flatter. If she had any doubt that she was a strikingly attractive woman, it no longer existed.

"It's a nice place to live," she replied. Maggie turned back to the baseball diamond and the two boys. Neither had noticed the arrival of their coach.

And Tom Darby was in no hurry to make them aware of his presence. That fact produced another warm glow of satisfaction in Maggie.

"Are you staying to watch the practice?" He asked in a way that revealed he'd be pleased if she did.

"I'm afraid I can't." A rueful smile tugged at one corner of her mouth. "I have a bunch of errands to do this morning. I promised Mike I'd only stay for a few minutes," Maggie said.

She didn't want him to think he had been the sole reason she had waited. At the same time she didn't want to totally rebuff the interest he was showing in her.

This time Tom was the one to glance at the two boys playing catch. "Your little brother is a very good ball player."

"He isn't my brother," Maggie corrected him with a laughing gleam in her green eyes. "Mike is my son."

Startled hazel eyes flicked a surprised look back to her. "You must have been a child bride, Mrs. Rafferty," he said with a smile that let her know he was only half-kidding.

"No, I wasn't. And the name is Maggie."

"Tom Darby," he introduced himself, his gaze sliding to her ringless left hand.

Maggie saw the question forming on his face and was about to tell him she wasn't married when a shout of recognition from Mike eliminated the chance.

Both boys came racing to the wire fence.

"You said if we came early, Coach, you'd give us some tips on switch-hitting," Mike reminded him on a breathless note, all eagerness and enthusiasm.

"I did," Tom smiled indulgently. "The bats are in the back of my jeep. Why don't you two go get them?"

As they started to dash off to do his bidding, he called them to a halt.

"Wait a minute—it's locked. I'll have to get them for you."

The opportunity for private conversation was gone.

But Maggie wasn't concerned. There would be others.

"I'd better be going," she told everyone in general, but Tom in particular, as she started for her own car. Her parting remark was directed at her son. "I'll pick you up after practice."

"Okay."

He absently waved a goodbye.

* * *

There wasn't another chance that week for the personal discussion the boys had interrupted. That day Maggie was late getting back to the ball park to pick up Mike, and Tom Darby was already in his car by the time she arrived. At Mike's next practice Maggie brought him early but couldn't stay, and again picked him up late.

It couldn't be helped.

There was so much she wanted done before Wade returned this Sunday. The biggest task was spring-cleaning the house from top to bottom. She intended it to be spotless when he came. She wanted to show him how much the space had changed. Plus, there was shopping to be done for new kitchen and dining-room curtains. She even bought a new outfit and managed to squeeze in a visit to the beauty salon.

She was perfectly aware that she was doing all this because of Wade.

It was deliberate, if a trifle vindictive. She wanted him to see how very well she managed on her own. In some ways, she wanted to impress him and wasn't ashamed to admit it to herself.

CHAPTER TWO

"Hey, Mom, are you going to sleep all morning? I'm hungry!" Maggie opened one eye to see Mike standing in the doorway of her bedroom.

She groaned and pulled the covers over her head, trying to shut out her son and the daylight streaming through the window.

"Get yourself some cereal," she mumbled. "You're old enough to get your own breakfast."

"It's Sunday," he protested.

Maggie groaned again. It had become a Sunday morning ritual that breakfast was a special meal. No hot cereal and toast, nor a quickly fried egg on this day. No, it was pancakes with blueberry syrup and bacon, eaten at leisure with neither of them rushing off anywhere, not to school or work.

"Come on, Mom, get up," Mike insisted when she failed to show any signs of rising. "Dad's going to be calling anytime now."

That opened her eyes as the full significance of the day hit her like a dousing of cold water.

Maggie tossed the covers back and rolled over to sit on the edge of the bed. She yawned and paused to rub the sleep from her eyes. Mike was still at the door, as if he expected her to slide back under the covers any minute.

"All right, I'm up. Go and put on some coffee." Maggie waved him toward the kitchen. "I'll be right there."

Mike hesitated, then trotted off.

She slid her feet into a pair of furry slippers and padded to the clothes closet. Ignoring a newer robe hanging inside, she removed a faded quilted one.

"Old Faithful" had seen better days. A seam was ripped out under an arm. Two buttons were off on the bottom. But it was as comfortable as a pair of old shoes, cozy and warm and dependable.

She touched an inspecting hand to her hair to be certain all the clips and hair rollers were in place.

She hated sleeping with rollers but she was anxious about keeping the bounce in her hair.

Most of the time, her thick red gold hair did whatever it wanted and it was hard to keep any kind of style in it. As much tossing and turning as she had done last night she was surprised they'd even stayed in place.

She hadn't been able to forget that Wade was coming. She kept trying to imagine how she would treat him, what her manner would be.

She couldn't make up her mind whether she would be cool and polite or indifferently friendly. How, exactly, did one treat an ex-husband?

Even now the answer eluded her.

At the door to the bathroom, she paused. Shrugging, she walked toward the kitchen.

There would be time enough to fix her hair and put on makeup after Wade had telephoned to say when he was coming.

The coffeepot was perking merrily in the kitchen. Maggie inhaled the aroma wistfully and took out the skillet to begin frying the bacon.

While it sizzled in the pan, she mixed up the pancakes and heated the griddle, putting Mike to work setting the table. As she stole a sip of the freshly brewed coffee she had poured, she noticed the way Mike kept eyeing the telephone by the cupboards. She knew he was anxious, but made no comment.

When she put the food on the table, Mike didn't eat his favorite meal with his usual enthusiasm. He did more playing than eating, his gaze constantly straying to the telephone.

Half a pancake was drowning in blueberry syrup, slowly disintegrating under his pushing fork.

"There's more bacon." Maggie offered him the platter.

He shook his head in refusal.

"Why hasn't he called yet? He said he'd call Sunday morning."

"It's a little early." The wall clock indicated a few minutes after eight o'clock. "Maybe he thinks you're still sleeping."

"But he knows I'll be waiting."

"He also said he'd be arriving late last night. Maybe your father is sleeping late this morning," Maggie suggested.

"Him? Dad never sleeps late." Mike dismissed that, knowing his father never slept in.

Maggie had to admit Mike was probably right. Wade had always been a disgustingly early riser, constantly chiding her for being such a sleepyhead. Wade had always been punctual, if not early, for appointments, while she had been habitually late.

There was a long list of differences between them

and they had been a continual source of conflict during their marriage.

"You'd better eat that pancake before it turns into mush," Maggie advised.

She turned her mind from the long-ago problems that had been resolved by a divorce.

"I'm not hungry anymore." Mike pushed his plate back. His dark eyes gazed at the phone as if willing it to ring.

"You've heard the old saying, haven't you, Mike? 'A watched pot never boils.' Why don't you see if the Sunday paper is here, yet?"

When he hesitated, Maggie added, "You can hear the phone ring outside and it won't take you a minute."

"Okay," he agreed, but reluctantly.

As Mike walked to the side door, Maggie rose to begin clearing the table. Leaving the dirty dishes for the moment, she covered the butter tray and put it in the refrigerator.

The door closed behind Mike.

Blueberry syrup had trickled down the side of its container. She wiped away the sticky substance with a dishcloth from the sink and put the syrup jar in the refrigerator.

As she picked up the bottle of orange juice, the lid wasn't on tight and skittered off onto the floor. It rolled into the narrow slit between the refrigerator and the cabinet.

"Damn!" Maggie muttered beneath her breath, and stooped down.

She could see the lid in the shadowy aperture. Kneeling, she worked her hand into the slit, just barely, and tried to reach the lid. Her fingertips touched the edge. She wiggled her arm a little farther inside and hooked a fingernail in the inner rim. Slowly and carefully she pulled her arm, her hand, and the lid out.

"Hey, Mom! Look who brought the paper!" Mike's excited voice cried.

Maggie was on her hands and knees, twisting her head to see the door open. "Dad drove in just as I went outside." Mike glanced upward at the tall, dark man who had followed him into the house.

She was mortified. Here she was on her knees. With her tattered old robe on. There were rollers in her hair. Syrup and pancake crumbs all over her face. She was shocked for a second, but quickly recovered. "I thought you were going to call first."

"I was," the familiar, deep-pitched voice answered. "Since you were expecting me anyway, I decided not to bother, so I came over instead." Eyes equally black as his hair looked at Maggie. "Hello, Maggie."

The room spun crazily for a moment when she heard his voice. She was paralyzed, unable to move.

There was a familiar leap of her pulse as she stared up at him.

Wade looked achingly the same as when she had first seen him.

That shaggy black mane of hair, those virile, rugged features, that self-assured carriage, all made an impact on her.

A cream silk shirt was opened at the throat, hinting at the perfectly toned muscles of his chest and shoulders. The long sleeves were rolled up almost to the elbows, a look indolently casual and relaxed.

A whole assortment of disturbing memories came rushing back.

Her flesh remembered the evocative caress of

those large hands. The warm taste of his mouth and the male scent of his body was strong in her memory.

Her ears could hear the husky love words Wade used to murmur to her.

He was there, standing in her kitchen, his dark eyes glinting with silent mockery.

There were dirty dishes on the table. The room smelled of bacon, thanks to the skillet on the stove and the grease splattered over the enameled range top.

The place was a mess.

And most importantly, so was she.

This wasn't how she had planned it.

The house was going to be spotless, her appearance immaculate. Her new outfit, the two precious hours at the beauty parlor, all to prove how beautiful she still was, and here she was looking like a caricature of a housewife in the morning. Bitter frustration sparked her highly combustible temper.

"Damn it, Wade!" Maggie pushed herself to her feet, stepping on the hem of her robe and nearly tripping. She accidently dropped the orange juice lid she had struggled so hard to reach. "You did this on purpose. You deliberately came here without calling just to make me look . . . Only you could be that rude and inconsiderate! You can't just show up!"

She was so angry and embarrassed that she was almost choking on her tears.

During the course of her tirade, the glittering light of mockery never left Wade's eyes, although they hardened somewhat.

They became a brooding black, narrowing a bit. His mouth thinned, bringing his harshly masculine features even more into focus.

His hand had remained on the back of Mike's

neck in a gesture of affection, but at that moment, neither of them looked at Mike.

Until he called attention to himself.

"Mom!" he said in a wavering voice.

His stricken look quenched Maggie's irritation.

But the damage was already done. Her outburst had spoiled Mike's reunion with his father and there wasn't anything she could say to take those first moments back. Her fingers curled into the palms of her hands as she strived to obtain some measure of dignity. She hadn't even decided how she was going to deal with his presence.

"I would appreciate it if you would have Michael back home by ten this evening."

Without allowing Wade an opportunity to respond, Maggie walked from the kitchen, her head held high. Her cheeks burned with the knowledge of the picture she made, acting like a lady of the house and looking like a hag. The first thing she did, upon reaching her bedroom, was take off her old, comfortable robe and jam it into the small wastebasket in her room. Then she began tugging the curlers and silver clips from her hair and flinging them on her dresser. She fought back tears.

She didn't stop until she heard the front door close, indicating Wade and Mike had left.

Then she slumped onto her bed, burying her face in her hands.

Yesterday she had been positive Wade no longer had the power to stir up any emotions in her. Yet, she'd been so wrong. She couldn't even control herself around him. Why did he always manage to succeed in making her lose it? And in front of Mike, too. Maggie groaned in despair.

There was only one lesson to be learned from the

incident. Things were just as volatile between them as they always had been. From now on she would have to be on her guard. He wouldn't catch her unawares again.

In the meantime, she still had the task of facing both of them tonight.

CHAPTER THREE

That evening Maggie sat in a living-room chair. The house was once again spotlessly clean. Not a single dirty dish was in the sink. She had perfectly applied her makeup and there was hardly a hair out of place on her head.

She was wearing an elegant jersey dress. Except for the tightly clasped hands in her lap, she appeared calm and completely controlled.

A car pulled into the driveway and she unconsciously held her breath. She heard a car door slam shut, but only one door.

As the kitchen door opened, the car reversed out of the driveway. Maggie slowly began breathing again.

"Hey, Mike!" Her greeting was determinedly bright as she rose to meet him.

She glanced pointedly behind him. "Your father is not coming in with you?"

"No. After the way you acted this morning, I didn't think he'd want to." He didn't quite meet her eyes, but there was no malice in his tone, only the hurt of disappointment.

"No, I guess he didn't," Maggie admitted. "I baked a cake this afternoon—chocolate with chocolate frosting. Would you like a piece?"

"No, thanks." Mike wandered into the room and slumped into the twin of the chair Maggie had been sitting in. "I'm not hungry."

"Did you and yo—Wade have a good time together today? Where did you go?"

She longed to ask if Wade had made any reference to her outburst or her appearance, but she doubted he had. He had always possessed much more control over his emotions than she had.

"Yeah, we had fun." He shrugged. "We went down to the harbor and took a ferry to one of the islands."

"Did your fa—did Wade say how long he'd be staying in Seattle?"

"No."

Mike was usually more talkative than this. She took a deep breath and plunged into an apology. "I'm sorry about this morning, Mike. I really am."

"Weren't you happy to see Dad?" He sounded both puzzled and hurt. "All he did was say hello. You really don't like him that much?"

"Oh, Mike." Maggie sighed. "I don't know how to explain it to you. Maybe you'd have to be a girl to understand." She attempted a teasing smile, but he wasn't put off by it.

"It's been five years since I saw . . . Wade."

"I know, and the minute you see him you start shouting."

"That's because I had curlers in my hair, no lipstick on, dirty dishes all over the table and I was wearing that horrible old robe. I didn't want him to see me like that. I wanted to be all dressed up and perfect. I was embarrassed and because I was embarrassed I became irritated. It doesn't excuse the way I spoke to him, but I hope you understand why."

Mike considered her words for a minute, then nodded uncertainly.

"Yeah, I guess I do."

"I just wanted to be prepared. After not seeing someone for so long, you don't want to look a complete mess. I guess I also felt like he just walked into my life without announcing himself. It's like someone opening the door while you're in the bathroom."

That made Mike laugh. "Yeah, well, the next time you see Dad—"

"I'll apologize." She'd do it for Mike's sake.

"He was anxious to see you, that's why he came first instead of calling. He misses you just as much as you miss him."

Maggie didn't have any doubt about that.

"Which reminds me, what are you two planning for tomorrow?"

"Dad's busy all day tomorrow. He said there were some things he had to do."

"Oh." Maggie frowned. "I thought you'd be spending the day with him, or at least part of it."

"I'm not. Why?"

"Aaron called this afternoon and asked me to work tomorrow."

"But you're on vacation," Mike protested.

"I know, but Patty's sprained her ankle and can't come in. Since it's only for Monday, I told Aaron I could. I thought you'd be with Wade."

She did some quick thinking. "I'll call Denny's mother." Shelley Bixby lived next door and kept an eye on Mike while Maggie worked.

"But what about the game?"

Maggie started for the telephone and stopped. "What game?"

"My baseball game tomorrow afternoon. It starts at five and Coach wants us to be there no later than four-thirty. You don't get home until after five. If I'm late, I'll probably have to sit on the bench the whole time. I won't even have a chance to play."

"Don't start thinking the worst. I'm supposed to be on vacation, so, I'll just tell Aaron that I have to leave by four."

She picked up the telephone. "It's a pity Denny isn't in Little League. Then Shelley could take you both."

"You won't forget to tell him, will you, Mom? You won't be late coming home?" Mike repeated skeptically.

Maggie's fingers hovered above the telephone dial. "I won't forget, and I won't be late."

But she very nearly was.

She didn't leave the office until five past four the next day. A traffic light failed to function properly and there was a snarl of cars at the major intersection where she had to turn.

Five minutes before Mike had to be at the ball park, she turned into the driveway and honked the horn. Mike was waiting on the front doorstep and was halfway to the car before she had stopped it.

He was wearing his striped baseball player's uniform, complete with the billed cap, socks and shoes. He looked cute, but he would have blushed scarlet if Maggie had told him so.

Mike shot her an impatient glance as he hopped into the passenger side of the car.

"You're late."

"Only a couple of minutes," Maggie hedged, and put the car in reverse when his door was shut.

"Dad said I should set all our clocks ahead an hour and then you'd be on time."

She felt a surge of annoyance at the unrequested suggestion, but squelched it.

"I haven't been doing too badly."

Luckily there was little traffic to slow her up. Several other parents were just arriving with their children when she reached the ball park.

There was a faint smugness to the smile she gave Mike. "See? You aren't the last one here." She stopped the car at the curb so he could get out.

He stood outside by the door. "Aren't you going to watch me play?"

"You said the game didn't start until five. I'm going home to change my clothes, then come back. This outfit—" Maggie touched the ivory material of her skirt and its matching top "—isn't what I want to wear if I have to sit in those dirty bleachers."

"Okay. See you later."

And Mike dashed off to where his team was congregating. Maggie smiled wryly as she drove the car away from the curb.

Parking in the driveway, she climbed out of the car and dug into her purse for the house key.

She unlocked the front door and held it open with her foot as she took the mail out of the box.

Once inside, she let the door shut on its own and walked into the living room.

She sifted quickly through the mail as she went,

kicking her shoes off and letting her bag slide from her shoulder onto a chair.

Halfway to her bedroom, the doorbell rang.

Doing an about-face, Maggie walked back to answer it. With a brief glance at her wristwatch, she opened the door and stopped dead.

It was Wade, and her heart fluttered madly against her ribs.

She had forgotten how overpowering he could be at close quarters.

Not because of his height, although he was tall. Her forehead came to the point of his chin and no higher. Nor because of his bulk, since his brawny shoulders and chest were in proportion to his frame. His hands were large and his fingers long, easily capable of spanning her waist. No, the sensation was all wrapped up in the sheer force of his presence.

The years had made few changes, adding character lines to his sun- and snow-browned face. They hadn't blunted the angular thrust of his jaw nor softened his square chin.

There was a closed look to his Celtic black eyes, although the shutters could be thrown open at any time and they would be alive with expression.

Alaska suited Wade, a land raw and untamed, demanding a man capable of compromising with the elements. It required intelligence, keen insight, and a large measure of self-confidence.

These were also the very traits needed to succeed in a so-called civilized society. Wade could slip in or out of either world at will.

Then Maggie noticed Wade had cocked his head slightly to one side.

She realized she had been staring and hadn't spoken a word of greeting.

The day's mail was still in her hand. She stood in her stockinged feet, her hair windblown, her makeup fading. Wade had again caught her off-guard. She managed to curb part of the rush of irritation, but some of it slipped through to make her voice curt.

"Wade, uh, Mike isn't here. He has a Little League ball game tonight."

"Aren't you going to watch him play? Children like to have their parents there, cheering them on."

Maggie bristled. "What are you trying to say? I'm somehow not there for him?"

"I merely asked a question." Wade elevated a dark brow. "I can't control the way your conscience interprets it." He added a smirk.

"My conscience?" Maggie breathed in sharply "What about yours? I've attended every function Mike has participated in. Can you say the same?"

"I never said that I could."

"Before you start throwing stones, you'd better check to see if your windows have shatterproof glass," she warned.

"I wasn't throwing stones. I asked a question that you still haven't answered." His smirk turned into a smile.

"As a matter of fact, I am going to watch him play. I came home to change my clothes first. The game starts at five—" Maggie glanced at her watch, the seconds ticking away "—so I better get going. Why don't you come along? I'm sure Mike would love to have us both there."

"I've been planning to go to the game ever since Mike mentioned it to me yesterday."

"Then what are you doing here? Oh, you don't know where the game is being played." She stepped onto the threshold to point out the directions, her arm brushing his shoulder. "You go down to this next corner and turn—"

"I know where the ball park is," Wade interrupted.

"What's the point of coming here, then?" Maggie stepped back, the brief contact jolting through her like the charge of a lightning bolt.

"I wanted to speak to you privately, although preferably not on the doorstep."

He pointedly drew attention to the fact that she had not invited him in.

A different sort of tension raced through her nerve endings. "You want to talk about Mike. Well, come in, then." She stepped aside to let him in, but he didn't budge. "He's doing just fine. He's healthy and active, as normal as any boy his age. Unless—" her worst fears suddenly surfaced "—you intend to sue for custody of him. I'll fight that, Wade."

His mouth quirked in a humorless smile.

"I wouldn't try. That would be like trying to take a cub away from a tigress. You can sheathe your claws, Maggie. I have no intention of doing that."

She was confused, and still wary.

"Then why—"

He smiled a slow smile that melted most of her resistance despite her better judgment.

After a moment's hesitation she swung the door open wider and backed away from the opening. She walked into the living room, pausing to pick up her discarded shoes and bag and set the mail on the coffee table.

She didn't glance at Wade, although all of her

senses were aware he had followed her after closing the door.

A glance at her watch showed that she was running out of time. "Is there any way this could wait? I really don't want to be late for the game."

She needed a few minutes alone to collect her wits before engaging in any conversation with Wade. "I have to change my clothes. It won't take long. If you want something to drink while you're waiting there's beer, Coke, and iced tea in the refrigerator and instant coffee in the cupboard. Help yourself."

All of that was issued over her shoulder as she walked across the living room toward her bedroom. Wade's refusal drifted after her.

"No, thanks."

"Suit yourself." She wasn't going to force . . . or serve him. She ducked into the hallway, sparing a moment of gratitude that the living room was in order and not strewn with Mike's things, or hers. Tossing her shoes and bag on the bed, she walked to the closet and began rummaging through the hangers for a pair of jeans.

Wade's statement kept running through her mind. He wanted to speak to her about Mike, yet it had nothing to do with custody.

What could it be? School? Perhaps a private one? Not a boarding school—she would never agree to that. If it didn't have to do with his education, what did that leave?

CHAPTER FOUR

A sound in the hallway caused her to turn around and her pulse rocketed in alarm at the sight of Wade lounging in the doorway, dark and innately powerful like a predatory beast.

She turned back to the closet, grabbing the first pair of jeans her fingers touched.

"I told you I wouldn't be long."

"Don't forget I was married to you." He straightened from the doorjamb and wandered into the room. "I know how long it can take you to dress. 'Long' becomes a relative term. When you say you won't be long, I always wonder, compared to what?"

His blandness bordered on indifference, yet his comment irked Maggie. "I never claimed to be as speedy or punctual as you. I doubt if anyone can meet your standards."

She glanced at the pants in her hand and began searching through the closet for a shirt.

"What is this?"

At his question, Maggie looked over her shoulder. He was pulling out the old robe she had stuffed in the wastebasket. There was a hint of mockery in the ebony depths of his eyes.

"You know very well what that is." She yanked a pale blue blouse from its hanger. The color intensified the green of her eyes. With her change of clothes in hand, Maggie stalked to the bed.

"I promised Mike I would apologize to you for that outburst yesterday, but it's not okay for you to show up unannounced like that. If you knew how much trouble I went through to . . . and you find me looking like something out of a comic strip. It wasn't fair!"

"So in a burst of temper you threw Old Faithful away." Wade gave the quilted robe a considering study. "It has seen some better days. Still, it was my favorite. You always look great, Maggie. Even when you think you don't."

Maggie was silenced by the fact that Wade had recognized her favorite robe, even to the point of recalling the name she had given it. She mentally shook away the feeling of surprised pleasure at his compliment. So he had a good memory and was trying to humor her. What did it matter?

"I threw it away."

She tried to act indifferent to the memories attached to the garment. "I have a beautiful new robe in the closet."

"You could've looked a lot worse." He let the robe fall back into the wastebasket.

"Are you trying to console me?" Maggie snapped.

"Remember the Sunday we went looking at boats and you fell off the dock into the water?" Wade recalled with a husky laugh. "I think you were wearing a new dress."

"I didn't fall!"

With jerky movements Maggie began unbuttoning her blouse.

"My heel hooked in one of the boards and I lost my balance. I don't remember you helping me. You just stood there laughing!"

"What could I do? I was holding Mike. Good thing, too, or you'd have drowned him." He was still chuckling, maliciously, Maggie thought. "God, you were a sight! Water dripping from everywhere, your hair looking like a red floor mop."

"I didn't think it was funny then! And I don't think it's funny now!"

Impatiently she tugged at the buttons on the cuffs of her sleeves, finally freeing them and shrugging out of the blouse.

It fell to a crumpled heap on the floor. "Your sense of humor was missing when you waded ashore. You did a slow boil all the way home. We had one whale of an argument when we got back."

"And you slammed out of the house and didn't come back until after midnight," Maggie reminded him.

"Yes." The faint smile left his mouth. "Our fights always ended one of two ways—either me slamming out of the house or right here in this bedroom."

The waistband of her skirt fastened behind. She managed the button, but in her agitation she caught the zipper in the material of her skirt, then in the silk of her slip.

"Damn!" she whispered in an angry breath.

"Most of the time the arguments ended in the bedroom," Wade corrected himself. He saw the difficulty she was having with the zipper. "I'll fix it for you. The way you're going at it, you're going to break the zipper."

Before Maggie could object or agree, he was pushing her hands out of the way.

The touch of his fingers against her spine brought instant acquiescence as a whole series of disturbing sensations splintered through her.

The warmth of his breath trailed lightly over the bareness of her shoulders, his head bent to his task. The musky fragrance of his cologne wafted in the air, elusive and heady. She suddenly realized that she was actually undressing in front of him as if they were still married. As if it were the most common thing to change her clothes in front of a man she'd not seen in five years.

From the corner of her eye Maggie could see the glistening blackness of his hair and experienced a desire to slide her fingers into its thickness.

His physical attraction was compelling. She was on dangerous ground.

She wished she had objected to his presence in her bedroom, or steered the conversation away from how their arguments had often ended. It aroused intimate memories it was better to forget.

There was a slight tug and her skirt zipper slid freely. In proportion to its downward slide, her pulse went up. There was a crazy weakness in her knees, muscles tightening in the pit of her stomach.

"There you are, with no damage." His hand rested lightly on her hip, momentarily holding the skirt up. Maggie couldn't move, couldn't breathe. "I had forgotten how little there is to you."

In a thoughtfully quiet voice, Wade referred to the slightness of her build and how easily his hands could span her waist.

Maggie searched for a quick retort, saying the

first thing that came to mind in order to deny that his touch was disturbing her.

"There was always enough of me to satisfy you," she insisted with a husky tremor, and immediately wanted to bite her tongue.

"Yes."

His hand slid to her waist to turn her around, releasing the skirt and letting it fall around her ankles. "There was always more than enough of you to satisfy me, wasn't there?"

Both hands rested on her waist, sliding up to her rib cage. The silk of her slip acted like a second skin, the imprint of his hand burning through.

The smoldering light in his eyes stole the breath from her lungs.

"And you received an ample share of satisfaction, too," he added.

That look awakened all the sleeping desires that had lain dormant.

As his mouth descended toward hers, Maggie trembled. Would his kiss be the same? Could it still spark the blazing flame of her passion?

Curiosity and familiarity overpowered any thought of protest. She was caught up in the sweeping tide of the past when kissing Wade had been as natural as arguing with him.

Her lips yielded to the possessive pressure of his kiss. That same fiery glow spread through her, hot and brilliant. His grip on her tightened, threatening to crack her ribs, as if he, too, experienced the same glorious reaction. Her arms glided slowly around his neck, her fingers seeking the sensuous thickness of his hair.

The sweetly pagan song in her ears was the wild drumming of her heart while the heat coursing through her veins turned her bones to liquid. Her slender curves fitted themselves to the hard contours of his length, firing her senses with ecstasy.

There had never been any lack of skill in Wade's lovemaking before, but it was better now. More wonderful. More destroying.

Because now that Maggie had been without that special thrill for these past years, she realized the worth of what she had lost. Having lost it, it was even more beautiful to find it again.

His kisses were like rare wine, and they went to her head. She was spinning away into a rose-colored dreamworld where only the crush of his hands and mouth held any reality.

Then the kiss was ending, before her hunger was satisfied. Wade was lifting his head, staring deeply into her slowly opening eyes, which were as yet unwilling to return to the present.

Gradually her vision focused on the frown darkening his face.

"Old habits die hard, don't they?" he mused with a trace of cynicism.

His hands were still supporting her passion-limp body. A flurry of new questions raced through her dazed brain. The fresh memory of his kiss wiped away others that dealt with the bitterness and anger of their divorce. She wondered if she had deliberately blocked out the good times of their marriage, needing to remember the bad to keep from missing Wade.

He had said that he wanted to speak to her about something in Mike's interest. An entirely new possibility presented itself to her. After that shattering kiss, could it be that he wanted a reconciliation between them?

Yesterday Maggie would have found the suggestion appalling. But what about now?

"Why, Wade?" There was an aching tightness in her throat. "Why are you here? Why did you want to see me?"

He let go of her and pulled her arms from around his neck. A muscle twitched along his jaw, constricting in sudden tension.

Not until all physical contact between them had been broken did he answer her question.

"I came to tell you that I'm seeing someone again." Maggie went white with shock, but Wade was already walking toward the door. "I think I'll take you up on that offer of a drink while you finish changing."

He disappeared into the hallway.

She thought she was going to be violently sick. That possibility had never occurred to her. He hadn't said he was getting married again, but the woman must mean something to him if he wanted to bring it up.

Although why she hadn't thought of that possibility, she didn't know. That supremely male aura of his had always drawn women. Besides that, he was eligible and successful. Those two reasons alone were sufficient cause for many women to want him.

Hysterical laughter welled in her throat, and she jammed a fist into her mouth to choke it back. It was all so pathetically funny! After that kiss, she'd actually thought he might have wanted to come back to her.

How stupid! Physical desire hadn't been able to keep their marriage afloat before. Why would it now?

It would never bring them back together. Besides,

she'd created a great life for herself in the past five years. She was a great mother, self-sufficient and happy. It wasn't right that Wade could come back and make her doubt herself. Still, knowing that he was serious about another woman bothered her.

Maggie moaned and buried her face in her hands. She wanted to rush over and shut the door, close out the fact of Wade's announcement until she had the strength to cope with it, to face and accept it. But it couldn't be done.

There wasn't time to pull her scattered feelings together. He was waiting for her.

"Old habits die hard," Wade had said after he had kissed her. Maggie knew that was how she had to regard it.

A kiss between two ex-lovers who had found themselves in familiar positions on familiar grounds. The kiss had been a natural progression of events, but without the meaning it had held in the past.

In a numbed state, Maggie finished changing her clothes. She added a brush of shadow and mascara to her eyes and a coating of tinted gloss to her lips, a splash of color in her otherwise pale face.

She ran a quick comb through her flame red hair. Drawing deeply on her reserve strength, she walked out of the bedroom to rejoin Wade.

He wasn't in the living room. She continued through the dining room into the kitchen.

He was standing at the counter, turning when she entered, a glass in his hand.

"I decided I needed something stronger than beer." He lifted the glass, a lone ice cube clinking against the side, amber liquid covering the bottom.

On the counter behind him, Maggie saw the opened bottle of Scotch.

Wade caught her glance. "You still keep it in the same place—behind the flour canister."

"Yes." Was that raspy sound her voice?

"Do you want me to pour you a drink?"

"No."

God, no! Maggie thought vehemently.

As wretched as she felt, one drink wouldn't be enough. She'd want to drown herself in the oblivion of alcohol and it would probably take more than one bottle. "I'd rather have coffee, thanks."

Walking to the sink, she partially filled a saucepan with hot water and put it on the stove.

Then she reached into the cupboard and took out the jar of instant coffee.

Normally she disliked it, but she kept it on hand for mornings when she overslept and didn't have time to make coffee in her old-fashioned percolator. Now, she realized, she was using it for a different kind of emergency as she spooned the brown crystals into a cup along with three teaspoons of sugar.

"You never used to sweeten your coffee," Wade observed.

His memory was much too good.

"It's the only way I can stand drinking instant coffee," Maggie lied.

The truth was she had heard that black, sweetened coffee was good for shock, and at the moment she felt numbed to the bone.

CHAPTER FIVE

She felt the penetration of his gaze between her shoulder blades, but she hadn't yet the composure to face him squarely.

There was an indefinable tension in the air, even a second's silence hanging heavy. Bubbles formed quickly in the pan of water on the stove. Maggie removed it from the burner before it came to a boil and poured the steaming water into her cup.

As she stirred the coffee, she took a deep breath and exhaled the words, "So it looks as if congratulations are in order, then."

Although she turned to lean her hips against the counter, she again avoided directly meeting his steady gaze, holding the cup in one hand and continuing to stir the coffee with the other.

"We agreed to seek our happiness elsewhere."

"It was obviously the right decision, wasn't it?" Maggie countered, much too brightly. "I mean, you've found someone else. She must make you happy."

"That's right. I needed to, Maggie. I deserve to be happy with someone."

There was a certain grimness in his answer as he lifted his glass to his mouth. But the admission brought a sharp, stabbing pain in the region of Maggie's heart. It glittered briefly in her jewel green eyes before she lowered her lashes to conceal the reaction.

"Who's the lucky girl?"

Maggie sipped at the coffee and nearly scalded her tongue.

"Her name is Belinda Hale."

"Belinda," Maggie repeated, and lied, "that's a pretty name. Is she from Alaska?"

"No, from Seattle, but I met her while she was visiting some friends in Anchorage."

"It sounds like a whirlwind courtship." As theirs had been. She couldn't help saying dryly, "Is that wise?"

"Don't worry—" there was a wry twist to his mouth as he swirled the liquor in his glass "—I don't intend to make the same mistake twice. I've known her for over a year now."

"Oh. Well, I'm glad." Maggie nearly gagged on the sweetness of the coffee. "I hear that you're doing quite well. Mike mentioned something about you getting a promotion."

"Yes, I'm a vice-president in the firm now. I have total charge of the Alaskan operation, pipeline, terminals, new drillings, everything."

His description somehow held no trace of boast; he wasn't trying to impress Maggie.

It had always seemed destined to Maggie that he'd head some big operation.

Wade had always enjoyed challenges and responsibilities. Since he was aggressive and ambitious, it was the natural outcome.

"She must be very proud of you. Of course, dating an executive isn't easy. I hope Belinda is up to the task."

She couldn't care less. In fact, part of her hoped she would prove inadequate. That realization surprised Maggie.

"Belinda can handle it. Her father is chairman of the board."

Maggie's eyes widened at that, sarcasm coating her tongue.

"How convenient. Did your vice-presidency come before or after you put the moves on her?"

That brought Wade out of his languid pose. "The promotion came a year ago. I met Belinda for the first time at a cocktail party celebrating my promotion. I stand or fall on my own ability. You know that, Maggie."

"Sorry, that was a cheap shot," she replied. She took another sip of the heavily sweetened coffee and began to feel its bracing effect.

"I do wish you happiness, Wade. You know that, too." In a more rational moment, she would mean it very sincerely, even if the words did stick in her throat now.

"I didn't come here just to get your okay on this, Maggie. I could have done that with a long-distance phone call from Alaska."

"So, why are you here?" Then she remembered. "You said you wanted to speak to me about Mike."

"Yes. I haven't told him yet that I'm seeing someone again."

Her interrupting laugh was short and humorless.

"I hope you aren't planning to ask me to tell him."

"No. I'm telling you first because I want your support. I know it won't be easy for Mike to accept the fact that I'm seeing someone else.

"From some of the things he's said, I know he isn't going to welcome this," Wade said.

"And how am I supposed to change that?" she demanded.

"By remaining calm. I want him to feel that you're fine so that he doesn't react negatively when he meets her."

"I'm entitled to my feelings, Wade. Whatever they may be. I'm not emotionless and our son isn't either!" Maggie replied.

"I've accepted your emotions, Maggie. I've just chosen not to live in your tempestuous teapot."

Maggie turned away. That remark had hit below the belt. She took a large swallow of coffee. "That was unnecessary, Wade," she said.

"Yes," he sighed heavily, "it was. Look, Maggie, we've managed to have a fairly civil relationship since our divorce, and I don't want anything to change that. Maybe I'm asking too much, but I'd like you to extend the same distantly friendly terms to Belinda. For Mike's sake, I think it would be best."

"Oh, yes, the four of us can be just one great big happy family," she mocked.

After all these years, she couldn't believe her reaction. It was as if she couldn't help herself and was thereby proving him right.

"I'm not suggesting anything of the kind."

Maggie pivoted around to him. "What are you suggesting?"

"That you provide some moral and physical support," he explained.

"What do you want me to do? If you marry her,

walk down the aisle with you and give you away?" she quipped, hiding behind wit to conceal the pain of this conversation. She tried to smile to show that it was meant in good humor.

"Maggie, please."

"Well, I'm sorry. But I don't know what you expect me to do. I have no intention of interfering with your personal life in any way. As for Mike, I'll encourage him to welcome your girlfriend. I don't see how I can do more than that. And I doubt if your Belinda would like it if I interfered more than that."

Wade shook his head and downed the rest of his drink. "One thing is certain—" he set the glass down hard on the counter, his control stretching thin "—Belinda is a hell of a lot more open-minded than you are."

"I suppose you've discussed me with her." That thought didn't set well. "As well as all my little short-comings."

"I discussed our marriage and incompatibility, but I didn't go into detail. Belinda is an intelligent and sensible woman."

"And I'm not." Maggie stated what she felt he had implied.

The line of his jaw hardened. "I didn't say that."

"You didn't have to."

"Once you meet Belinda, I know you'd like her if you would let yourself—" there was irritation in his voice and the glittering black of his eyes "—and not become jealous."

"Jealous! I would never be jealous of her!" The denial leaped from her throat. "Don't forget I divorced you because I didn't want you anymore."

So why did that feel like a lie? Maggie realized

that she hadn't permitted herself to admit still wanting him after the divorce. Subconsciously she had compared every man she met with Wade, and they had all been lacking.

Moreover, if his darling Belinda were in the room at this minute, Maggie would probably want to claw her. It angered her that Wade had been so accurate in guessing that.

"Don't pretend you won't be jealous. It's a normal reaction for anyone whose former mate starts seeing someone else."

"Don't be so damned logical!" Maggie turned and set her cup on the kitchen counter, where some of the coffee spilled. In agitation she grabbed for the dishcloth and wiped up the spill.

As she started to throw it into the sink, Wade's hand closed around her upper arm. "One of us has to be," he said. "I was hoping both of us could be logical about this."

Maggie jerked away from his hold. Her eyes were blazing with green fires, the toss of her head making her hair ripple like liquid flame around her shoulders.

"I'm more than aware that you're free and can remarry or not, as it suits you. I've even offered you my congratulations and wished you every happiness. As for Mike, I've even agreed to help him become adjusted to the fact that he'll not only have a mother but quite possibly a stepmother, as well."

There was a flashing glimpse of the thinning line of his mouth before he was turning his back to her, his hands on his hips. He ran his hands through his hair.

"Maggie, I couldn't let go of you for a long time. I wanted you to be happy with me, but when I realized that you couldn't, that you didn't want to be, I had no choice but to let you go."

Maggie sensed rather than saw the control he was exercising over his own words.

He shook his head and emitted a sardonic silent laugh. "I'd forgotten how easily you can rile me. When we weren't making love, we were fighting, weren't we?"

The embittered question deflated Maggie's anger. The stiffness of defiance and challenge left her shoulders and spine, and she felt the sagging weight of defeat. Tears stung her eyes, acid and burning.

She didn't want to talk about that. At the moment, the memories of that time were too poignant and too vivid. "When are you planning to introduce Mike? You haven't said."

"Soon. Maybe within the month."

Her mouth dropped open. "It must really be serious."

She had expected his response to be autumn or Christmas.

The pain of loss splintered through her, followed by relief that at least this wouldn't be drawn out.

"That isn't much time," she recovered to say. But it wasn't Mike she was thinking about, it was herself. "You should have told him sooner, let him know there was someone you were seriously interested in. You've had over a year."

"How?" Wade glanced over his shoulder, his mouth twisting in a cynical line. "In a letter? Over the telephone? No, that's too impersonal for something that's so important in his life. I wanted us to be face to face when I told him.

"And I wanted him to meet Belinda, get to know

her in case . . . there's a wedding in the future. I couldn't do that from Alaska."

"You shouldn't have waited so long," Maggie persisted in the thought, realizing that Wade wanted to prepare her as well.

"Unfortunately I couldn't get away before now. I considered having Mike visit me, but I knew he would want you around once he learned I was serious about someone else. I did the best I could to arrange to spend this time with him before I go any further with this. Belinda is very understanding about . . ."

"She sounds like a really nice woman," Maggie muttered. Wade shot her a look full of emotion before glancing at the heavy gold watch on his wrist. "Mike's ball game started ten minutes ago. My car is outside. Do you want to ride with me? There's no point in taking two cars."

"No, thanks, I prefer to drive my own. Besides, it will save you having to make the trip back here after the game," she refused his offer briskly.

Common sense told her that it was better if she didn't spend too much time alone in his company. The time would be too bittersweet.

Chapter Six

A silver-gray Mercedes was parked in the driveway behind her small car, the luxury model a sharp contrast to Maggie's economy one. She eyed the Mercedes somewhat resentfully.

It seemed to emphasize the chasm that gaped between them. They were poles apart, as they always had been.

"Your company is generous to its executives, furnishing them with a car like that," she remarked dryly as she walked ahead of Wade to the driveway.

"It isn't a company car. It belongs to Belinda," Wade corrected. "Since I was without one, she offered me hers."

"What's she driving, then? Her father's Rolls-Royce?" Maggie sounded catty and she knew it.

It wasn't that she envied the obvious wealth of Belinda's family. She envied the woman because she would soon have Wade, something all the money in the world couldn't buy. Maggie realized it was easier to just embrace her mixed feelings for him, rather than pretend they weren't there. She'd choke on them.

"She's probably driving her mother's Rolls." His mouth quirked briefly in a mocking smile that didn't make Maggie proud of her remark.

She tried to change the subject. "Which hotel are you staying at? In case there's an emergency and I need to reach you," she tacked on.

"I'm staying with the Hales in their home, not a hotel," Wade said with a glint of amusement in his dark eyes.

"Oh." Was the man purposely trying to kill her?

How foolish of her to have fallen into that! Where else would a prospective son-in-law stay but in the home of his intended's parents? Maggie tried not to think how much time that gave him to spend in Belinda's company.

Their paths diverged as they walked to their respective cars.

Maggie's was closest, so she reached hers first and had to wait until Wade had reversed out of the driveway into the street. Jealousy was a demeaning emotion, she realized as she followed the silver Mercedes to the ball park.

Mike's team was at bat when they arrived. Wade waited to walk with Maggie to the bleachers, occupied by only a scattering of other parents. The rest of the boys on the bench with Mike were shouting encouragement to their teammate at bat.

Mike watched him but was silent, a faintly disappointed expression on his face. His gaze strayed to the bleachers.When he saw Maggie, and a second later Wade, he immediately broke into a wide smile and waved. Maggie returned the salute as she sat down on the second row of the bleacher seats.

Mike poked his teammates and pointed to his parents in the stands.

With all the emptiness in the bleachers, Maggie wished Wade had sat somewhere else other than beside her. Though, it was only right that he did. After all, they were both there to see Mike play. He was their son. Not even Wade's possible marriage changed that.

At the end of the inning Mike dashed to the protective mesh fence near where Maggie and Wade sat. The rest of his teammates were taking the field.

"Hi!" His shining dark eyes gazed at the two people he loved most in the world. "You're late."

"My fault," Wade took the blame. "I had something to discuss with your mother and we lost track of time."

"That's all right."

Mike shrugged away the explanation as unnecessary now that they were here. Glancing over his shoulder at the ball field, he added a hurried, "I gotta go. I'm playing first base." He raced to join his teammates and take his position.

"You do it, too," Maggie murmured. She caught the lift of a black eyebrow in question and explained, "Mike gets upset when I say 'your father' and keeps insisting you have a name. You just said 'your mother.'"

Wade paused and rubbed his face. "It's easier."

"Yes, I know," she responded quietly.

Their gazes locked for a long span of seconds, each knowing why they wanted to forget the first-name intimacy in referring to the other. It kept the memory of their once shared love at bay. Maggie felt the tugging of her heartstrings. Her heart hadn't forgotten that song of savage ecstasy, not a single note of it. Had Wade?

He turned to watch the game before Maggie could find the answer in his dark eyes.

She chided herself for being so foolish. What did it matter if he did remember? She'd divorced him and he'd found another woman whose love played a sweeter melody. It was his right to be happy. It was best if Maggie's heart forgot the love song.

The ball game was close, but in the end Mike's team lost.

In contrast to the marked jubilation of the winning team, there was noticeable silence among Mike's teammates. The corners of Mike's mouth were drooping and his shoulders were slumped by the defeat as Maggie and Wade walked around the wire fence to the team bench.

"It was a good game," Maggie offered in consolation.

"We could have won," Mike grumbled, "if I hadn't struck out every time I was at bat."

Tom Darby approached as the defeated words were spoken. He smiled briefly at Maggie before clamping a hand on Mike's shoulder.

The coach was as handsome as Maggie remembered, but even he stood in Wade's shadow.

"You'll have to work harder at batting practice, Mike, so you can change that," he said. "But you did a very good job at first base. If it hadn't been for you there, the other team might have scored higher."

The words of praise bolstered Mike's spirits and he managed a smile. "At least they didn't clobber us, did they, Coach?"

"They sure didn't," Tom agreed, smiling down at the baseball-capped boy.

He glanced at Maggie. "Mike played a good

game. All the boys did." His gaze strayed to Wade, swift and assessing in its sweep of him, as if measuring the strength of his competition.

Mike caught the look, as Maggie had, and quickly supplied the information.

"This is my dad," he declared with a considerable amount of pride.

In the blink of an eye, Tom's startled gaze darted from Maggie's face to the ringless fingers of her left hand. Then his surprise was hidden by a mask of professionalism as he extended a hand to Wade.

"Mr. Rafferty. I'm Tom Darby," he introduced himself.

Maggie stole a sideways glance at Wade as the two men shook hands.

She saw the aloofness in Wade's expression, his dark eyes cool and withdrawn. Yet behind that chilling veil of indifference they were just as sharp and assessing as Tom's had been.

"It's a rare treat for Mike to have his father attending one of his games," Maggie heard herself saying. "His father works in Alaska and is only here on a short vacation."

She realized she was talking about Wade as if he weren't standing there beside her, but she couldn't seem to stop herself.

Her explanation brought a cloud of confusion to Tom's hazel eyes. Maggie cleared that up with an abrupt, "We're divorced."

There was a moment of awkward silence in which Maggie silently cursed her tactless announcement.

"Don't mind her," Wade said. "She's always said exactly what was on her mind. One of the reasons I married her was because she was so refreshingly honest. After a few years it wasn't so refreshing anymore."

The joke made Tom laugh, but Maggie knew there was more than a measure of truth in it.

She felt the sting, but forced a smile onto her face. "If you have no objections," Tom began, "I thought I'd treat the boys to some ice cream before they go home. Parents are more than welcome to come along."

"Will you?" Mike asked eagerly, wanting to be with his father yet wanting to be with his team-mates, and hoping Wade would say yes so the two pleasures could be combined.

"Of course," Wade agreed, a slow smile spreading across his darkly tanned face.

It only took a second for Maggie to consider her answer.

"Not me," she refused.

She didn't want to spend any more time with Wade, certainly not with the complication of Tom Darby around.

She wanted time to be alone and think, to come to grips with her feelings and Wade's announcement. "I have some housework to do." She turned to Wade. "You will bring Mike home afterward, won't you?"

At his nod, she glanced at Mike. "Have a good time."

"I will."

He was sorry, but not disappointed that she wasn't coming. Why should he be when he saw her virtually every day?

"I wish you'd come, Maggie, but I know I'll see you again." Tom seemed happier now that he was assured she was single.

"I'll see you soon, Tom."

It was only when she was in her car on the way

back to the house that Maggie wondered whether Wade had noticed that Tom called her Maggie and how easily she'd used Tom's name.

Nothing escaped Wade's notice for long. What had he thought? It was obvious that Tom hadn't been aware she was divorced until now.

Sighing, Maggie shook away such questions. Why did she care? Wade couldn't care less.

His only interest in her was as the mother of his child. Any interest in her private life stopped there. He was seriously seeing someone else, and could even soon be marrying. And yet, he'd kissed her. That was still a difficult thing to accept.

There was housework to do. Also, Maggie hadn't eaten. A cold sandwich and a helping of cottage cheese were singularly unappetizing, but she forced herself to eat them. She washed the dishes and put them away—not that there were many to do, a couple of juice glasses and a cereal bowl from this morning, a plate from tonight, and the cup from her instant coffee and Wade's glass, which she'd held a second longer than she needed to.

With the dishes done, she had eliminated all trace of Wade from the kitchen, but she couldn't banish his specter from the rest of the house, especially the bedroom. She found herself glancing out the windows for a glimpse of the silver Mercedes bringing Mike home. The telephone rang and she ran to it.

"May I please speak to Wade, if he's available?" It was a feminine voice on the other end of the line.

A chill went through Maggie. "Wade doesn't live here. Who's calling, please?" She knew what the answer would be.

"This is Belinda Hale. Are you . . . Maggie?" the polite but falsely friendly voice inquired.

"Yes, I am."

She was stiff, on guard, disliking intensely the cultured, musically pitched voice in her ear.

"Has Wade . . . mentioned anything to you about me?"

Again there was an infinitesimal pause, calculated to be secretive.

"Yes, he has, Miss Hale." Her teeth were grinding against each other, but Maggie was determined not to sound like a bitchy ex-wife.

She would be pleasant and nice, even if it killed her. Even if she couldn't understand why this woman had her home number and actually dialed it to look for Wade. The man had a cell phone.

"I'm glad to meet you, at least over the phone," Belinda answered, so very graciously that it grated. "Wade had said he was going to speak to you about us before he told Michael. But I wasn't certain if he'd had an opportunity. He also mentioned some baseball game or other that Michael was playing in, so I didn't know whether he'd talked to you privately yet."

"Yes, we spoke before the game started." Maggie's fingers tightened around the receiver.

If it had been the woman's throat, she would have been strangled by now.

As it was, there was little Maggie could do to silence her, short of hanging up.

Wade had at some point mentioned that Belinda was blond. Hearing her voice, Maggie could almost picture her. Blond, probably with blue eyes, always wearing the right clothes with just the right amount of makeup, always poised and prepared for any contingency.

Wade would never find his Belinda with rollers in her hair, wearing an old bathrobe, on her hands and knees.

Belinda was the opposite of Maggie, and listening to the cool, unflustered voice, Maggie believed it.

"Oh. Is the game over?" Belinda Hale asked smoothly, with the proper note of innocent surprise.

"Yes." Maggie's answer was curt.

"I imagine Wade is on his way home, then, and it was needless for me to call."

Maggie wondered if the other woman knew how stinging it was to hear Belinda's home referred to as Wade's. She decided it had been deliberate.

"He's not on his way home," she said with a trace of smugness. She'd just about had it with this charade.

"Oh?"

"Mike's coach is treating the team to ice cream, and Wade went along. He promised to bring Mike home afterward. Could you please explain to me why you're calling my home? Wade has a cell phone."

"Oh, well, he left me the phone number in case of an emergency and well . . . apparently, his cell phone is turned off."

"Is this an emergency?" Maggie asked.

"Well, uh . . . no, not exactly. I apologize for the inconvenience, but I was a bit worried about him. We speak frequently and I'm just not used to him being incommunicable for this long," Belinda answered in a voice full of fake sugary sweetness.

"I'll let him know you called, Belinda. Maybe his cell phone ran out of battery," Maggie answered, eager to get off the phone and back to the privacy of her thoughts.

"Would you, please, if it isn't too much trouble?" So polite, so courteous, so pseudowarm. "One of my very dearest friends stopped by this evening. I'm hoping that Wade will come back in time to meet her."

"I'm sure he will if he can."

"Yes. Wade can be such a darling at times, and," Belinda added with a throaty laugh, "so infuriatingly stubborn at other times. But, of course, I don't need to tell you that. You *were* married to him."

Again Maggie felt the prick of a sharp blade jabbing at her while her assailant smiled benignly and placed emphasis on their past tense marriage.

"That was a long time ago, Belinda," Maggie replied. She wanted to add "so why don't you get over it," and then realized that would've been mighty hypocritical. It didn't seem that long ago at all. Maybe because it hadn't been very long since he'd held her in his arms and kissed her and all that old magic had come racing back, more potent than before.

"I really am looking forward to meeting you, Maggie. I know that must sound strange, but I do mean it. It's just that I don't see any reason for there to be any enmity between us. Obviously we aren't in competition for anything. Both you and Wade wanted the divorce. For Michael's sake, I think it would be very important for us to be friends."

"I'm looking forward to meeting you, too, Belinda." For once, Maggie held her usually candid tongue.

A suspicion was beginning to form. Open-minded, Wade had described her. Almost ridiculously so, Maggie decided. Not for a minute did she believe a hand of friendship was being extended to her.

More than likely the gesture was part of Belinda's act to impress Wade with her unselfishness, her lack of jealousy and possessiveness.

While it cemented her relationship with Wade, Belinda would know it'd put any red-blooded ex-wife on the defensive. If she rejected the attempt at friendliness by Belinda, Wade would view it as spite and ill temper on Maggie's part. The woman was clever, very clever.

"Wade has promised we'll meet sometime soon," Belinda went on. "And I can hardly wait to meet Michael. Wade has talked about him so much that I almost feel I know him already. I just don't want things to be difficult for him after Wade and I are married."

"I wasn't aware that you were engaged, Belinda. Wade didn't mention that, but I know that he's very serious about you." Maggie bit her finger after that one.

"Oh, well, it's not official, but of course it's the natural progression of our relationship. My family simply adores him. I naturally want Michael to continue to visit us, just as he always has visited his father in the past," Belinda cooed.

"Well, Mike has always enjoyed visiting his father," Maggie returned. "I doubt he'll enjoy it any less with you around."

"You and I should get together for a private little chat. I want to learn what Michael's favorite foods are and the things he likes to do, his pet peeves, and so on."

"Mike is a normal boy, easier to please than most."

Maggie was not up to the task of making a list of her son's likes and dislikes.

"I'm certain he's a darling. Every photograph I've seen of him, Michael has had a striking resemblance to Wade."

"Yes, he has Wade's dark coloring," Maggie agreed. "His personality is very much his own, though."

"After Wade formally introduces us, we shall have to get together and have that little chat. You can sort of forewarn me about the things that irritate Michael . . . and Wade, for that matter.

"I don't mean any offense, but I don't want to make the same mistake you did in your marriage to Wade. Perhaps you can steer me right."

The woman was insane! This was really about Wade, not her wanting to make her son feel comfortable. "Look, Belinda. I have to go. I look forward to meeting you," Maggie dryly answered.

"So do I." Belinda laughed, and again it was that practiced laugh that sounded in the throat, rich and husky like velvet. "But you probably do know more about Wade's darker side than I do. I'd be grateful for any tidbit you would want to share."

Maggie couldn't tolerate any more of the phone conversation. "I'm sure you want to get back to your friend. I'll let Wade know you called as soon as he brings Mike home."

"Thank you, I do appreciate that. I hope I'll be talking to you again very soon, Maggie."

"Yes—me, too, Belinda," Maggie lied through her teeth, and waited until she heard the disconnecting click before she slammed the receiver onto its cradle out of sheer frustration. There was no solace in the fact that she hadn't exactly lost her composure. All she felt was a growing sense of despair.

The only way to cope with the situation seemed to be to get through it with as much grace as possible, which wasn't one of her fortes, and to take each day after that as it came.

A car door slammed outside. Maggie guessed it was Wade bringing Mike back.

Remembering the last time when he had dropped Mike off and left, she was tempted not to go outside and tell him that Belinda had called. But what good would it do? She didn't want to be accused of not passing on her message.

Wade was just stepping out of the car when Maggie opened the front door. "There was a telephone call for you, Wade."

An absent frown creased his forehead. "Who?"

Maggie hesitated for a fraction of a second, aware of Mike slowly making his way up the sidewalk to the house. "Miss Hale asked you to call her."

Wade grabbed his cell phone out of his jacket pocket and sighed. "May I use your phone?"

No! Maggie wanted to scream, but she controlled the impulse and nodded. "Of course. Come in."

At that moment Mike ducked under her arm and slipped into the house. Automatically she prompted him, "Change out of your uniform."

"I will," was his desultory murmur.

Her nerves grew taut as Wade drew closer, his nearness vibrating them like a tuning fork. He gave her a warm, open look of appraisal before walking past her into the house. She closed the door, fighting the weakness in her knees.

"You can go in the kitchen if you'd like some privacy," she offered, but Wade was already walking toward the beige phone in the living room.

"It isn't necessary." He picked up the receiver and began dialing the number with an economy of movement. Maggie wanted to make herself scarce, but his indifference trapped her into listening to a one-sided conversation.

"This is Wade." While he waited, his sharp gaze swerved to Maggie. "Did she say why she called?"

"Something about a friend she wanted you to meet," she answered.

He seemed somewhat relieved. His attention was suddenly diverted by a voice on the other end of the phone. "Hey." He was returning a greeting, his voice intimately quiet.

A pain twisted through Maggie at the sensual softening of his mouth. "Yes, she did. Is everything all right?" Wade asked. "I'm here now—" he glanced at his watch "—about twenty minutes, depending on the traffic." With penetrating swiftness his gaze slashed back to Maggie. "You did? I'm glad."

There was a skeptically mocking lift of one eyebrow, and it didn't require much deduction for Maggie to guess they were talking about her. "Yes, I'll be there soon." Maggie's fingers curled into her palms. She couldn't believe that after five years, the waves of jealousy and envy washing through her nearly swamped her control.

She turned her back to Wade, her stomach a churning ball.

"Belinda said she had a 'nice' conversation with you. The adjective was hers, not mine," Wade commented.

"What did you think I would do? Hang up on her?" Maggie snapped.

"I wouldn't have been surprised if you had," he countered dryly.

She spun around.

Her temper had been held in check too long, and it flared now as fiery as her red hair. "No, you shouldn't have been surprised. Belinda said you gave her my home number in case of an emergency. I don't think her wanting you to meet her friend qualifies as an emergency, Wade. This is my house. My telephone. You don't live here anymore, remember? You can't just go handing out my telephone number to people without speaking to me about it first!"

"My cell phone had no battery left. She was worried. I'm sorry about that, Maggie."

"Look, Wade, I've had a long day, okay? I just want to finish it." Maggie sighed.

She decided that telling Wade about Belinda's interrogation wasn't worth it. She'd come off sounding like a jealous fool. She didn't like Belinda; she never would, but she didn't doubt that the woman was going to attempt to be all things to Wade.

A nerve twitched convulsively in Wade's jaw as he took a step closer.

Maggie just wanted him to leave, but held her ground.

"I want you to explain why you're still single. I don't see anybody beating a path to your door. From what Mike has mentioned, you don't date frequently. Why?"

"I have as many dates as I want, when I want them and with whom! Besides, after wiggling out from underneath your thumb, I value my freedom."

"No commitments, is that it?" He towered above her, male and dominating.

"That's it!"

"Men like Mike's coach must like that. You make it easy for them."

Maggie was now trembling with rage.

"You above all people should know that's one thing I'm not!" she hissed.

"No, you're not easy," Wade agreed, "so, am I right about Mike's coach? He wants you, Maggie?" His hand shot out to imprison her wrist and twist it behind her back. The move wasn't painful, it was meant to bring her into sudden close contact with him.

The volatile atmosphere changed to something as elemental as time eternal. Maggie was trapped by that searing desire and couldn't escape its velvet snare. The black coals of his eyes burned over her face, catching that breathless look of expectancy in her expression.

"I may have brought out the worst of your temper," he growled, "but I also brought out the best."

"Yes."

The admission crumpled some inner defense mechanism and Maggie's head dipped in defeat to rest against the solid wall of his chest.

"Maggie, I . . ."

"Wade, please stop."

His hand released her wrist and hesitated on her back, his touch not quite a caress nor totally impersonal. But in the next second he was withdrawing his hands and walking away. His gaze was hooded when he glanced at her, making it difficult to tell whether the fires were banked or out completely. "Belinda is waiting for me—I have to leave."

Her backbone stiffened. "Of course."

Wade started for the door and paused. "I was late bringing Mike because we stopped somewhere to talk. I told him about Belinda."

"What did he say?"

"Nothing. Not a word. He didn't say he was sorry or glad. He didn't ask if or when I was getting married. Nothing." Wade breathed in deeply. "Absolutely nothing."

"It was a shock."

She, too, had been speechless when Wade had first told her. Unlike Mike, she was an adult and had had time to recover.

"I hadn't realized what a shock it would be," he murmured.

"I'll talk to him," said Maggie.

"Tell Mike I'll call him tomorrow afternoon. If it's nice, we'll go boating. I've arranged . . . oh, hell, what does that matter?" Long, impatient strides carried him to the door. Without glancing back, he repeated, "I'll call him tomorrow."

The door slammed shut before Maggie could find her voice to acknowledge his statement. She stared into the emptiness of the room, still filled with the ghost of Wade's presence. When the powerful engine of the Mercedes growled outside, she slowly turned toward the bedrooms of the house.

CHAPTER SEVEN

Mike's bedroom door was closed. Maggie hesi
tated outside, then knocked once.

Silence was her only answer. She knocked again,
more loudly the second time. Several seconds later
she received a reluctant response.

"Yeah?"

"It's me. May I come in?" She waited, holding her
breath, dreading these next few minutes probably
as much as Mike was.

"Yeah."

Turning the doorknob, she pushed the door
open and walked in.

Mike was lying on his bed, his hands behind his
head, staring at the flat white of the ceiling. He was
still dressed in his baseball uniform, the cap on his
head, dirty tennis shoes on his feet.

He didn't glance at her.

"I thought you were going to change your
clothes," Maggie reminded him.

"I forgot." Mike didn't make any move to correct
the oversight.

Maggie didn't want to force the subject, not yet.

She walked to the foot of the bed. "The uniform can wait, but these shoes have to go." She began untying the laces.

"You already know, don't you?"

His gaze ended its study of the ceiling to dart accusingly at her.

"If you mean do I know that your father is seriously dating someone else, then—yes, I do." She kept her voice calm with effort. "He told me before the game. That's why we were late."

"Why? Is he going to marry her? Why can't things stay the way they are?" Mike protested.

"You don't want things to stay the way they are."

"Yes, I do!"

"If they did, you'd never be able to improve your hitting," she reasoned. "You'd never grow up. Everything changes, people, places and things. That's part of growing up. So is accepting those changes."

"He doesn't have to get married. You haven't."

"That doesn't mean I might not someday." She pulled off the tennis shoes and set them on the floor at the foot of his bed. "Your father has met someone he cares about very much, so it's only natural that he would want to marry her, someday."

"I don't care!"

"You want your father to be happy, don't you?"

"Getting married doesn't mean he's going to be happy. He was married to you and neither of you were happy," Mike reminded her, a low blow in Maggie's book.

"That isn't fair, Mike. Just because your father and I couldn't work it out, it doesn't mean he won't be happy with Belinda. Besides, this isn't really that big of a change."

Maggie diverted the subject. "It only means there may be a woman living with your father. You might even like her after you meet her."

"Have you met her?" Mike wanted to know, skeptical.

"No."

"Do you think you're going to like her?"

"How do I know? I haven't met her." Maggie avoided the question, knowing that she, too, was already prejudiced against the woman.

"Dad says she's young and pretty. They might have kids of their own," he speculated. He stared again at the ceiling, eyes troubled and increasingly dark. "They'd be living with him all the time."

Maggie could not believe that Wade told Mike Belinda was "young and pretty." But her son's concerns took precedence over her own pettiness. "Your father would continue to love you, no matter how many children he and Belinda might have." That, too, was a thought that didn't bring joy into her heart.

"Besides, when you go to visit him, you would have a brother or sister, or both, to play with. When they get older, you can teach them how to play baseball and things like that."

"Aw, Mom, that's boring!"

"How do you know? It might be fun," she argued.

"I just wish he wasn't thinking about getting married."

"He is, so you might as well accept that." *So had I,* Maggie thought.

"I don't have to like it, though." There was a stubborn set to Mike's chin as he unclasped his hands from behind his head and sat up, curling his sock-covered feet beneath him.

"No, you don't have to like it," Maggie agreed, "but you should keep an open mind about it. You haven't even met the woman your father is seeing."

"Stop calling him that!"

Mike began unbuttoning the shirt of his baseball uniform, his head bent to the task.

"All right." Maggie accepted the reproval. "You haven't met the woman Wade is seeing. You could like her. She might be a lot of fun."

If the impression Maggie had gained from the telephone conversation was accurate, with her poise and sophistication Belinda would not easily relate to a ten-year-old's idea of a person who is a lot of fun. There were enough negatives buzzing around in Mike's head without adding more.

"Why couldn't he marry you again?" It was more a protest than a question.

Mike tugged his shirttail from the waistband of his pants.

"Because he loves somebody else. Besides, maybe I wouldn't want to marry him again."

"I'm not blind, Mom. I know you and Dad still love each other. I see the way he looks at you."

Where had that come from, Maggie wondered.

"Even when you're arguing, I know that it's because you miss each other."

Maggie wasn't certain how to handle that, so she decided to avoid it.

"Which reminds me, your fa—Wade said he would call you tomorrow afternoon. He mentioned something about going boating."

"Boating! Oh, wow! That's great!" Mike declared exuberantly, completely diverted from his previous subject. Maggie understood his enthusiasm. Most of his friends went on short trips with their parents almost every weekend. Mike's friends were always talking about what they did. Now he would have a story of his own to tell the others.

"That's tomorrow." Playfully Maggie pulled the bill of his cap low on his forehead. "Tonight, it's out of that uniform and into the tub."

"Cut it out," he grumbled in protest, but there was a grin on his face as he pushed her hand away.

The next morning Maggie was in the utility room, folding the clean clothes from the dryer.

The washing machine was in its spin cycle, and its thumping roar combined with the music from the radio and the whir of the dryer drowned out all other sounds.

It wasn't until the washing machine stopped that Maggie heard the phone ringing in the kitchen. She dashed quickly to answer it.

"Hello," she rushed, half expecting to hear a dial tone to indicate the caller had hung up.

"Maggie? It's Wade."

Her already racing pulse redoubled its tempo. Determinedly she tried to check its thudding rise. "Mike's outside. I'll get him for you."

Before she could put the receiver down, Wade was ordering, "Wait a minute."

"Yes?"

A self-conscious hand touched the flaming silk tumble of hair on top of her head, secured there by a green ribbon. It was crazy—Wade couldn't see her.

"Did you talk to Mike last night?"

"Yes, I did." She tried to order her scattered thoughts. "He was upset, naturally. No child likes things to change unless they initiate it. This just makes him a little insecure."

"Mike's life isn't changing that drastically because of my love life."

"But Mike sees that it potentially could," Maggie pointed out. "His main worry seems to be that you might have other children and forget him."

"Maggie, you know . . ." Wade began impatiently.

"I'm not saying it would happen," she interrupted. "I'm saying that it concerns Mike. He isn't an impulsive boy. It's going to take him time to adjust. You've known her for more than a year, Mike hasn't even met her. One or two meetings aren't going to be enough for him, either."

"No, it will take time," Wade agreed in a grimly resigned voice. "How was he after your talk?"

"Eager for today to come so he could go boating with you." Then Maggie realized the time. "You haven't had to change your plans, have you? You said you'd call this afternoon."

"I haven't changed my plans. I thought Mike might like to leave sooner, have lunch on the boat."

"He'd love it."

"Do you mind?"

"No, I don't mind," Maggie insisted, and wondered where the silly lump came from in her throat. "You'll want to talk to him. I'll tell him you're on the phone."

Once again Wade stopped her. "Just tell him I'm leaving now and to be ready when I get there."

"I will."

"Maggie? Thanks," he said simply.

She hesitated. "You'll have to do the same for me someday when I decide to get married." The idea seemed so remote at the moment that it was laughable. Instead, Maggie felt tears pricking her eyes.

The silence on the other end was palpable. At last, she heard, "You can count on it."

It was several minutes after he had said goodbye before Maggie had enough composure to walk to the back door to call Mike inside.

He was ecstatic over the change of plans. When he ran to his room to change shirts and put on a clean pair of sneakers, Maggie freshened her makeup and took the green ribbon from her hair.

Then it was back to the utility room and the clothes in the dryer.

As she was pairing the socks, Mike poked his head around the door.

"I'm going outside to wait for Dad."

"Have a good time," Maggie smiled.

"You bet!"

"I'll see you tonight."

But Mike was already gone and her words bounced forlornly off the walls of the utility room. Trying not to dwell too much on what she was going to do with herself all day, Maggie methodically folded the socks and put them with the stack of clothes in the wicker basket.

When it was filled, she picked it up. It was heavy and she hurried in order to bring a quick end to the weight tugging at her arms.

As she rounded the archway into the living room, she was hit broadside by a tall, hard form. The collision wrenched the basket from her straining hands, flipping it upside down and dumping the folded clean clothes onto the floor. The force of the collision staggered her, but a pair of large hands immediately steadied her.

Wade's hands—her senses recognized his touch immediately. On impact, she had issued a startled cry. Her heart was lodged in her throat as she stared at Wade and not a sound could get past it.

A white knit shirt, unbuttoned at the throat, contrasted with the navy pants and Windbreaker he wore. The dark blue color intensified the jet blackness of his attractively unkempt hair, looking as if it were freshly rumpled by a sea breeze. A concerned look was etched in his harshly vital and male features, his dark eyes piercing in their scrutiny.

With an effort Maggie forced her gaze from his compelling face, fighting the breathless waves of excitement that engulfed her.

Her glance fell on the once neatly folded clothes scattered over the floor. They would all have to be folded, separated, and stacked in the basket again. Angry exasperation at the wasted time she'd spent overtook the rest of her tangled emotions and her hands slid to her hips in an attitude of temper.

Before she could speak, Wade was saying, "I'm sorry."

She turned on him, her green eyes flashing. As her mouth started to open, his fingers closed it.

There was a wicked twinkle in his dark eyes. "I said I was sorry," he reminded her. His thumb lightly caressed the curve of her mouth before he took his hand away and glanced at his son.

"Come on, Mike. Let's help your mom pick up the clothes."

That vague caress had turned away her anger. Maggie was left standing there while Mike and Wade bent to begin picking up the scattered clothes. It was several seconds before she recovered sufficiently to help them.

"We were just coming in to tell you we were going," Mike explained.

"You'll be home before dark, won't you?" Maggie hadn't asked Wade how long they intended to be gone.

"We'll be back to the marina before dark." He satisfied her mind on that worry. "Don't wait dinner for Mike, though. We'll probably have something to eat before I bring him home."

"Oh."

That meant two meals she would have to eat alone, lunch and dinner.

"Dad, are we going out on the boat alone, just you and me?" Mike bunched a group of socks together and stuffed them in the basket. Maggie rescued them and tried to sort them into pairs.

"Yes, it will just be the two of us."

"Why can't Mom come along?"

CHAPTER EIGHT

"Mike!"

She was startled by Mike's unexpected request to include her in their plans. She was mortified that Wade would think she had no plans.

Color rouged her cheeks for fear Wade might think she had previously hinted to Mike for the invitation. A sideways glance at Wade showed his curious frown.

Mike pursued his request, ignoring her outburst.

"She's on vacation and she doesn't have anything to do, especially with me going places with you." He continued without giving Wade a chance to reply, "I know Mom likes boats 'cause I've seen the pictures of the boat you two used to have."

"Mike," Maggie interrupted sharply, "your father wants to spend time alone with you. You and I will have time to do things together later."

"Yeah, but—" he was struggling for the words "—we've never done things together like a family. At least, I was too little to remember if we did. And—"

"But," Maggie protested.

"He's right," Wade said in a quiet but firm voice. "You are the mother, I am the father and Mike is the son. A divorce doesn't change that."

"No, but . . ." She felt panic.

"Can she come along, Dad?" Mike interrupted eagerly, his eyes alight with cautious hope.

"Of course she can come along," Wade agreed, and glanced at Maggie. "Will you go boating with us?"

She was thrown into confusion. He couldn't really mean it, but there wasn't any reluctance in his voice or his expression.

"Oh, but I—" she began.

"Please, Mom!" Mike inserted to ward off her refusal.

"Please, Maggie."

Wade lent his voice to Mike's. His expression was serious, not a hint of mockery to be seen.

She might have resisted Mike's plea, but to deny Wade's was impossible.

Her head was bobbing in agreement before she could get the words out.

"Very well, I'll come with you." Not without misgivings. Her glance went down the crisp blue Levi's she wore and plain knit top. "I'll have to—"

Wade saw the direction her thoughts were taking and interrupted.

"There's nothing wrong with what you're wearing. Just get a pair of sneakers and a Windbreaker. Mike and I don't want to wait."

This time there was a glint of mockery in his dark eyes.

"It doesn't take me that long," Maggie denied with a defiant tilt of her chin.

"Only forever," Mike exaggerated.

"That isn't true!" There was an indignant gleam in her look.

"The invitation was issued with the proviso to 'come as you are,'" Wade told her. "Mike, go and get her shoes and a Windbreaker."

"Right, Dad."

Common sense agreed that there was nothing wrong with what she was wearing. Her Levi's and top were neat and clean. Vanity, however, insisted there were outfits in her wardrobe equally service-able and much more fashionable. But between Wade and Mike, they had taken the choice out of her hands.

Wade added the last of the clothes to the basket and set it aside. Maggie watched him. He lifted the heavy basket so easily.

All thought of clothes was pushed from her mind, the void to be filled by recognition of his powerfully muscled frame and his innate virility.

She realized how dangerous it was to spend an afternoon or an hour with him.

"I don't think this is a good idea," she murmured aloud.

"What?" He cocked his head at an inquiring angle, a brow lifting slightly, a half smile touching his mouth. "Not changing clothes?" he mocked.

"No, my going with you." In self-defense, Maggie hastened to disguise the truth of her answer. "The idea is for Mike to spend time with you alone and adjust to your relationship. My coming along is just going to confuse the issue."

"I don't agree." He eyed her steadily. "Since Mike has grown up, he's either been with you alone, or with me alone—never in the company of a couple where he isn't the sole object of attention. Today he's going to see what it's like when there are three people together."

"That's very logical," she murmured.

His motives for wanting her along became obvious. It wasn't a desire for her company, or for a last time to be together as a family.

No, Wade was sparing his darling Belinda from any outright rejection by his son. Some of the inner joy that Maggie had hardly dared to let herself feel faded at the discovery.

"What's very logical?"

Mike returned with her sneakers and yellow Windbreaker. For a split second Maggie was at a loss for an answer. "For your father to invite me along so he won't have to cook."

"Yeah, that is pretty smart, Dad," he agreed with a grin.

"I thought so."

Stepping out of her slippers, Maggie put on the shoes and tied the laces. The thin, slick jacket she let drape over one shoulder. When she was ready, Mike led the way outside. If Maggie needed any further reminder that she was only a stand-in for Belinda, the silver Mercedes provided it. She began to wonder if the boat, too, belonged to his future bride.

For once, she didn't have the audacity to ask. She chose to sit alone in the back. It saved making innocuous conversation.

"What do you think of the car, Mike?"

Wade turned it onto a busy street, the luxury car accelerating into the flow of traffic.

"It's nice." Mike was obviously unimpressed by the plushness of the interior. "But I like that four-wheel-drive car you have in Alaska a lot better. It can go anywhere!"

Wade chuckled and admitted, "There are times when you can't get around unless you have that kind of car."

Personally Maggie thought Wade was more suited to the type of vehicle Mike had described. Not that he didn't look perfectly at home behind the wheel of this luxury model. But the plush, elegant car seemed to shield its owner from the realities of life, whereas Wade was the kind of man who met life head-on, taking the knocks and driving forward, going anywhere he pleased.

But such admiration for the character of the man was not wise.

Maggie turned her attention to the city sprawling around them. Like the Eternal City of Rome, Seattle had originally been a city of seven hills. Shortly after the turn of the century, Denny Hill was leveled to permit the city to expand.

Water dominated the city, not just because it was a seaport, but because of the two lakes within its limits and a ship canal, as well as its being flanked by Lake Washington on the east and Puget Sound on the west.

Considering that fact, it wasn't surprising that there were more boats per capita than anywhere else in the country. Maggie was positive they were all crowded into the marina where Wade stopped. Unerring, he led them past the rows of boats, all shapes, sizes and kinds, to a sleek powerful cruiser.

It was larger and a later model than the one they owned when they were married. Maggie felt she was stepping back in time when she stepped aboard. As he helped her onto the deck, her flesh tingled at the impersonal grip of his hand.

"Where are we going? Just anywhere?" Mike

wanted to know their destination, at the same time not caring.

"We'll decide when we reach open water. How's that?" Wade loosed the mooring ropes. "Or maybe we won't go anywhere special."

"I suppose it's too far to go all the way to the ocean."

"No, it isn't too far, but I think we'll find enough to see and do without that."

The inboard motors roared to life and Wade began maneuvering the cruiser out of the crowded marina waters. Mike was right at his side observing everything he did. There was a tightening in her throat as Maggie saw how strong the resemblance was between father and son, Mike a young miniature of Wade.

The breeze coming off the water was cool. Maggie started to slip her Windbreaker on, then decided, "I'll go below and start lunch now."

"Good idea," Wade agreed, and combed his fingers through his wind-ruffled hair. "We're well stocked with food, so fix whatever you like." As she started down the open hatchway, he called after her, "Maggie? There's some bait shrimp in the refrigerator. I didn't want you to mistake it for the eating kind."

She heard the teasing laughter in his voice and retorted, "Are you sure you wouldn't like a shrimp cocktail?" reminding him of the time the first year they were married when she had unknowingly used bait shrimp for that purpose.

His rich laughter followed her below.

The private joke was beyond Mike, but he was more interested in the use of the shrimp. "Are we going to fish?"

"I thought we might. Fishing is supposed to be good."

"Hey, Mom! Why don't you wait to fix lunch until after we catch some fish? Then you can cook what we catch."

"No, thanks. I might starve before then," Maggie called back.

"It doesn't sound as if she thinks too much of us as fishermen, does it?" she heard Wade say.

"That's because she's never been fishing with us," Mike replied.

"Didn't you tell her about any of the fish we caught?"

"Oh, sure."

Maggie walked from the galley to the bottom of the steps. "Mike told me all those fish stories about the times he went with you in Alaska. You only brought back three fish apiece and each of the three fish weighed thirty pounds," she teased.

"It's the truth, Mom, honest," Mike insisted.

"The next time we'll have to take a camera along, won't we?" said Wade.

"Then she'll have to believe me, huh?"

"Right."

Maggie went back to fixing lunch, listening to the bantering between father and son. It made her feel warm and secure inside, as if they were really a family. She wished it could always be this way . . . or that it had always been like this.

But it hadn't and it couldn't.

The lunch was simple fare, a mug of hot soup and a cold meat sandwich served on deck. Wade anchored the cruiser in a sheltered cove of Whidbey Island.

A beautiful wilderness beach stretched invitingly along the shore.

"Boy, this soup sure warms up your stomach," Mike declared.

"Tastes good, doesn't it?" Maggie sipped the hot liquid in her mug.

The breeze remained cool and a thickening layer of clouds shut out the warmth of the sun. She eyed the matte gray sky and glanced at Wade. Perceptively he read her thoughts.

"I checked the weather a few minutes ago. There's a front moving in—overcast skies, cooler temperatures, but very little rain is expected with it," he reported.

"That's pretty normal for the area, isn't it?" she smiled.

The Olympic Mountains to the west sheltered the islands in Puget Sound, as well as Seattle, from the brunt of weather fronts moving in from the Pacific. The mountains divested the clouds of most of their moisture, keeping the rainfall inland to nominal amounts. Few storms of any intensity ever reached the protected sound.

Chapter Nine

After lunch was over, Mike was designated cabin boy and ordered to clean the dishes. He grudgingly obeyed, after trying unsuccessfully to enlist help from either of them. The boat remained anchored in the cove, with Maggie and Wade relaxing on the cushioned seats of the aft deck.

Her yellow Windbreaker was zipped to the throat, her hands stuffed in the front pockets. Thus protected, she leaned back to enjoy the brisk air, tangy with the scent of the sea.

All was quiet except for the lapping water against the boat's hull and the whispering breeze talking to the rustling leaves on the island's wooded interior. And, of course, there was the clatter of dishes in the cabin galley below.

"You've made a good job of raising Mike," Wade remarked quietly.

"I haven't done it alone. You've contributed, too." Maggie met his look, aware of its gentleness.

"The credit belongs to you. He's with you much more than he is with me. But thanks for making me feel I've had a hand in it."

Looking away from her, he took a deep breath and let it out slowly, like a sigh. "Today you said you would want me to talk to Mike before you got married. Are you planning to marry again?"

"Someday, when I find the right man." The prospect looked dismal. "Like you, I don't want to make another mistake. The next time I want to be very, very sure."

"You don't have anyone in mind, then?" His gaze returned to her, dark and impenetrable.

"Not any one person. There are a few prospects on the horizon, but—" Maggie shrugged "—I'm not going to rush into anything."

"You said something the other day that's been bothering me."

His expression was thoughtful, slightly distant.

"What was that?"

"You said that after you'd wiggled out from under my thumb, you learned to value your freedom. What did you mean by that?"

Before she attempted an answer, Wade went on. "Granted, you were irritated when you said it. But you rarely say things in the heat of the moment that you don't mean.

"When we were married, you were always free to do as you pleased."

"In theory, I was."

At his gathering frown, Maggie tried to explain.

"All day long you gave orders to your employees. When you came home, you continued to give orders. You never seemed to ask me to do anything, you were always telling me.

"Instead of giving orders to the people who worked under you, you gave them to me—and I was much too independent to stand for that." A wry smile dimpled her cheeks.

"I never intended them to be orders."

"You probably didn't, but that's the way they came out. I just felt like I didn't have control of my own life."

"I'm . . . sorry."

"Don't be. It's in the past and forgotten."

But Maggie guessed he was filing it away for future reference, something he didn't want to repeat in his new marriage to Belinda.

It hurt.

"I'm done!" Mike popped up the steps. "Can we fish now?"

The quiet interlude was over. Wade straightened from his comfortable position with obvious reluctance. "Get the bait out of the refrigerator while I find the rods and reels," he directed.

"Are we going to fish here?"

"Why not? If the fish aren't biting here, we'll move someplace else," Wade reasoned.

As far as Maggie was concerned, she found Mike's presence, his steady stream of chatter and expectant excitement, better than the confiding quietness when she and Wade had been alone.

He kept her mind from thinking intimate thoughts and envisioning hopeless dreams.

The fishing turned out to be not very good in that cove and Wade moved the boat to another. Early afternoon was not the best time of day for fishing, but at the second place they stopped, Mike did catch one that was big enough to keep.

They all threw several back. After they had moved again, Wade caught the next.

A fine mist began to fall, but despite their partial

success, the weather didn't interfere with their sport. It dampened their clothes, but not their spirit. The water in the third cove was fairly deep.

A fish nibbled on Maggie's baited hook, then took it. She began reeling it in, feeling it fight and certain this time she had got a big one.

"Got a fish, Mom?" Mike glanced over his shoulder from his position on the opposite side of the boat next to Wade.

"A fish or a baby." She had reeled in too many small ones that she thought would be large to brag about this one.

"At the rate your mother is going, you and I are going to be the only ones with food on our plates tonight, Mike," Wade teased.

"Yeah, and she's got to cook it for us."

Maggie kept her silence with an effort, ignoring the way they were ganging up on her. The fish broke surface and she had to swallow back her shout of glee. It looked big enough to keep. Now all she had to do was land it. A few minutes later she had it in her lap—literally, its tail flapping on her jeans while she tried to work the hook out of its mouth.

"What ya got there, Mom? A goldfish?" Mike teased.

"No, I have a real fish." She struggled some more but couldn't work the hook free. "He's swallowed the hook."

"It's the only way she could have caught it," Wade laughed.

"Watch my rod while I help your mother." He walked over and Maggie surrendered her catch, a shade triumphantly, to him.

"You really hooked him. That's too bad." He

crouched on the deck beside her and gently began working the hook in the gaping fish's mouth.

"Why is that too bad?" Maggie demanded to know.

"Because it isn't big enough to keep."

"It is, too!" she declared indignantly. "It's just as big as yours was."

"No, it's a couple of inches smaller," Wade replied.

"You have to throw it back, Mom," Mike inserted.

She turned to Wade. "You get out your fish and we'll see if mine is smaller."

He smiled. "I don't have to get out my fish. I already know yours is smaller—too small to keep." He freed the hook and tossed the fish over the side.

"My fish!" Maggie wailed, and dived toward the rail, as if thinking she could catch it before it reached the water.

There was a splash before she even reached the side of the boat. Her hand went out for the railing to stop her progress.

The steady mist had coated the railing with slippery beads of moisture and her hand found nothing to grip on the wet surface of the rail and slid beyond it. The unchecked forward impetus carried her against the low rail, pitching her body over it.

Her startled shriek of fright and alarm was echoed by Mike's "Mom!"

Something grabbed at her foot and in the next second she was tumbling into the water. Immediately instinct took over. Holding her breath, she turned and kicked toward the surface, taking care to avoid the hull of the boat.

She came up spluttering, gasping in air. She was shaking all over, more from cold than the initial fright. The first sound she heard was laughter, Wade's deep, chuckling laughter.

When he saw Maggie was safe and unharmed, Mike joined in.

"Have you found a new way to fish?" Wade mocked.

"You . . ." In her surge of anger, Maggie forgot to tread water and ended up swallowing a mouthful of the salty stuff.

Coughing and choking, she resurfaced and struck out for the boat ladder. The weight of her saturated clothes pulled at her body.

His hand was there to help her aboard. With the fingers of one hand around the lowest rung, Maggie paused in the water to glare at him and the dancing light in his black eyes. Ignoring his offer of his assistance, she pulled herself aboard unaided.

Standing on deck, a pool of sea water at her feet, water streaming from her sodden clothes, she looked first at Mike, who was giggling behind his hand. Her hair was plastered over her forehead, cheeks and neck. Water ran into her eyes and she wiped it away to glare again at Wade. A smile was playing with the corners of his mouth, regardless of his attempts to make it go away.

"You think it's all very funny, don't you?" she accused, her teeth chattering with an on-setting chill. "I could have drowned while the two of you were laughing!"

"That's hardly likely, Maggie. You're an excellent swimmer," Wade reminded her in a dry, mocking tone.

"I could have hit my head on the boat or a rock or something!" she sputtered.

"The water is fairly clear," Wade pointed out. "I

could see you weren't in trouble. Here." He reached down and picked up a sneaker from the deck—Maggie's. "When I grabbed for you, all I got was your shoe. At least it's dry."

Maggie snatched it from his outstretched hand. "What good is one dry shoe—" she waved it in front of his face "—when I have one wet one? Not to mention that my clothes are soaked! A dry shoe just doesn't go with the rest of my outfit!" In a fit, she hurled the lone, dry tennis shoe over the side, where it floated on the quiet surface. She knew she was being silly, and borderline overreacting, but here she was looking like a drowned rat in front of her ex-husband and it reminded her of when Wade first walked into her kitchen that Sunday morning.

Mike broke out laughing, finding the scene uproariously funny.

It didn't help Maggie's growing sense of frustration one bit.

"You'd better practice your casting, Mike, and see if you can't hook that shoe before it sinks," Wade advised, keeping the amusement in his voice at a minimum. "As for you, Maggie, I think you'd better go below and get out of those wet clothes before you get chilled."

"Chilled! What do you think I am now?" she cried angrily. "My legs are shaking so badly now that I can hardly stand up."

"I'll help you."

Wade took a step toward her.

"No! I don't need any help from you. You take one more step and I'll push you over the side; then you can see what it feels like to be drenched to the skin," she threatened. "And stop giving me orders!

I'm an adult. I know I have to get out of these wet clothes. You don't have to remind me of that."

The latter half of her statement wiped the gleam from his eyes. They were flat black as he stepped to the side, indicating by his action that he would make no move to help her.

Maggie swept by him to the steps with as much dignity as her dripping figure could muster, but her chattering teeth destroyed much of the effect.

Below, she tugged the clothes from her body and piled them in the sink.

Taking a towel from the lavatory, she rubbed her skin dry until it burned. A second towel she wrapped around her straggly wet hair, securing it on top of her head with a tuck in front.

Then came the problem of something dry to wear. She opened a drawer, looking for a blanket. Inside were folded flannel shirts, men's shirts. A red and black plaid was on top. At this point Maggie wasn't particular. Anything that was warm and dry and permitted movement would do.

The shirt engulfed her, the tails reaching to her knees, the sleeves almost as far. After a few awkward attempts she managed to roll the long sleeves up to her forearms and button the front.

With that accomplished, she began trying to towel her hair dry.

"How are you doing?" Wade called down.

"Fine," she snapped. She was still shivering.

After glancing around, she called, "Is there any cocoa?"

Instead of answering, Wade descended the steps as soundlessly as a cat. "If there isn't cocoa, there's instant coffee. With sugar, it will probably do you more good than cocoa."

"I know there's instant coffee. I would have made a cup if you'd told me there wasn't cocoa."

"You'll feel better in a second." He walked to the cupboards above the galley sink.

"I'm freezing," Maggie muttered.

"I don't see any cocoa."

Wade moved items on the shelf around. "You'll have to settle for coffee."

"I can fix it myself," she insisted when he filled the kettle with water.

"Shut up, Maggie." It was said quietly but no less firmly. "Stop trying to show me that you're so damned independent and go sit down." He saw the flashing green fire in her eyes and added, "Yes, that's an order. I'm just trying to help you. There's nothing wrong with that."

"Thank you," she said.

He lit the gas burner and set the kettle over the flame. Shaking his dark head, he murmured, "You have the most beautiful eyes I've ever seen."

Maggie paused and didn't argue any more about making the coffee herself.

Neither did she go sit down as he had ordered. She resumed the brisk rubbing of her hair, deep red gold wavelets rippling over her head.

"I still can't believe I fell overboard," she muttered.

"All because of a silly little fish." The corners of his mouth deepened.

"That you threw away," Maggie reminded him.

"It was too small."

"It was almost big enough to keep," she argued.

"There, you just admitted it yourself." Wade smiled, without triumph.

"Okay, so I admit it."

She tossed the towel aside.

"What are you doing in that shirt?"

The change of subject startled her. Her winged brows drew together in a frown and a short, disbelieving laugh came from her throat.

"I'm wearing it," she retorted.

A raking glance swept her from head to foot. "You think you look sexy wearing a man's shirt that comes to your knees, with shoulder seams that practically reach your elbows?"

"It never occurred to me how I might look wearing it!" she answered defensively. "It was warm and I could move around freely while I was wearing it. If it reminded me of anything, it was a flannel nightgown. I wasn't even thinking about being sexy. The only male around here that I care about is Michael."

And she denied the thudding pulse racing in her slender neck.

"Believe me, you don't look a bit like my grandmother did in her flannel nightgown." Wade spooned coffee crystals into a mug and gave her a black, smoldering look. A muscle stood out along his jaw. "When a man sees you like that, dressed in a man's shirt without a stitch of clothing under it, looking lost and vulnerable, he wants to hold you in his arms and—" He snapped off the rest of that sentence.

"I don't know if that's a compliment or a sin."

Confusion tempered her as she turned aside.

His hand gripped her elbow to turn her back.

"The only place you're supposed to have in my life is as the mother of my child."

The brutally frank statement stung.

"I know that," Maggie retorted, choking, unable to shrug out of his hold.

"Then explain to me why I can't forget that you're my wife?"

His grip shifted to clasp both her shoulders in hard demand.

CHAPTER TEN

Her lips parted to draw in a fearfully happy breath. As she gazed up at him, a fine mist of tears brought a jewel-like intensity to the green color of her eyes. She heard the groaning sound he made before his fingers tightened to dig into her flesh and draw her to him.

The soft sweep of his mouth ignited a sweet fire that raged through her veins.

Curving her arms around his neck, Maggie slid her fingers into his shaggy mane of black hair. The drifting mist of rain outside had left his hair damp and silken to the touch.

Behind the spinning wonder of his kiss, the recesses of her mind knew it couldn't last.

The knowledge that Wade belonged to someone else made her hungry response more desperate, savoring every fragment of the stolen embrace.

The driving possession of his mouth bent her backward while the large hand on her spine forced the lower half of her body against him. His muscled legs were hardwood columns, solid and unyielding.

The wideness of the shirt's collar made the

neckline plunge to the valley between her breasts. With masterful ease he unfastened the single obstructing top button. His hand slid inside to mold itself to the mature curves of her breast, swallowing its fullness in the large cup of his hand.

Maggie shuddered with intense longing. His searing caress burned her already heated flesh.

The male smell of him was a stimulant more potent than any drug. Her heart was beating so wildly that she couldn't think.

Wade ended his imprisonment of her mouth, leaving her lips swollen with passion, and began a sensuous exploration of her curving neck. Desire quivered along her spine as he found the pleasure points that excited her, and Maggie couldn't stop the moan of delight from escaping her throat. The fanning warmth of his disturbed breathing caressed her skin.

"God help me, Maggie, I want you."

His husky, grudging admission sent tremors through her limbs.

She felt the pressure of his growing need for her. It was echoed by the empty ache in her loins. There was only here and now; nothing else existed, and this moment would never come again.

"Don't you think I feel the same, Wade?" she whispered.

With blazing sureness his mouth sought her lips. There was only one ultimate climax to the crushing embrace. But before a move could be made in that direction, a young voice jolted them back to reality.

"Mom! Dad! Look at the size of the fish I caught!" Mike's excited cry tore their kiss apart.

Almost immediately he came tumbling down the steps, holding the fish aloft.

There was no time for Wade to withdraw his arms from around her. A trembling Maggie was glad of their support. Her head dipped to hide behind the protective shield of Wade's wide shoulders, concealing her love-drugged expression from her son.

She felt Wade take a deep, controlling breath before glancing over his shoulder.

"It's the biggest one yet!"

Instead of holding the fish by the gills, Mike was trying to hold it in his hands. It slipped through his grasp onto the cabin floor, giving both of them a momentary reprieve from his gaze.

"It is a big fish," Wade agreed.

"See it, Mom?"

This time Mike picked it up correctly.

A supporting arm remained around her as Wade moved to one side.

"It's a beauty, Mike." Even to her own ears, her voice sounded strange.

It earned her a curious look from Mike. "Are you all right, Mom?"

"I'm fine."

Maggie shivered in late reaction.

"She's just a bit chilled, that's all," Wade said.

Chilled. It was directly the opposite. Her whole body was suffused with heat, the heat of regret, of shame and of love.

"I'm freezing now, Mike, but I'll be fine in a minute."

Mike seemed satisfied with the answer and let his attention return to the fish he held. "Actually I caught it on your pole, Mom." He grinned at Wade. "I guess we'll have to say it's hers."

"I guess we will." Wade nodded in concession.

"I'd better go put this guy on the stringer and see if anything's biting on my line."

As quickly as he had come, Mike left, scurrying back on deck.

His departure left an uncomfortable void. Aware of Wade's piercing study, Maggie turned away from it. Her emotions were still too close to the surface. A bubbling sound provided the necessary distraction.

"The water's boiling," she said. "I'd better get that coffee before it boils away."

She turned her back on him as she shut off the gas to the burner.

"Maggie . . ."

She could hear the beginnings of an apology in his voice. No doubt it would be followed by a reminder that he was engaged to someone else and that the desire they had shared moments ago was all a mistake, and they were the very last things she wanted to hear. The tears weren't that far away. Maggie sought refuge behind the excuse Wade had offered the last time.

"We were following the pattern of a memory. It didn't mean anything." Not to you, her heart qualified the last statement.

There was a long silence that left her with the uncanny feeling that Wade didn't believe she meant what she said. He took a step toward her and then abruptly turned and opened a drawer beneath one of the bunk beds.

"After you drink your coffee, it probably wouldn't hurt if you wrapped up in a blanket and stayed below."

"I think I will."

Maggie didn't fight his suggestion.

There was another pause before she heard Wade mounting the steps to the deck.

Her hand shook as she added the boiling water to the brown crystals in the mug. Now she did feel cold, and terribly lonely.

Carrying the mug to the bed, she wrapped herself in the blanket Wade had laid on the bunk.

Within minutes after she had curled herself into a ball of abject misery, Maggie heard the engines start. She knew Wade wasn't going to look for another fishing hole; he was returning to the marina. She closed her eyes and tried to forget.

Maggie didn't emerge from the cocoon of the blanket until the boat was docked, the mooring lines tied and the engines silent.

She wadded her wet clothes into a bundle and started up the steps.

The instant she set foot on deck, Wade's voice barked, "Where do you think you're going?"

"I'm assuming you're taking us home." Poised short of the top step, she lifted her chin.

"Not dressed like that."

Wade softened his tone, but it was no less lacking in determination.

"I hope you don't think I'm going to wear these." She indicated the wet bundle of clothes in her hand. "They're wet. It may not bother you, but I'm not going to stain the upholstery in that expensive car by wearing these wet things."

He stood in her path, blocking it as effectively as a tall gate.

"You're not wearing that shirt."

"For heaven's sake, Wade—" his attitude rankled "—this shirt covers more than if I were wearing a bathing suit."

"I don't care how much it covers." There was a hardening set to his jaw. "My wife is not going to parade down these docks half-dressed."

His statement seared through her, but Maggie realized that Wade was unaware of what he had said. The swift rush of heat was quickly replaced by a chilling depression.

Avoiding his gaze, she made a bitterly mocking reply. "I'm not your wife anymore. Or had you forgotten?"

Out of the corner of her eye, she saw the startled jerk of his head. Taking advantage of the moment, she climbed the last step and brushed past him. Wade didn't try to stop her.

Mike was on the dock, standing by one of the mooring lines. "Are you taking us straight home, Dad? What about the fish?" He had seen them talking, but hadn't heard the substance of their conversation.

"Your mother needs some dry clothes," Wade answered. "As for the fish, we'll take them with us."

"You'll help me clean them, won't you? I'm still not very good at it." Mike scrambled back aboard to get the fish.

Maggie heard Wade agree as she stepped ashore. Within minutes the three of them were making their way to the silver Mercedes in the marina parking lot. Most of the looks that Maggie received focused on the bare length of her legs, rather than the oversized flannel shirt and what was, or wasn't, beneath it. Maggie ignored the mostly admiring glances, but it wasn't so easy to ignore Wade's growing aloofness.

At the house, Maggie carried her wet clothes to the utility room while Mike and Wade gathered what they needed from the kitchen to clean the fish. As they walked out the side door to the backyard, Maggie went to her bedroom to dress.

When they returned to the kitchen with the cleaned fish in a pan of water, they were laughing about something. A pain of loss and regret splintered through Maggie and she turned away to conceal it.

Mike came rushing forward. "Will you cook the fish tonight?"

"If you like," she agreed, taking the pan from him and setting it on the counter.

"Great!" He turned back to his father. "Now we can eat what we caught, like real outdoorsmen."

"You can."

"Aren't you staying?" Mike was surprised, but Maggie wasn't.

"I can't. I have a few things to do tonight." Wade's voice was smooth, his words cutting.

"But—" Mike searched for a protest "—this morning before Mom agreed to come along, you said we might not get home until dark and we'd eat somewhere before you brought me home. Why can't you stay now?"

He was standing close to her. Maggie turned and quickly but affectionately placed her hand across his mouth, silencing him before his innocent remarks made the situation more awkward than it already was.

"Your father said he had to leave, Mike. That's final." She took her hand away and saw the resigned droop of his mouth.

"I'm sorry, Mike. I'll be busy tomorrow, but I'll call you Thursday," Wade promised.

"I have baseball practice in the morning," Mike told him.

"I'll remember. Between now and Thursday afternoon, you can be thinking about what you'd like to do," Wade suggested.

"Okay," Mike agreed with halfhearted enthusiasm.

The exchange was prolonged for a few more minutes before Wade finally left.

Maggie's only acknowledgment from him was a curt nod of goodbye. She turned to the sink when the door closed and began rinsing the fish in cold water. Mike watched.

"You know where he's going, don't you?" Mike said glumly.

"Where?"

"He's got a date with her." The feminine pronoun was emphasized with scorn as Mike wandered away from the sink.

Chapter Eleven

Maggie wiped the perspiration from her forehead with the back of her gloved hand. She hadn't realized there were so many weeds in the flower bed when she'd started. The muscles in her back were beginning to cramp from constantly bending over. But she was almost done. Arching her shoulders briefly to ease the stiffness, she again stooped to her task.

A car turned into the driveway. Her backward glance recognized the jeep as being familiar, but she couldn't immediately decide why.

Her brows drew together in a frown as she straightened up.

The passenger door opened and Mike scrambled out, baseball and glove in his hand. "You forgot to pick me up."

Her green eyes widened in disbelief. "Practice can't be over this soon?"

"Well, it is," he declared. "Coach gave me a ride home since you didn't show up."

Embarrassed, Maggie glanced at the bronzed man sliding out from behind the wheel of the car.

"I'm sorry, I honestly didn't realize it was so late. I started weeding the garden and lost all track of time."

"That's all right. Things like that happen. We actually ended things a bit early today." Smiling away her apology, Tom Darby walked around the hood of the car toward her.

"All the time," Mike mumbled in good humor, but thankfully not loud enough for Tom to hear.

Denny, the neighbor boy, called to Mike, wanting him to come over. With his coach there, Mike refused, shouting, "Later!"

"Denny has a new puppy he wants you to see," Maggie told him.

"Oh!" That changed things. He shoved his baseball and glove into her hands and raced off.

Self-conscious about her oversight, Maggie tried to make amends.

"Thanks for bringing Mike home. I really appreciate it. I know it was out of your way."

"It was no trouble at all," Tom insisted. "In fact, I sort of ended things early so that I'd have the perfect excuse to see you again."

His boldness took her by surprise. It shouldn't have, she realized. Her actions in the past had encouraged him to show this interest.

It was just in the last few days all her thoughts had been concerned with Wade. Tom Darby had ceased to exist in her mind as anything but Mike's coach.

"Oh." It was a small sound, revealing Maggie's inner confusion.

The initial attraction she had felt toward Tom had faded into insignificance in the face of the overwhelming emotion that consumed her. How could she handle the change?

Tom appeared not to notice her hesitation. His hazel eyes looked steadily into her green ones.

"I would like you to have dinner with me one night this weekend. Friday or Saturday night, maybe?" His technique was excellent, not giving her a chance to say no, only to choose which night to accept.

"I'm sorry, but my schedule is all screwy right now. I don't know when I'll be free this weekend . . ." Maggie stalled for a moment. "With Mike's father here, it's difficult for me to make plans until I know what his are. I'll have to take a raincheck on the invitation."

"Whatever you say." He wasn't happy with her answer, but he seemed resigned to it. Glancing up at the clear, blue sky overhead, he remarked, "I'm glad it's warm today."

Maggie sensed a hint behind the comment. Regardless of his motives, Tom had done her a favor by bringing Mike home. The least she could do was repay him with some measure of hospitality.

"You've been on the ball field with those boys all morning. Why don't you come in and let me get you something cold to drink since I can't accept your dinner invitation. Iced tea, beer, Coke?"

"A beer would be good if it isn't too much trouble," Tom said.

"No trouble at all. Come on." Tom followed her into the house. She set Mike's ball and glove on the kitchen table and paused to remove her cotton work gloves.

Tom strolled along a few paces behind her, seeming to appear perfectly at home. She walked to the refrigerator.

"How is Mike doing?"

Maggie sought to establish a less personal topic of conversation, discuss Tom's work and steer away from his social life and whether it would or would not include her.

"He's doing fine, shows a real aptitude for the game."

As she opened the refrigerator door, she cast him a brief, smiling look. "Well, except for his hitting. He was upset about not getting a single hit in the game the other night."

"His hitting will improve before the summer is over," Tom replied with a certainty that revealed a firm belief in his teaching prowess. "Mike has to learn to keep his eye on the ball and stop swinging blindly at anything that comes over the plate."

"It must take a lot of patience to teach how to play baseball."

Along with the can of beer, Maggie took the pitcher of iced tea from the refrigerator shelf. "Would you like a glass for your beer?"

"The can is fine."

He took it from her and popped the tab. "I suppose it does require patience, but the end results are rewarding. I enjoy sports and I enjoy working with kids. For me, it's natural to combine the two."

"That's good."

Taking a glass from the cupboard, Maggie filled it with tea from the pitcher for herself.

"Listen, Maggie . . . there isn't any reason why I can't bring Mike home after practice. You don't need to keep making special trips to pick him up."

He walked over to stand next to her, leaning a hip against the counter edge.

"It's very generous of you to offer, but I couldn't let you do it."

Maggie shook her head in refusal. The sunshine streaming in through the window above the sink glinted on the fiery sheen of her hair.

It caught Tom's attention and he reached out to touch it as an innocent child would reach out for a dancing flame.

"Your hair is an extraordinary shade of red." A lock trailed across his finger. His voice was musing and absent. "Beautiful."

"Thank you." Maggie would have moved to the side to elude his involuntary caress, but the kitchen door leading outside opened.

She froze as Wade crossed the threshold and stopped, his gaze narrowing darkly, slashing from her to Tom. The curling strand of hair slid off Tom's finger. They were standing so close together at that moment that the scene didn't look as innocent as it had been: the hard glitter in Wade's eyes told Maggie that.

"Mike is at the neighbors'." Maggie took the step from Tom's side.

Her head assumed a defiant angle; she was irritated by the criticism and condemnation she saw written in Wade's features. She was single, thus free to have male friends.

"I know." Wade's attitude continued to be silently intimidating. "I saw him when I drove in and he told me you were in the house. I wanted to speak to you."

Maggie mentally braced herself. The last time he had wanted to speak to her privately it was to tell her about Belinda. What was it about this time? Something equally shattering, she was sure.

Tom realized that it was a rather awkward situation and set his can of beer on the countertop.

"I'd better be moving along. Thanks for the beer, Maggie. Good to see you again, Wade."

Wade could only nod to acknowledge his greeting.

"I'll walk you to the door," Maggie said.

She was trying to postpone the inevitable conversation with Wade, if only for a few minutes. "Help yourself to something cold to drink, Wade. I'll be right back."

There was no response, but she hadn't expected there to be one.

Ignoring the side door Wade had entered, she led Tom through the living room to the front door.

"Thanks again for bringing Mike home."

"Maggie—" he paused at the door, his thoughtfully curious gaze resting on her face "—is there a reconciliation in the works between the two of you?"

"No, hardly," she answered with a bitterly rueful twist to her mouth.

"Are you sure? Because I had the impression when he walked in that I was being confronted by an outraged husband." His head tipped skeptically.

"You're wrong, Tom," Maggie said in a tone that signaled her discomfort with the conversation.

"Maybe he hasn't let you go, Maggie. Maybe you haven't let him go, either. I don't know . . ." Tom was still hesitant.

"I do." Maggie smiled. "You see, Wade is seeing someone else." Tom stood there and continued to study her face.

"I guess I did make a mistake, then." He shrugged. "I'll be seeing you, Maggie."

"Thanks again, Tom."

When he left, Maggie returned to the kitchen. Wade had helped himself to a glass of tea and was putting the pitcher back in the refrigerator.

"What was he doing here, Maggie?" he asked.

"Practice ended early and he brought Mike home. But it's really none of your business, Wade."

"Are you seeing him, Maggie? Does he want you?" Wade asked and he took a step forward eyeing her like prey.

"Tom and I are getting to know each other. He's a nice man as far as I can see and Mike really enjoys the time with him," Maggie answered.

Maggie picked up her glass, glad to have something to do with her hands to hide her apprehension about this conversation.

"Have you kissed him?" His voice was a near whisper and he ran his hands nervously through his thick hair. "No . . . I don't want to know. I'm sorry if I interrupted anything."

"No, you're not," she retorted. "If you were, you would have suggested we talk another time and left." But she didn't confirm or deny his suspicions about the scene he had interrupted. He was seriously seeing someone else and it wasn't fair of him to question her actions or for her to feel that she had to comfort him in any way.

"What I came to discuss with you is important. I didn't think it was wise to put it off," Wade said.

"I'm sure it's important by your standards, but I might not think so." Maggie was still trying to stall. She knew whatever was coming would not be good.

"It's about Mike, and unless I'm greatly mistaken, he's always important to you."

It was almost a challenge.

She didn't like the sound of it any more than the portentous feelings that made her so uneasy.

"Yes, Mike is important," she agreed warily. "What about him?"

"Belinda is anxious to meet him," he said.

"Naturally."

Her voice was dry, tinged with cynicism, and it drew her a sharp look from Wade.

"I want to arrange something for this weekend."

"You know what, Wade? That's fine," Maggie nodded. "Feel free to have Mike whichever day suits you best. You know I'm not going to make any objections. Let's just get this over with so I can go back to my life."

"It isn't as simple as that," Wade sighed heavily in exasperation.

"Isn't it?" Mockery twisted her mouth.

"No. I want Mike to be on familiar ground when he meets her. I think it's going to be difficult enough for him without it occurring on alien ground."

"It won't be easy for Belinda, either," Maggie reminded him, not liking the direction his comments were pointing.

"She's an adult, more capable of handling a difficult situation than Mike is. It's more important for him to feel as comfortable as possible," he said.

"What is your solution?" she challenged. "I'm sure you've already thought of one."

Wade breathed out a silent laugh, his mouth quirking cynically.

"Why do I have the feeling that the minute I answer that question this kitchen is going to turn into a battlefield?"

"Maybe because you already know I'm not going to like it." Her nerves were tensing, her fingers tightening their grip on the moist glass, its coolness matching the temperature of her blood.

Wade held her gaze, refusing to let her look away.

"I want to bring Belinda over here to meet Mike.

He would be here, in his own home, where he would be comfortable and relaxed, and it would give you an opportunity to meet her at the same time. Your presence would also ease some of the pressure Mike might feel."

She didn't want that woman in her home. "You can't be serious?"

"I'm very serious."

"I can see it now, the four of us sitting around with our hands in our laps staring at each other." Maggie laughed aloud at the thought, but she didn't think it was funny, only preposterous.

"Granted, it may be awkward. It's bound to be no matter when or where it takes place," he argued, then suggested, "perhaps it would be better if we came for dinner."

"Dinner!"

"We could come in time to have a drink before we sit down to the table. There wouldn't be time for a lot of awkward silences before there'd be the distraction of the meal. Coffee afterward and then we'd leave."

"No!"

"Why?" Wade countered.

"Are you out of your mind? First you give her my home number without my permission and now you want her over for dinner? How accommodating do you expect me to be? Should I prepare the guest room for both of you?" Maggie sputtered helplessly, unable to control herself.

Wade ignored that last incendiary comment. "Mike has to meet her sooner or later. Why not when you're with him to lend moral support?" Wade tried to drive home the logic of his suggestion.

But there was no one around to give her moral

support, she argued silently. She was tempted to ask if Tom could also join them, but that wouldn't be fair. They were not seeing each other and she didn't want to give Tom the wrong idea. Instead, she sought refuge behind a weak protest.

"Mike has to meet her, Wade, but I don't!"

"Do you mean you would leave him in the care of a total stranger? Because that is exactly what you would be doing. I spend a lot of time with Belinda. When Mike visits me, he'll also be visiting her. Are you seriously trying to tell me you don't want to meet the woman who'll be around our son? I don't believe that, not for a minute."

Maggie turned away, because everything Wade had said was true.

For Mike's sake, she had to meet Wade's fiancée in order to have peace in her own mind when Mike visited Wade. She was trapped in a corner and she resented Wade for maneuvering her there.

"You don't have to like her, Maggie. I just . . . want you to be comfortable with her. I just want Mike to be comfortable. That's all I'm asking."

"Which night would you and your darling Belinda like to come for dinner?"

Cloying sarcasm rolled from her tongue, the only weapon she had left in her arsenal.

"Is Friday okay with you?" he asked tentatively.

"What time?"

"Seven. There's no need to plan anything elaborate," he added.

"In other words, you don't want me to use our wedding china and crystal?" she asked sweetly.

"Maggie, please don't make this more difficult," he said.

"Easier? What do you know about making something easier?" Her temper flared. "The only one who's finding any of this easy is you! It's going to be difficult for Mike, Belinda and myself. All you have to do is just sit back and wait for us to adjust to your vision!"

"What would you like me to do? Break up with her?" His look was cold, a dark brow arched in threatening challenge.

Yes! Instead Maggie cried, "No! I wouldn't presume to tell you what to do with your life. I want you to stop telling me what my attitude should be!"

"I'm not telling you anything!" Wade snapped. He rubbed his hands over his face. "We're on for Friday, then."

"Friday," she replied quietly.

"Bye, Maggie."

In the next second Wade was slamming out the side door and Maggie was alone in the kitchen.

There was nothing to vent her anger on. It turned inward onto herself. The pain was agonizing.

Tension throbbed in her temples and she pressed her fingers to them, their tips cool from holding the icy glass. The cool pressure brought temporary relief, but it came pounding back when she took her hands away. The side door opened and her head jerked up as she tried to regroup her defenses to face Wade. It was Mike who dashed in.

"Hi, Mom. Dad said I was to come in and tell you I was going with him. I'll be home by five." He started back out, then paused. "Okay?"

"Yes, it's okay." She nodded with a stiff smile.

"Bye!"

CHAPTER TWELVE

Maggie glanced through the glass door of the oven to check the roast, something she had done half a dozen times in the last hour.

At the same time she checked her dim reflection in the door, an unconscious gesture to be sure her makeup didn't need retouching.

She rubbed her palms together, surprised to find them perspiring. She wiped them dry by smoothing the long black skirt over her hips.

She was nervous, her throat dry, her stomach churning. She felt like the harried image of a wife about to entertain her husband's boss—and the thought made her laugh aloud.

Mike walked into the kitchen. "What's so funny, Mom?" He wore a clean white shirt and dark blue pants. His face was scrubbed so clean that it practically shone.

"Nothing." She didn't attempt to explain the piece of irony that she had found amusing. Wade's boss could possibly also be his future father-in-law. Instead of his boss, she was about to entertain what could be his future bride. The whole thing seemed ludicrous.

The doorbell rang. But for once Mike didn't race to answer it.

He gave her a sideways glance, and his dark eyes were filled with many of the apprehensions Maggie felt. She held out her hand to him.

"Come on, let's go and answer the door."

"I know I have to meet her," he mumbled, and moved reluctantly to walk with her, "but I wish she wasn't staying for dinner."

There wasn't any response she could make to that, so she just smiled her understanding.

"Don't you feel kinda funny about meeting her?" Mike asked as they neared the front door. "I mean, because she's dating Dad?"

"Yes, I do feel kinda funny," Maggie admitted, and that was putting it mildly.

They shared a quick smile before Maggie opened the door. She saw Wade first, standing tall and dark, dressed in a dark suit and tie, so casually elegant, and her pulse rocketed.

There was a breathless tightness in her chest. The two combined to make her feel weak at the knees.

He paused and swept his gaze over her, then said, "Hello, Maggie."

The gentle warmth in his gaze seemed to set her aglow. "Hello, Wade." She returned the greeting with a slow smile. Suddenly she realized this was the way she had visualized their first meeting, not the horrendous episode with hair curlers and old robe that had occurred. This was how she had imagined it—seeing each other and having the bitterness of their divorce fade under the mounting pleasure the reunion brought.

There was a movement by his side that compelled

her attention, and her gaze focused on what seemed like a stunningly attractive blonde.

Belinda Hale was exactly as Maggie had pictured her to be, tall and willowy, her fairness a perfect complement to Wade's darkness.

Her hair was an unusual, and probably unnatural, shade of creamy toast, worn long and caught in a clasp at the back of her neck.

Every elegant bone reeked of smooth sophistication and poise. Her eyes were as blue as a clear Seattle sky, their color accentuated by the dress she wore in a subtle blue print.

There was only one thing about her that Maggie had not guessed—her age. "Woman" seemed a premature term. At the very most, Maggie suspected Belinda might be in her early twenties.

It had never occurred to her that Wade might choose someone so much younger than himself.

The shock of seeing Belinda in her icy beauty kept Maggie silent.

Belinda Hale had no such difficulty finding her voice. "Maggie, I've been looking forward to meeting you," she declared with husky sincerity and offered her hand.

Maggie managed the handshake. "Nice to meet you,Belinda." In comparison to Belinda's friendliness, she knew she sounded stiff and polite. "Please come in."

Moving out of the doorway, she nearly stepped into Mike, who had managed to stay well in the background and silently observe his future stepmother. Now it was his turn to be thrust into the limelight.

"You must be Michael," Belinda deduced. "What does everyone call you? Mike or Mickey?"

He cringed at "Mickey" and quickly told her it was Mike. Then he copied Maggie and greeted her. "Nice to meet you, Miss Hale."

"Please call me Belinda."

She shook hands with him while Wade looked on. "You look so much like your father, Mike, I think I would have recognized you anywhere." Her gaze swung adoringly to Wade. "He's a handsome boy. No wonder you're so proud of him."

Mike shifted uncomfortably at this praise from a stranger.

Maggie tried to rescue him and wondered why Wade hadn't. Was he going to leave all the conversation up to the three of them?

Of course, Belinda seemed to have enough poise to overcome any awkward silence.

"Let's head to the living room and sit down." Maggie moved toward the collection of sofas and chairs. "What can I get you to drink?" She threw a dagger at Wade for his silence. "You still drink Scotch and water, don't you?"

"Yes."

He inclined his head in agreement, nonplussed by her irritation.

"And you, Belinda?" Maggie inquired, and was stunned to hear herself add, "Mike is having a Coke. Would you like the same?" as if Belinda weren't old enough to drink.

The blonde seemed to miss the subtle insult, although Wade hadn't. His gaze narrowed dangerously, and Maggie knew it was a remark he wouldn't soon forget.

She bit down on her tongue and hoped she could control it.

"A glass of white wine would be nice, if you have it," Belinda answered.

If she had it. Maybe Belinda hadn't missed that barb after all. "Of course."

This time Maggie was properly demure and didn't attach anything to her reply. "Make yourself at home. I'll be back in a sec."

As she started for the kitchen, Wade separated himself from Belinda's side.

"I'll help you. Mike can entertain Belinda for a few minutes."

Startled by his unexpected offer of assistance, Maggie stopped. Mike cast her a beseeching look, partly accusing her of deserting him in the face of the enemy.

But before Maggie could attempt to help him, Wade's hand was on her elbow, propelling her toward the kitchen. She didn't attempt to twist out of his hold until the door was swinging shut behind them and they were out of view.

"You left her slightly in the lurch out there," she accused.

"I think Belinda and Mike can survive for a few minutes on their own." He knew her concern wasn't for Belinda.

Irritated, Maggie walked to the cupboard for the glasses. "The Scotch is—"

"I know where the Scotch is," he interrupted.

Pink warmed her cheeks as she remembered it hadn't been very many days ago that he had drunk from the bottle.

She walked to the refrigerator and took out the chilling wine, as well as a Coke for Mike. Wade followed to get ice from the freezer compartment.

"Well?"

The cubes made a clinking sound as he dropped them in his glass.

"Well, what?" she retorted.

"Out with it."

"With what?" Maggie said.

"It's tripping all over the tip of your tongue. You might as well say it and get it out of your system." Wade poured a shot of Scotch over the ice cubes while Maggie filled the wineglasses.

She debated silently with herself, then finally abandoned all caution.

"When you were listing all of Belinda's virtues, you didn't mention her youth."

"She'll be twenty-five next month. It doesn't classify her as being fresh from the crib."

"But you have to admit, Wade, that Mike is closer to her age than you are."

It sounded so catty that Maggie wished she hadn't said it.

"It might make it easier for her to relate to him, and vice versa. Is her age the only objection you have to her?" he questioned.

"It wasn't an objection." She rushed to correct. "It just took me by surprise. I expected the woman you're seeing to be older, more mature. It didn't occur to me you would be attracted to a . . . woman so young."

"Why not? You were younger than Belinda is when we were married."

Her fingers trembled as she recorked the wine bottle. She didn't want to be reminded of their marriage, since it also reminded her of their regrettable divorce. Without responding to his comment, she returned the wine bottle to the refrigerator, conscious of his hooded gaze watching her.

"Belinda is very mature. Her head is squarely on her shoulders. She's practical and logical in her relationships with other people. I suppose you could describe her as sensible," he concluded.

"How very dull," was Maggie's first reaction, and naturally she said it.

"After our tumultuous years, I think it will be a refreshing change of pace." His retort was quick and intended to cut.

"I hope the two of you will be very comfortable together." She arranged the glasses on a serving way. "Now, Belinda may not need rescuing, but I think Mike does. Shall we go back?"

"After you. And, Maggie—" the hard line of his mouth was tempered by forced patience "—try to hold your tongue."

"I do try, Wade. Believe me, I do," she said, taking a deep breath and picking up the tray.

Maggie had expected their return would be met with a searching look. In Belinda's place, she would have been curious and a little jealous to have Wade alone in the kitchen with his ex-wife. But there wasn't a trace of either emotion in the blonde's smiling look. Belinda was either very understanding or very confident that Wade loved only her.

"I hope we didn't take too long." Maggie felt their return demanded some remark from her as hostess, then immediately realized the words she had chosen might intimate that they had been doing more in the kitchen than fixing the drinks. And after she had just promised Wade she would watch what she said!

She felt doomed.

"Not at all." Belinda seemed indifferent to their absence. She smiled at Wade as he sat on the sofa cushion beside her. "Mike and I have been talking about different things."

"Oh?"

Maggie glanced at Mike. He didn't look as if he'd been doing very much talking. But she felt a curiosity for their subject. "What about?"

Belinda answered, "He was telling me about the fishing trip the three of you took this week. He said each of you caught a fish."

"That isn't exactly true," Maggie corrected the impression, and wondered if Wade hadn't mentioned that she had accompanied him and Mike. "I didn't actually catch a fish. Mike caught one on my rod and gave me credit for it."

"You would have caught it," he came to her defense, "if you hadn't fallen overboard."

"You fell overboard?" The blonde's expression was all concern.

Maggie wished Mike hadn't offered that piece of information.

"Yes. It was nothing."

"How did it happen?"

"Mom caught this fish," Mike started to explain, "and she couldn't get the hook out of its mouth, so Dad had to do it for her. He said it was too small to keep and they started arguing."

Maggie wished he wouldn't go into such detail, but there didn't seem to be any way to stop him. "When Dad tossed it back into the water, Mom tried to catch it. She slipped and went headfirst over the side. Dad tried to grab her, but all he got was her shoe. It was the funniest thing you ever saw!"

Mike was beginning to smile at the memory.

In retrospect, Maggie could see the humor of the incident.

"Mom was soaking wet when she climbed back on the boat. She really got mad when she saw me and Dad laughing at her," Mike confided. "When Dad gave her the tennis shoe he'd grabbed off her foot, she threw it in the water. I hooked it with my line and got it back before it sank."

"You didn't laugh at her, did you, Wade?" Belinda glanced at him with reproach.

"I'm afraid I did," he admired, a devilish, unapologetic light dancing in his dark eyes.

"That wasn't kind. No wonder you lost your temper, Maggie," Belinda sympathized.

"I imagine I looked pretty comical."

Maggie found herself defending their amusement at her expense.

"You looked even funnier in that shirt," Mike piped up.

"What shirt?" Belinda asked.

"All her clothes were wet, so Mom had to wear this shirt. Only it was too big for her," Mike explained.

"How awful for you, Maggie! It must have been a trying experience."

Again Maggie dismissed the offer of sympathy. "Now that I'm warm and dry and on land, I've recovered my sense of humor. I was more embarrassed than anything else."

"Do you like to fish, Miss Hale?" Mike wanted to know.

"Call me Belinda," she corrected him. "Yes, I do like to fish. Wade has taken me with him several times in Alaska. When you come to visit us, the three of us will have to go fishing together."

"It could be fun, huh?" Mike seemed to consider the possibility.

"Not the same kind of fun as you have with your mother."

Belinda was making an attempt to show she didn't intend to try to take Maggie's place—a commendable gesture. "At least, I hope I don't fall into the river," she joked. "The water up there is very cold."

"I wouldn't worry about that." Wade's arm was draped over the back of the sofa, lightly brushing the girl's shoulders.

The affection in the implied caress sent a wave of jealousy through Maggie.

"There's only one Maggie. The things that happen to her aren't likely to happen to anyone else." He looked intently into Maggie's eyes.

"Yes, only one of me, Wade." Her murmured response was dryly sarcastic, directed at Wade. "Do you ski, Miss Hale? With all that snow in Alaska, it would be a shame if you didn't."

"I love to ski. Unfortunately, I don't get the chance to do it often."

"I'm sure that's true, but what a perfect excuse to drape yourself in furs."

Maggie sipped at her wine, hating the image of the young blonde wrapped in sables.

"I wouldn't wear animal fur," Maggie said. "I can't stand the idea of an animal being killed just so its fur can be used for a coat."

"Oh, yes, of course you would. Wade may have mentioned this," Belinda mewled.

Belinda didn't seem human. She was a perfectly coiffed, trust-funded Barbie doll. Even now, confronted by Wade's ex-wife, Belinda was gracious and charming and disgustingly friendly—even if she draped herself in animal skins.

"I do hope you're not a vegetarian. I have a

beautiful rib roast cooking in the oven," Maggie heard herself murmuring with false concern.

Belinda just laughed at the comment, a throaty, genuinely amused sound.

"No, I'm not a vegetarian. Maybe it's the practical side of me that abhors waste. I've never been able to understand why people in India have to starve when there are all those sacred cattle roaming around. It's so senseless and tragic."

"Yes, I know what you mean." She set her wineglass down.

"Excuse me, I think I'd better check on the dinner."

"May I help?" Belinda offered.

"She's an excellent cook," Wade inserted, smiling when Belinda beamed at his compliment.

"I don't doubt it," Maggie said with a quick smile. "Thank you, but I can manage. Excuse me."

Chapter Thirteen

In the kitchen she wanted to bang pots and pans, slam cupboard doors, release all this pent-up frustration. How could anyone possibly compete with a woman who was so perfect?

She forced herself to control the anger she felt, but it seethed inside her, bubbling like a volcano.

To make her feel worse, she didn't think there was a gram of jealousy in Belinda's body. If there was, the ice princess hid it quite well.

She herself was torn apart by the emotion, and it made her feel small and mean.

When she was satisfied that everything was in order in the kitchen, Maggie decided it was better to begin dinner now than wait and risk overcooking the meal. She carried the servings of spinach salad to the dining-room table before returning to the living room to suggest they come to the table.

"Spinach salad, one of my favorites," Belinda remarked as she sat in a chair opposite from Wade. "Did you tell her it was?" she asked him, and Maggie immediately wished she had chosen something else for the salad course.

"No, I didn't mention it to her."

"It's one of our favorites," Maggie explained grudgingly.

"Do you like spinach, Mike?" Belinda smiled at Mike sitting at the head of the table.

"I like it this way, but I don't like it when it's cooked."

"I don't think many children do," Belinda replied with understanding.

Maggie suspected she was a veritable paragon of understanding.

"This is a beautiful set of china, Maggie."

"A wedding gift." Now why had she volunteered that information, Maggie wondered. Why hadn't she simply accepted the compliment with a thank-you? Her irritation increased.

"If you and Dad get married, will you have kids?" Mike blurted out the question.

Maggie felt her cheeks flame in an attempt to match the color of her hair, but she was the only one who registered any embarrassment. Belinda seemed to find nothing wrong with it.

Wade shot Maggie an apologetic look.

"I'd like to have a family, yes," Belinda answered. "Wade and I both love children and if our seeing each other leads to marriage, I hope to have several babies. What do you think about becoming a big brother?"

"I don't know," Mike shrugged and attacked his salad.

Maggie's fork extracted vengeance from the innocent green leaves. Several babies. One big happy family. The only thing wrong with the picture was that Belinda would be in her place. The need to destroy the image consumed her.

"The two-o'clock feedings, the croup and teething are definitely not for the faint of heart." She hid her jealousy behind the words. "Wade's probably a little too old for that now. You should have children when you're young and your nerves are more capable of taking the strain. Of course, Belinda is still young and can handle it, but you . . ." Maggie let the sentence trail away unfinished, and laughed. There was a dangerous glitter in his dark eyes, but Wade responded with marked evenness.

"I'm certain I'll be able to cope, Maggie. Don't you think I did a good job with Mike?"

"I think Wade will make an excellent father," Belinda remarked. "You've already had proof of that."

Again, it was a calm statement of fact, with no envy.

"Wade was a very good father, and still is," Maggie agreed, mimicking the blonde's tone. "I was only concerned that when your children are grown, Wade will practically be in his dotage."

"What's dotage?" Mike frowned.

"It's a diplomatic way of saying 'old age,'" Wade explained, his mouth twisted wryly. "Your mother is trying to point out that I'm getting older."

"You are old, aren't you?" Mike countered with perfect innocence.

It was all Maggie could do not to laugh.

Wade managed to maintain his composure, however tightly held. "I'm just approaching my prime."

"That's so very true in our society," Belinda expanded on his answer. "A man's attraction increases when he's over thirty, but when a woman reaches that age, she's considered over the hill. I think it's terribly unfair. But haven't you found it to be true, Maggie?"

Maggie was so outraged she couldn't speak. It was a unnecessary reminder of her own age.

Wade recognized the danger signals flashing from her. "That opinion is changing. Women over thirty are still very desirable, and people are recognizing that."

He salved her wounded ego.

Maggie had never been particularly sensitive about her age until that moment. Despite Wade's comment, she still felt slightly raw. She managed to bring her temper down to a low simmer. Maggie used the excuse that she had to bring the rest of the food from the kitchen in order to make a discreet exit and regain control of her turbulent emotions. As she transferred the meat from its roasting pan onto a platter, she thought of the way Wade had kissed her and his appraising looks.

Maggie laid the carving knife and fork on the meat platter and carried it into the dining room, where she set it in front of Wade.

"Will you carve the meat?"

"Yes," he agreed, and eyed her with quiet speculation. Gathering the salad plates, she carried them to the kitchen.

With an ominously steady hand she dished up the potatoes and vegetables to take them in.

Over and over in her mind she kept repeating that she wouldn't lose her temper no matter how sorely she was tried.

"Maggie, I think the relationship you have with Mike is quite remarkable," Belinda declared.

"Oh? Why is that?" She set the bowl of potatoes beside Mike's plate.

"I believe it's difficult to raise an only child, especially when the parents are divorced. The tendency for a single parent is to become overprotective. Yet Mike shows no signs of that, even though you are very close. I think it's marvelous that it's turned out that way, since you're nearing the age where it isn't wise to have more children."

It was sheer misfortune that Maggie was standing beside Belinda's chair when she said it.

And it was even worse that she had a bowl of cream peas and pearl onions in her hand.

With no conscious direction from her mind, her hand tipped the bowl and poured the creamy vegetables in Belinda's lap. The instant she heard the other girl's startled shriek and saw what she had done, Maggie was horrified.

"I'm so sorry! I don't know how it happened." She was grabbing for a napkin as Belinda pushed her chair away from the table. "I'm sorry," she repeated, and dabbed ineffectually at the spreading stain of cream sauce and smashed peas.

"Maggie!" Wade rushed around the table to help.

While it hadn't been exactly deliberate, Maggie didn't try to protest her innocence. She wasn't entirely convinced herself that it had been an accident. She felt wretched. Belinda recovered sufficiently from her stunned dismay to murmur, "It's all right. I'm sure it was an accident."

Maggie thought she would have felt better if the young woman had yelled at her.

All this magnanimous forgiving and understanding was becoming too much.

Mike wasn't helping matters. Both hands were clamped over his mouth in an attempt to hold back his convulsing laughter.

One glance at Maggie and Mike turned away, his shoulders shaking all the harder.

"Come on, Belinda."

Wade was helping the girl to her feet, but Maggie

had the distinct impression that he, too, wanted to laugh. The worst of the cream sauce and peas were absorbed and blobbed on a once white napkin.

But they had left a large, ugly stain down the front of the blue dress. "I'll take you home," he told her.

"I'm sorry," Maggie repeated, helpless to undo what she had done.

"It will clean, don't worry," Belinda assured her, still slightly in a daze.

"Please send me the bill," Maggie insisted as she followed the couple to the front door. "I'll pay for it."

"Don't worry about it, Maggie. I'll take care of it." Wade sighed.

"It was nice meeting you," Belinda called over her shoulder as Wade hustled her out the door.

That convinced Maggie the girl wasn't human. No ordinary mortal could have a bowl of peas spilled on her and still say with sincerity that it was nice to meet the person who did it.

Maggie walked numbly back into the dining room and stared at the peas and onions on the carpet beside Belinda's chair.

Mike no longer tried to contain his laughter as tears rolled from his eyes.

"Stop laughing, Mike! It isn't funny."

"Yes, it is. It's the funniest thing I ever saw!"

"Just help me clear up this mess before the peas get ground into the carpet."

Maggie bent down and began picking up the vegetables drenched in cream sauce.

Mike joined her, wiping the tears from his cheeks and trying to choke back the laughter. "Mom," he declared, "you're priceless!"

Chapter Fourteen

Maggie folded the damp dish towel and hung it on its rack to dry.

Apart from the leftover roast and potatoes in the refrigerator, there was nothing about the house to suggest she had entertained guests that evening.

All the dishes were washed and put away. The carpet in the dining room had been spot-cleaned of its cream sauce. The linen tablecloth was buried in the clothes hamper, along with the napkins.

This elimination of any hint of entertaining extended even to herself. Her face was scrubbed clean of all makeup. The long black hostess skirt and silver lamé blouse were hanging in her closet once again. The onyx earrings were in her jewel box, and the black evening shoes were in her shoe bag.

In their place she wore her new forest green house robe. Barefoot, Maggie walked to the coffeepot and filled a cup with the fresh brew.

The doorbell rang and she didn't need a magic genie to tell her who it was. She had known all along that Wade would be coming back, probably to tell her off, after he had seen Belinda safely home.

She walked into the dining room toward the living room. Mike answered the door, as she had known he would. "Mom? Dad's here!"

Wade had not changed his clothes. But the knot of his tie was loosened and the top button of his shirt unfastened. The small change seemed to remove the veneer of civilization to expose a ruthless quality.

As wrong as she was, Maggie wouldn't bow her head to him.

"Hello, Wade." Her voice was amazingly steady. "I've been expecting you. The coffee is fresh. Would you like a cup?"

"No."

Wade glanced at Mike, who was watching them both with silent expectancy.

"Go to your room, Mike. I want to speak to your mother in private."

"Okay." Mike didn't argue. "Don't be too hard on her, Dad. Mom feels pretty bad about what happened."

"On second thought, call your friend next door and see if you can spend the night with him," Wade told him.

Mike glanced hesitantly at Maggie. With a silent nod, she gave her permission. The strained silence over the next few minutes, during which Mike telephoned and got an invitation to spend the night with his friend, was an ordeal.

Maggie drank her coffee and tasted none of it. Both she and Wade were too tense to sit down. They wandered aimlessly around the living room like circling combatants until Mike left.

Then finally, when they were alone, they confronted each other.

Maggie took the initiative. "There's no excuse for what I did tonight," she began.

"I'm glad you realize that."

The fact that she took the blame didn't appease Wade's anger.

"I didn't do it intentionally, I swear," Maggie continued.

"Well, I'm not so sure it was an accident," he said.

"It wasn't an accident, but it wasn't on purpose, either."

She set her cup down and twisted her fingers together. "I didn't even know what I was doing until it was too late."

"Why did you do it?" Wade raked his fingers through the side of his hair.

"It just happened," Maggie protested.

"Nothing 'just happens.' She must have really annoyed you. I don't think she meant what she said. It's not like you're much older than she is, anyway. She was just trying to make conversation."

"If you feel that way, you never should have brought her over here in the first place!" She struck back. "It was too soon for us to meet. Why do we all have to be on your timeline?"

"That's typical!" Wade declared with an exasperated sigh. "Blame me because you can't control your temper."

"I'm not blaming you—I blame myself. It was unforgivable and I know that! But I just couldn't take it anymore."

"Take what? Don't tell me you let all that talk about age get under your skin? Why should that bother you?"

"Oh, yes, I remember all you said about women over thirty still being desirable," Maggie said caustically.

"It was nothing but talk."

"Look at you—you're seeing a twenty-year-old woman."

"Twenty-five."

"Twenty-five," she repeated.

"For God's sake, Maggie, I meant every word I said!" He took her by the shoulders and shook her hard. "Haven't my actions since I came back proved that I find you a very desirable woman still?"

"I'm nothing but a habit to you?"

She flung back his words that had stung her before. "Like when a person quits smoking and keeps on wanting a cigarette."

"Yes," Wade agreed tightly, "even when he knows it's bad for him.

"The problem is when he lights up a cigarette again, all he remembers is how good it is. That's how it's been for me ever since I made the mistake of kissing you again. All I can think about is how good it is."

"Sure," she mocked. "That's why you're seeing Belinda."

"It's confusing, isn't it?" One corner of his mouth curled in a cynical smile. "You ought to be in my shoes if you want to know what real confusion is like. Belinda is a girl in a million, yet—"

"I don't care if she's a girl in ten million. I'm sick and tired of hearing about her!" Maggie was nearly in tears as she struggled futilely to break out of Wade's hold. "I don't want to hear about her virtues—or the children you're going to have!"

"Are you jealous, Maggie?"

Maggie hesitated for only an instant before abandoning all pretense to the contrary. "Yes! Yes, I am jealous. I didn't want to be, I told myself I wouldn't be. But I am jealous of her!"

"Why?" His dark gaze seemed to bore deep into her very soul. "We're divorced. Remember?"

"I know that. And I know I should want you to be happy, but . . . Why should both of us be alone and miserable?"

"Are you miserable, Maggie? You didn't look miserable when Tom was here running his hands through your hair." His hands tightened, drawing her a few inches closer.

Her fingers spread across his chest, slipping inside his jacket to cover the thinness of his shirt. She strained to keep him at a distance.

Conscious of the subtle change in the atmosphere, her pulse behaved erratically.

She could only stare at the hairs curling near the hollow of his throat.

"Don't you like being alone?" Wade demanded.

"No."

"My independent, stubborn little Maggie doesn't like being free?"

His faint skepticism made it a question. "That's a change. Six years ago that was the one thing you wanted above all else."

"I know."

"Maggie—" his large hand curved around her throat and under her chin, lifting it up "—did we give up too soon? Could we have made our marriage work?"

A tear collected on the tip of her eyelash. "I don't know."

"What do you know?"

There was a mocking lilt to his low voice that was oddly pleasing.

"I . . . I know that I'm sorry for spilling those peas all over Belinda. I never meant to do it, honestly."

An attempt at a smile trembled over her lips. "There, you have your apology from me. Now you can go back to Belinda and tell her how very contrite I am. In a few days you'll both be laughing about what a termagant your ex-wife is."

"I never laugh about you, Maggie. I never have."

His hard features were composed in a serious expression. "When we were divorced, I immediately asked my company to transfer me to Alaska because I knew I would never be able to stay away from you unless thousands of miles separated us. Each month, each year, the separation became easier to bear until finally I met Belinda. Then I came back here." Wade took a deep breath and released it in a long sigh. "And I find I still can't stay away from you."

"It hasn't been easy to get you out of my system, either." Maggie was moved by his words into admitting her own impossible position.

His hands relaxed on her shoulders and slid around to cross her back. It happened so gently and without force that she barely realized she was being enfolded in his arms.

Her head rested against his shoulder. She felt the feather-light brush of his mouth against her hair, but she didn't object.

"What are we going to do about us?" he mused.

"There isn't any us."

She slid her hands the rest of the way inside his jacket to wind her arms around his middle, unconsciously hugging closer.

"Isn't there, Maggie?"

He kissed the corner of her eye.

She lifted her head and his mouth found her lips.

It was a warm, drugging kiss, slow to passion, allowing Maggie to enjoy the sensation as she moved toward the heights.

Wade was content to make the climb at a leisurely pace.

"Legally we may not be bound to each other," he murmured against the sensitive cord along her neck. "But we haven't broken that one tie that keeps pulling us back together."

"Not Mike?"

"No, not Mike."

His hands roamed with indolent ease over her slim figure, slowly but surely molding her to his granite length.

"We're like two pieces of flint, Maggie. Every time we rub up against each other, we strike sparks. We keep forgetting to put the fire out."

"It's just physical."

Her lips began to intimately trace the outline of his jaw, so strong and firm.

"That's what I keep telling myself." Wade nibbled at the lobe of her ear. "That you just know how to please me."

"That was a long time ago."

Maggie felt her heart hammering in response to the rapid beat of his.

Her legs felt shaky and weak.

"Was it?" He moved back to nuzzle her lips. "Or was it only last night in my dreams?"

His fingers located the zipper latch in the front of her robe.

It slid slowly down to her waist, the hair-roughened

back of his hand tickling her bare skin. She seemed to lose her breath as his hand slid inside.

"This is crazy, Wade. We argue all the time." But even as she made the protest, her lips were parting in anticipation of his kiss.

"We aren't having an argument now, unless you intend to start one." His mouth hovered close to hers, without taking it.

"I should." But Maggie hadn't the strength to resist, only to press her mouth to his and accept its hard possession. Flames leaped and soared around them. Their desire melted them together.

His hands burned over her skin, arousing her flesh to the demands of his.

They were reaching the corner where there would be no turning back.

To her surprise, Maggie found herself breaking away from his kiss. She was trembling, weak with her hunger for him. Yet she was resisting. It confused her.

"Maggie?"

His fingers sought her chin, trying to twist her head back to him.

"I can't," she answered his unspoken question.

"Why?" His bewildered demand echoed what she was feeling.

"I do want you to make love to me." Maggie looked at him at last, her heart in her eyes. "But I can't let you. I don't understand it myself, so don't ask me to explain."

"Is it because of Belinda?"

His hand continued its caressing massage of her lower back, an unconscious motion that was sensually disturbing.

"Maybe," she conceded without knowing if it

were true. "It's just . . . that I don't want this to happen for old times' sake. I don't want tonight to be one last fling before you go off into your new life with Belinda."

Although Wade didn't move, Maggie felt him withdrawing behind a wall of reserve. He was taking control of his emotions and his desires. She wasn't sure if she was glad about that or not.

"I understand," he murmured.

"Do you?" Maggie hoped he did. "We've always done things so impulsively, made decisions in the heat of the moment. Getting married, and getting divorced. Before we make another foolish decision, I—"

His forefinger pressed itself against her lips for silence. "Don't say any more." He smiled tightly. "I couldn't stand the shock of hearing practical, sensible statements coming from you."

With a reluctance that thrilled her, he withdrew his arms from around her and zipped the front of her robe shut all the way to her neck. Maggie stood there uncertainly, regretting that she had stopped him even though she knew she was right.

"I don't want you to go," she sighed.

His mouth crooked into a wry smile. "Don't ask me to stay and sleep on the couch."

"Okay, I won't." She copied his smile. "You sleep in the bed and I'll take the couch."

She was joking and Wade knew it, but he answered seriously.

"I need to think, Maggie, and I can do a better job of it if I don't have the distraction of knowing you are in another room."

"You're leaving, then?"

Maggie said it almost as if she were repeating a verdict.

"Yes."

"Tomorrow . . ." she began.

Wade bent and kissed her lightly on the lips. "We'll see what tomorrow brings.

"By then we'll both have time to be sure our decision is right."

Maggie could have told him that her decision was already made, but pride demanded that she remain silent. A shiver of apprehension chilled her skin. What if she had missed her chance for happiness?

He walked to the door and paused, not looking back. "Good night, Maggie."

At least it hadn't been goodbye. Not yet, anyway. "Good night, Wade."

What was she doing, Maggie wondered as he opened the door and walked out into the night.

Was she sending him back into Belinda's waiting arms? She hadn't told him that she loved him. Maybe it was better that way.

If his decision went against her, at least she could save face.

She had to accept the probability that Wade wouldn't choose her. He had to care a great deal for Belinda or he would never have wanted her to meet Mike in the first place.

Maggie had no such choice to make. There was only Wade. A car door slammed. Shortly afterward she heard the engine start and the car reversed out of the driveway. It was going to be a long night, the waiting turning it into an eternity.

She picked up her coffee cup and carried it to

the kitchen. She refilled it and sat down at the chrome table. It was three in the morning before she turned off the lights and went to bed.

She lay there for a long time, staring at the pattern the moonlight made on the ceiling. At some point in the aching loneliness of time, Maggie drifted off to sleep.

Chapter Fifteen

A bell rang. At first Maggie thought it was her alarm clock and swung her hand to the bedside table to shut it off. But it wasn't the alarm clock. She fumbled for the telephone, but there was a dial tone on the other end. The bell sounded again as she was about to decide she had dreamed it.

"Mike! Answer the door!" she called, and tried to bury her head under the pillow.

At this hour of the morning any visitor had to be one of Mike's friends.

Then she realized that Mike wasn't home. He had spent the night with Denny next door. And there was only one possible person who might be coming at this hour to see her.

Maggie shot out of the bed like a loaded cannon. She pulled on her robe as she raced down the hall.

"I'm coming!" she called as the doorbell rang again.

Breathless, her face aglow with excitement and hope, she pulled back the bolt and unhooked the safety chain. She jerked the door open, beaming a smile of welcome. But it wasn't Wade standing outside.

It was Belinda Hale.

Maggie stared.

The blonde looked immaculate, not a hair out of place, a sparing but efficient use of makeup. In comparison Maggie felt tousled and sleep-worn, her eyes puffy, her hair a tangle of red silk, too pale without makeup.

"May I come in?" Belinda asked.

Too startled to do anything else, Maggie stepped to one side to admit her.

"I'm a mess, I'm afraid," she apologized for her appearance. "I've just got out of bed."

"That's all right, I understand. I'm never at my best until I've had my orange juice and a morning cup of coffee."

Again, there was that smooth, understanding smile.

"About last night and your dress . . ." Maggie began.

"I think we would both feel better if we just forgot about last night and that little incident," Belinda suggested. "I'm convinced you didn't do it intentionally."

"I didn't, not exactly," Maggie responded. "You must be dying for some juice and a cup of coffee. Why don't we go into the kitchen?"

"I wouldn't mind another cup myself, if it isn't too much trouble." There was nothing pushy in her manner.

On the contrary, the young woman was acting

very thoughtful, although it was strange of her to just show up at this early hour.

"The kitchen is through here."

Maggie led the way. Her mind raced to find a reason for Belinda's arrival here this morning, but she was hesitant to ask.

"This is nice." Belinda glanced around the kitchen in approval. "Very efficient. It must be a pleasure to cook here."

"It is, when I have the time."

Maggie quickly made a pot of coffee and plugged it in before walking to the refrigerator for the orange juice.

"Where's Mike this morning?"

Was that the reason for Belinda's visit? "He's next door at the neighbors'."

"That's good. It will give us a chance to have a private talk."

"Talk?"

Her hand halted in midair, the orange juice glass poised short of her mouth.

"Yes. I made sure Wade's car wasn't here before I stopped. I knew he wouldn't like me coming to talk to you." Belinda smiled with faint conspiracy and sat down at the chrome table.

"Wade's car?" Maggie repeated.

"Please don't try to spare me. And please don't be embarrassed," the other girl insisted. "I know Wade spent the night with you last night. I'm not upset. In fact, I think it might be a good thing in the long run."

"You think Wade spent the night here with me?"

Maggie repeated the statement to be certain she had heard it correctly.

"Yes. It was fairly obvious. When he took me home, I knew he was coming back here. He came back because he was upset and angry about what had happened to my dress. You're a strikingly beautiful woman, Maggie. When Wade didn't come home, I knew that whatever sparks had flown between you hadn't all been from anger," Belinda explained.

Maggie couldn't believe what she was hearing. "You think he made love to me and you don't mind?" She found that impossible.

"No, I don't mind." Belinda shook her blond head, her expression indulgently gentle. "You see, I think I understand what happened. When a man sees his ex-wife again, it's natural for him to wonder if that old feeling is still around."

"And you think that last night Wade satisfied his curiosity?" Maggie was incredulous that Belinda could take that so calmly.

"It's better than having him marry me in the future and wonder about you," Belinda answered. "Don't you think so?"

"Oh, yes, much better, I'm sure," Maggie agreed dryly, and walked to the cupboard to take out two clean mugs.

"Do you take cream or sugar?"

"Both, please."

"Have you talked to Wade this morning?" She took the sugar bowl out of the cupboard and walked to the refrigerator for the cream.

"No, he wasn't back yet when I left the house. Naturally I'm not going to tell him that I know all about last night. He may volunteer the information on his own, but I won't admit that I know. I think it's the wisest thing. I don't want him to think that I'm the possessive type and will check up on him all the time."

"You are definitely not the possessive type," Maggie agreed with the faintest trace of sarcasm.

"It's a waste of emotion. A man is either going to be faithful or he's not. A woman can do all the worrying in the world about where he is or who he's with, but it won't change anything. It can make your life miserable," Belinda declared. "And I'm not going to let my life become miserable."

"It's a commendable philosophy, but difficult to live by, I would think."

The coffeepot stopped perking and Maggie filled the mugs.

"Not if you set your mind to it. It becomes amazingly easy."

There was an expressive lift to her shoulders. "It's a matter of not being distracted by harmful emotions."

"I see."

Maggie didn't see at all. By nature she was an emotional person. Belinda seemed the complete opposite. "What is it you wanted to talk to me about?" She carried the mugs to the table, set one in front of Belinda along with the cream and sugar, and carried the second to her chair.

"About Wade."

Mentally Maggie braced herself. This was the part she understood, where Belinda would ask her to stay away from him, that he no longer belonged to her.

"What about Wade?" Maggie sipped the steaming coffee.

"I want to know all about him—the things that irritate him, the things he likes. There are so many pitfalls in a relationship. I thought if I talked to you first, I could avoid some of the major ones."

Maggie set the cup down with a jerk, brown liquid slopping over the rim.

There would be no ultimatum for her to leave Wade alone, she realized.

"You can't be serious!" She choked on her disbelief.

"Oh, but I am. Don't you see how sensible it is?" the other girl reasoned.

"Sensible? You just accused me of having slept with Wade last night. Don't you realize that?" Maggie asked incredulously. "Now you're asking me to tell you all the dos and don'ts so your relationship with him can survive."

Belinda laughed away Maggie's outburst.

"Wade has always said that one of your greatest faults was your honesty. If anything, you have proved that to me this minute."

"Did it ever occur to you that I might want Wade back?" Maggie argued.

"Of course it occurred to me. But if there'd been any chance of a reconciliation between you, it would have happened before now. It's been six years. Surely you realize that."

The woman's confidence was unshakable. Belinda's total lack of jealousy put Maggie at a loss. It was impossible to be angry, or even irritated, in the face of this insanely "sensible" girl.

That left bewilderment.

"What if I told you Wade and I discovered that old special feeling was still there? What would you say?" Maggie wanted to know.

"That it's a good thing Wade found out before he married me."

Belinda's tone indicated that that was the only logical reaction.

Logic had never ruled Maggie's heart. She leaned back in her chair, completely baffled.

"I give up," she sighed in helpless confusion. "You can't be real!"

Belinda laughed, that throaty, practiced sound.

Chapter Sixteen

The side door opened and Wade walked in.

He let the door close behind him as he stopped and a puzzling frown of disbelief spread across his male features.

His jacket and tie had been discarded, but otherwise he was wearing the same clothes he had had on last night.

There was a shadowy growth of beard on his cheeks to indicate that he hadn't shaved yet this morning. His black hair was rumpled as if he'd run his fingers through it many times.

His dark gaze narrowed on Belinda.

"I saw your car in the driveway."

His voice indicated that he hadn't believed what he'd seen.

"Our little triangle is complete now," Maggie quipped. "Sit down, Wade. Join us for a cup of coffee, although you might feel the need for something stronger."

He slid a questioning glance at her before sharply returning his attention to Belinda. "What are you doing here?"

If Belinda found the situation awkward, she didn't show it. "I was in the neighborhood so I thought I'd stop by and assure Maggie that there was no permanent damage to my dress. I had no idea you were coming."

"When you weren't home, I had no idea you would be here, either."

His attitude was wary and suspicious. Maggie rose from her chair, a false smile, tinged with cynicism, curving her mouth. "I'm afraid the cat is out of the bag, darling." She walked past him to the kitchen cupboard.

"What cat? What are you talking about?" His frown darkened in confused anger.

Lack of sleep had deepened the lines in his face, highlighting his male attraction.

"Belinda knows you spent the night with me," she told him sweetly, and poured a third cup of coffee.

"What!" Wade roared after a stunned second.

"Don't raise your voice, darling," Maggie chided him with mock reproof. "I said Belinda knows you and I were together all night. Don't worry, dear, she doesn't mind."

"Wade, I don't want you to think I was checking up on you," Belinda inserted as he was momentarily at a loss for words. "Believe me, that's the last thing I would do."

"You see?" Maggie's green eyes rounded with innocent serenity. "She does understand."

She started to hand Wade the cup of coffee and paused. "Would you like it plain, or shall I lace it with a little Scotch?"

"I'll take it plain," he snapped, and reached for the cup. His accusing dark eyes impaled Maggie. "Perhaps you'd better explain to me what's going on? What have you been telling Belinda?"

"Me? I haven't told her anything." Mockingly Maggie placed one hand on her heart and lifted the other as if taking an oath.

Wade gritted his teeth, anger seething through.

"Don't be angry with Maggie," Belinda broke in. "She didn't tell me anything until she found out that I already knew."

"Knew what?" Wade turned roundly on the girl at the table.

"Darling, you aren't listening," Maggie taunted, and brushed past him to take her chair at the table.

He flashed her an impatient look. "Belinda, what makes you think I spent the night here? And what makes you think it's okay to just show up at Maggie's house?"

"It's fairly obvious, I think," Belinda shrugged. "After you left me, you came back here. And you never came home last night. I just wanted to speak to Maggie about my dress and to tell her that . . . well, we could talk about the situation like adults."

"Naturally, she reached the logical conclusion that—"

"Don't, Maggie." Wade cut her short and glowered at Belinda.

"You assumed I spent the night with Maggie. Belinda, I admit I was tempted. With the right encouragement, I probably would have."

"Oh."

For the first time, Belinda looked to be in water out of her depth.

"Then where were you?" Immediately her hand waved aside the question, indicating Wade should ignore it.

"No. No, you don't have to answer that. I don't expect you to report your every move to me. I have no intention of tying you down, or interfering in any way with the freedom of your movements."

"You certainly can't accuse Belinda of being possessive, Wade."

"Maggie!"

Wade warned her to keep silent.

"Sorry," she said with false innocence laughing in her green eyes. "If you like, I can leave you two to thrash this out on your own." Maggie grabbed her coffee and started to walk out of the kitchen. The situation was way too absurd for her not to make jokes.

"I feel so awful, Maggie. I owe you an apology for what I was thinking," Belinda insisted.

"No, you don't." Maggie's natural candor surfaced. "If I could live last night over again, it would probably turn out to be just the way you thought it had. Your assumption was wrong, but not because I didn't want it.

"I did, but I was afraid one of us, or both of us, might regret it in the morning. So don't apologize. If anyone is sorry, it's me," Maggie concluded and stared into her coffee cup, all her cynical humor at the situation gone.

"Now that you have that confession out of your system," Wade declared, "I think it's time Belinda was leaving. Come on," he told her and helped pull her chair away from the table. "You and I have some things to discuss."

"Of course, Wade," Belinda agreed. But he wasn't giving her a chance to disagree as he took hold of her arm and forced her to walk to the side door.

Over her shoulder, she managed, "Goodbye, Maggie. I'm sorry. Maybe we can have our talk another time."

Maggie nodded and suppressed a shudder of dread. "Another time," she agreed. "Goodbye," and hoped she never saw her again. But of course she would; Maggie was convinced of that.

As the door closed she heard Wade demand, "What were you going to talk to Maggie about?"

She didn't hear Belinda's reply, but she knew the answer. Their little tiff would work itself out; Belinda would see to it.

There was no doubt in Maggie's mind that Wade had chosen his fiancée.

A remark he had made when he first walked in had given his decision away.

He had said that when he hadn't found Belinda at home, he had wondered where she was. So he had obviously been returning to her.

A broken sigh came from her heart, and her fingers raked into her tousled red hair to support her lowered head. Being prepared for his decision didn't make the wrenching pain any easier to accept. The rest of her life yawned before her and Maggie wondered what she'd do. Tom was a wonderful man, but even without Wade around, he just didn't bring forth any passion from her. And she was a passionate woman.

She squeezed her eyes tightly shut and bit into her lower lip.

Car doors slammed and engines started. Sniffing back a sob, Maggie tossed her head to shake away the throes of self-pity.

Mike could walk in at any minute and she didn't want him to find her crying. There would be plenty of lonely hours to indulge in that.

CHAPTER SEVENTEEN

Briskly she rose to clear the coffee cups and juice glass from the table.

Returning the sugar bowl and cream to their respective places, she wiped the table and refilled her cup with coffee.

As she was walking back to the table, the side door opened.

When she saw Wade enter the kitchen, Maggie dropped the cup in her hand. It shattered on impact, spilling its hot contents on the floor amid the fragments of broken pottery.

"Damn, look what you made me do!" she cried to hide the leaping joy of hope in her heart. "Do you have to burst in on people all the time? Why can't you ever knock? You know, you and Belinda are more similar than I thought."

As she stooped to pick up the broken pieces, Wade was there to help.

"Be careful or you'll cut yourself," he muttered impatiently. "Let me do it. You get a rag to mop up the coffee."

Finding his closeness too disturbing, Maggie

obeyed. She took a rag from under the sink and began mopping up the floor, careful to avoid the fragments Wade hadn't collected yet.

"I thought you'd left with Belinda," she murmured to explain her shock when he had returned to the house. "I heard your car."

"I was parked behind her. I had to move my car so she could get out."

He put the broken pieces of the coffee cup in the waste bin.

"You could have gone with her. You didn't have to come back."

Maggie wished he hadn't.

"I didn't?"

A dark eyebrow lifted quizzically.

"No." She refused to meet his look. "I realized that you'd made your decision. You didn't have to come back to tell me or explain."

"You're as bad as Belinda about jumping to conclusions," he said.

There was an underlying grimness to his voice.

Maggie thought she understood the reason for it. "Look, I know you're upset with Belinda right now. But she's young and she's trying very hard to behave the way she thinks best."

Maggie made the mistake of glancing at him, and the look in his eyes confused her.

"What?" Wade prompted, still watching her in that bemused way.

"Where were you last night?" she asked instead of answering.

Belinda might have been reluctant to ask him, but Maggie wasn't.

"Driving. Thinking. I drank a lot of coffee at a

lot of different restaurants—I don't remember which ones."

"This morning you went to Belinda's home to see her. You said so," she reminded him.

"So you assumed that meant I was returning to her." Wade followed her comment to the conclusion Maggie had reached.

"Weren't you?" she asked, suddenly breathless.

"No, I was trying to do the proper thing. I wanted to tell her it was over before coming to you."

He took the wet rag from her hand and tossed it in the sink.

"I never dreamed she was here."

"Are you sure?" Maggie hardly dared to believe him. "What happened this morning didn't have anything to do with your decision?"

"It eliminated any doubts that might have been lingering." His hands gently settled on her shoulders.

"Belinda is very understanding. I doubt if she ever loses her temper or starts arguments," Maggie felt bound to point out the sharp contrast between them.

"Milk toast can make one feel better for a while, but a steady diet of it would soon make life very bland. Life with you was never dull, Maggie.

"I much prefer the road ahead of me to be filled with challenge. How about you?"

"Yes."

Maggie gravitated toward him. In the next second she was wrapped in the hard circle of his arms, his mouth crushing down on hers.

Joy burst from her like an eternal fountain, her happiness spilling over in the wild rush to give him all of her love. It was impossible. It would take a lifetime to do that. Wade seemed to recognize that, too. He broke off the kiss to bury his face in the lustrous thickness of her red gold hair.

His arms remained locked around her, and she felt the powerful tremors that shuddered through him.

"I love you, Maggie." The deep intensity of his emotion couldn't be muffled.

"I pretended I didn't, even to myself. But I never stopped loving you."

"And I never stopped loving you, but I was too scared to admit it," she responded.

"You? Scared?" Wade laughed softly at the thought. "My tigress has never been afraid to tackle anything."

"That isn't true, because I was always afraid of you. I realized that last night after you'd left." Her fingers outlined the angle of his jaw, free at last to caress him as much as she wanted.

Wade lifted his head to look at her, a frown creasing his forehead.

"Why should you be afraid of me?"

Her dimples came into play for a moment. "Whether you're aware of it or not, there's a certain quality about you that's dominating. But I don't think I was so much afraid of that.

"Subconsciously I realized that I loved you so much nothing else mattered. I was in danger of becoming totally absorbed in your personality, losing my own identity.

"I was constantly fighting that, which meant always arguing with you."

"Now?"

"Now I'm going to stop fighting the fact that I love you," Maggie promised, rising on tiptoe to kiss him.

His gaze roamed possessively over her face, the hands on her back keeping her close.

Faint, loving amusement glittered in the jet blackness of his eyes.

"Does that mean no more arguments?" he mocked.

"I doubt it," she laughed. "I'd hate to start boring you."

"I'd probably start picking fights if you did." His mouth teased the edges of her lips. "If only to have the fun of making up afterward."

CHAPTER EIGHTEEN

When Maggie could no longer stand the tantalizing brush of his mouth, she sought the heady excitement of his kiss. Wade let her take the initiative for a few breathless moments before taking over with a mastery that left her weak at the knees.

She clung to him, her heart beating wildly, as Wade forced her head back to explore the hollow at the base of her throat.

"Poor Belinda," murmured Maggie. "She's not going to take this too well."

"I already told her," he said against her skin.

"You have?"

"Yes, when I walked her to her car."

In the unending circle of his love, Maggie was generous enough to feel sympathy.

"Was she very upset?"

"Belinda?" said Wade as if it were impossible. "She took the news with her usual calmness."

"Don't tell me!" Maggie swallowed back a disbelieving laugh. "She didn't recite some platitude that it was better you found out before you married her, did she?"

"You took the words right out of her mouth," he admitted.

"She should be on exhibit in some museum. I can't believe she's for real. Honestly, Wade, I don't know how you weren't turned off by her plasticity," she sighed.

"Belinda has a lot to learn about life and people. It's easy to think you have all the answers when you're young."

"Yes," Maggie agreed. "I'm just glad, though, that we have a second chance."

"Our marriage will be better this time," Wade promised her.

"You want to marry me, again?"

"When do you want the wedding? Is next week too soon?"

"Tomorrow couldn't be too soon," she declared.

"For me, either."

His arms tightened around her.

"Dad?"

Mike's voice called from the living room.

The front door was closed and the sound of running feet approached the kitchen.

Maggie and Wade exchanged a smile as he burst in on them.

"I didn't know you were here, Dad, until I saw the car in the driveway." His dark eyes rounded as he took in the fact that his mother was firmly enwrapped in his father's arms. He seemed hesitant to draw any conclusion. "You aren't mad at Mom anymore, are you?" was the closest he would come.

"I was never mad at your mom." Wade smiled down on Maggie, then bent his head to kiss the tip of her nose.

"By the way, Mike, I've decided I'm not going to see Belinda anymore."

"You're not?" he repeated uncertainly.

"No, I'm not. I've decided that Maggie is the only woman I want to be with. I need to keep her out of trouble and I need her to do the same for me. I begged her and she's decided to give me another chance."

"Does that mean . . ." Mike began. "Are you and Mom going to get married again?"

"Yes, we are," Maggie answered.

"For good?" Mike asked.

Wade answered, "For good and bad, fighting and arguing and loving for the rest of our life." He looked at Maggie as he spoke, warming every inch of her with the love that shone in his eyes. "I hope you're as happy about it as we are, Mike."

"You bet I am!" he exclaimed now that he was fully convinced that they meant it.

"Oh, wow! I hoped—does this mean we're going to live in Alaska?"

"Yes. Would like that?" Wade watched closely for Mike's reaction.

"Would I? You could teach me how to ski! And maybe we could buy a sled and some dogs? And Mom could go fishing with us and catch one of those big fish like we did!"

Mike began making plans.

"With our luck, the fish will probably pull her into the water," Wade laughed.

"Wow! I gotta go tell Denny we're moving to Alaska!" Mike exclaimed, and shot out of the kitchen for the neighbors' house.

As the door banged shut behind him, Wade curved a finger under Maggie's chin and turned her head to look at him. There was a shimmer of tears in her eyes.

"What's the matter, honey?"

"Mike was so happy." She smiled at being so silly as to cry over that.

"I know."

He gently wiped the glistening tears from her lashes. "I never did ask you whether you wanted to live in Alaska."

"You know I don't care where I live so long as it's with you," Maggie told him.

"Careful! You're beginning to sound corny," Wade teased her.

"I don't care," she sighed, and rested her head against his shoulder.

Love was definitely sweeter the second time around.

"We'll call the real estate company on Monday and put the house up for sale. What about the furniture? Do you want to store it or take it with us?"

"We can take some of it and store the rest," Maggie decided, and sighed.

"What's that for?"

"I was just thinking about all the packing and sorting that has to be done. I have to give notice at my job. There's the utilities to call—there's so much to do."

"Would you rather not move?" Wade asked.

"No, it's not that. I just wish I had a genie who would do it all for me."

She laughed at her laziness. "How soon will we be going?"

"After our honeymoon."

"Are we going to have a honeymoon?"

"Don't all newlyweds?" he teased.

"Where are we going?"

Maggie was curious.

"I thought we'd take the boat and go up to the San Juan Islands in the sound, maybe all the way to Vancouver," Wade told her.

"What boat? You don't mean Belinda's?" Maggie pulled away from his arms, astounded by his suggestion. "Isn't that expecting rather a lot from her?"

"That wasn't Belinda's boat. Did you think it belonged to her family?" he queried in amusement.

"Yes. I mean, you'd borrowed her car, so I assumed you'd borrowed her boat."

"It's mine, Maggie. I bought it with my own hard-earned money," Wade explained.

"Oh."

"Do you feel better now?" He gently drew her back into his arms.

"Much better. I'm not as open-minded as Belinda," Maggie warned him. "The thought of spending my second honeymoon in her family's boat—"

"—touched a spark to your temper?" Wade finished the sentence for her.

"Something like that," she admitted.

"It's fitting, isn't it?"

"What?"

"For us to be leaving Seattle for Alaska, the same way the prospectors did, using this place as the jumping-off point on their way to the goldfields."

"I suppose so, except we aren't going to find gold."

"No. The only gold I'm interested in is a plain hollow circle to go around your finger." Wade found her left hand and carried it up to kiss her ring finger. Then he glanced at the bareness of it. "What did you do with your rings?"

"Don't ask." Maggie shook her head and tried

to withdraw her hand from his hold. "It's better if you don't know."

"Why? What did you do with them?" Her answer had fully aroused his curiosity.

Maggie knew he wouldn't leave the subject alone until she answered him. "I threw them in the river."

CHAPTER NINETEEN

"You did what? You threw your wedding band and your diamond ring in the river?"

"I told you it would be better if you didn't know," she reminded him of her warning.

"Why on earth would you do that?" he demanded.

"I was mad. That day you left for Alaska, you brought Mike home, but you never came in to say goodbye to me.

"The next day I was at my lunch break. There was the river and there were the rings on my fingers. I decided if you didn't think enough of me to say goodbye, I didn't think enough of you to wear your rings. So I took them off and threw them in the river."

"Oh, Maggie!"

His anger dissipated into a rueful smile. "I didn't come in to say goodbye because I knew I'd never be able to go if I did. It wasn't because I didn't want to see you. I couldn't."

"We must be the most stubborn people in the world. Neither one of us wanted to be the first to admit we'd made a mistake about the divorce."

"It's a communication problem that isn't going

to happen again. I love you, Maggie. Whatever else I say, for whatever reason, always remember that," he said.

"And I love you," she said. "From now on, I'll tell you that every day."

"We're going to have a lot of communication, but first there's a problem that needs immediate attention."

"Oh? What is that?"

Maggie challenged the thought that anything could be important.

"A place to stay. I can't very well stay at Belinda's home now that I've broken up with her."

"That is a problem," Maggie agreed. "I guess you could always move in here. You can always sleep on the couch."

"The couch, hell!" he growled against her lips.